編著

楊凡

U0061628

國際 IELTS 應考叢書

閱讀篇

中華教育

國際 IELTS 應考叢書
—— 閱讀篇

編著・楊凡

出版／中華教育

香港北角英皇道 499 號北角工業大廈 1 樓 B
電話：（852）2137 2338
傳真：（852）2713 8202
電子郵件：info@chunghwabook.com.hk
網址：http://www.chunghwabook.com.hk

發行／香港聯合書刊物流有限公司

香港新界大埔汀麗路 36 號 中華商務印刷大廈 3 字樓
電話：（852）2150 2100
傳真：（852）2407 3062
電子郵件：info@suplogistics.com.hk

印刷／美雅印刷製本有限公司

香港觀塘榮業街 6 號海濱工業大廈 4 字樓 A 室

版次／ 2020 年 5 月第 1 版第 7 次印刷
© 2020 中華教育

規格／ 16 開（230 mm x 170mm）
ISBN ／ 978-962-231-266-1

責任編輯：郭子晴
裝幀設計：李洛霖
印務：劉漢舉

閱讀，是 IELTS 考試中的難點。本書重在傳授解題技巧，作者以詳盡的分析性文字和大量例題對閱讀考試中出現的十幾種題型條分縷析，使解題思路一目了然。至今，還沒有一本 IELTS 閱讀指導教材有這麼詳盡周到的講解，因爲：

1. 現任北京多所 IELTS 培訓學校首席閱讀／寫作主講的本書作者厚積薄發，將三年 IELTS 教研和實踐經驗加以梳理、總結，才得以完成這本實用性極強的應考教材。

2. 本書首先重講解，其次重例題。一本優秀的參考書能通過生動而有條理的講解文字教會考生最重要的解題原理，隨之附加的試題則使講解形象化，使考生更快地領會作者意圖，並馬上檢驗學習效果，眞正將理論與實踐結合起來。

3. 本書例題與練習題均選自歷屆 IELTS 試題，目的是保證讓考生熟悉 IELTS 考題風格與出題思路，不至於因爲做了大量 "中國人製造" 的 IELTS 模擬題而反倒偏離了解題正軌。

4. 本書往往一題多例，考生可以了解同一題型在考試中出現的不同形式。各題型都有獨立章節介紹其實際操作的特點及竅門，以幫助考生在短期內提高閱讀成績。

5. 本書同時也爲考生提供了全方位的 IELTS 考試指導。由於本書作者在數次 IELTS 考試中百戰百勝，所以他總結的這些貌似瑣碎的細節非常值得重視。

祝您在 IELTS 考試中獲得成功！

目　錄

前 言

　　閱讀是 IELTS 考試中公認最難的部分,文章篇幅長,訊息量大,題型眾多。很多同學儘管做了不少題,但程度的提升仍不明顯。究其原因,除了字彙量和文法方面的欠缺之外,考生對閱讀方法和解題技巧掌握較差也是癥結所在。任何考試都是有規律可循的,本書的目的就是把這些解題技巧和出題規律清楚明白地展現在廣大考生面前,使同學們儘早走出"死背"的死胡同,達到事半功倍的效果。

本書有以下幾個突出特點:

1. 突出閱讀方法和解題技巧

　　閱讀方法和解題技巧是本書的核心,佔本書的大量篇幅。是先讀文章後看問題,還是先看問題後讀文章? IELTS 閱讀主要有哪些題型? 各題型有沒有操作性很強的解題方法? 做這些題型時,有沒有什麼需要注意的地方? 請同學們從第二章和第三章尋找這些問題的答案。

2. 所用材料最接近目前考試的風格和難度

　　為了說明閱讀方法和題型技巧,作者選用了一些和目前 IELTS 考試風格和難度最為接近的一些例題,同時,提供了每個題目的詳細解題過程,使同學們知其然,還知其所以然。閱讀本書的重點在於其解題思路,而不在於哪一個是正確答案,需要學習的是快速準確得到正確答案的過程。

3. 總結了 IELTS 閱讀的原則和規律

　　本書作者結合多年的教學實踐經驗,總結了 IELTS 閱讀的八大原則、二十條規律及十大出題原則。尤其是二十條規律,使得考生能夠不讀原文也能做對相當一部分題目。這些內容是本書作者的首創,詳細說明請見第六章。

4. 對閱讀中出現的難句進行句子結構分析

　　閱讀理解的困難在一定程度上是文章裏的難句造成的。因此,本書作者從

IELTS 考試風格的文章中選出了幾十個代表性的難句,提供中文翻譯,並對句子結構加以分析。同學們若對這些難句進行認真的分析和研究,必定會提高自己的閱讀水準。作者在提供中文翻譯的時候,並沒有使用標準的書面語言。畢竟閱讀不是翻譯,作者有意按照句子的結構來翻譯,是為了使同學們能夠更準確地學會分析句子的結構,這樣對同學們的幫助會更大。這部分內容詳見第五章。

　　本書的作者從事 IELTS 教學研究多年,課堂上所教授的學生人數已逾萬人。每期都有不少學員反映從閱讀課取得較大的收穫。但由於各種因素的限制,還有很多同學不能參加本書作者主講的培訓班。因此,作者基於多年講課而形成的筆記,編寫了這本書,系統完整地總結閱讀方法和解題技巧,使得考生通過閱讀本書能夠如同接受老師親自輔導一樣,迅速提高考試成績。

　　每當看到學生們埋頭苦讀,作者心中都會湧上強烈的責任感,決心要總結出最好的、最有效的方法和技巧,幫助這些莘莘學子實現他們的理想。正是這種激勵,促使作者幾年來潛心研究,不斷完善,精益求精,才有了這本書的誕生。如果它能給更多的人帶來幫助,那將是作者最欣慰的事。

祝廣大考生 IELTS 考試馬到成功!

CHAPTER I

IELTS 閱讀
概　述

READING

❖ 一、IELTS 閱讀概況 ❖

1. 考試時間

　　60 分鐘,包括將答案寫在答案紙上的時間。閱讀不像聽力那樣有額外的 10 分鐘,讓你將答案寫在答案紙上。

　　大多數同學會感到時間很急迫,很多同學題目答不完。

2. 試題分類

　　分為 A 類(Academic Training 即學術類)和 G 類(General Training 即移民類)兩類,兩類的閱讀試卷有相同之處,也有不同之處。

　　留學的同學要參加 A 類考試,移民的同學要參加 G 類考試。兩種考試不能相互代替,在報名時,必須確定。

3. 試卷組成

　　A 類、G 類都分為三部分。A 類是 3 篇長文章,每篇文章在 1000 字左右。G 類第一部分是 2－3 篇短文章;第二部分是 2 篇中等長度的文章;第三部分是 1 篇長文章,在 1000 字左右。A 類比 G 類要難一些。

4. 文章題材、體裁

　　G 類的文章主要來自於布告、廣告、小冊子、證明書、報紙、書籍和雜誌,主要涉及考生在英文國家必備的生存技能。

　　A 類的文章主要來自於報紙和雜誌,內容涉及文化、歷史、家庭、教育、交通、住家、環境、能源等社會方面的問題,也涉及到動植物、地質、海洋、遺傳、語言、空間、醫學等科技方面的問題。一般社會方面問題的文章有 2 篇,科技方面的文章有 1 篇。

　　體裁一般以議論文和說明文為主。

5. 題目數量

　　共 40 題左右。40 題是出現次數最多的情況,有時會有 38、39、41、42 題,一般而言三個部分平均分配,每部分 12 – 15 題。

6. 評分標準

根據答對的題數評定分數,不論難易,各題的分數都是一樣的。

學術類閱讀

正確題數	分數
13 ~ 15	4
16 ~ 17	4.5
18 ~ 20	5
21 ~ 22	5.5
23 ~ 25	6

正確題數	分數
26 ~ 27	6.5
28 ~ 30	7
31 ~ 32	7.5
33 ~ 35	8
36 ~ 38	8.5
39 ~ 40	9

移民類閱讀

正確題數	分數
15 ~ 17	4
18 ~ 19	4.5
20 ~ 22	5
23 ~ 24	5.5
25 ~ 27	6
28 ~ 29	6.5
30 ~ 32	7
33 ~ 34	7.5
35 ~ 37	8
38 ~ 39	8.5
40	9

上述評分標準只是一個參考標準，實際上會根據整套題目的難易略有變動。

7. 試題特點

最大的特點是題型眾多。傳統題型四選一只佔其中極少的一部分。大大小小的題型加起來共 10 種以上。

不同的題型有不同的解題方法。因此,解題技巧是 IELTS 閱讀的核心,也是本書最重要的部分,詳見第三章。

❖ 二、提高 IELTS 閱讀成績的四大要素 ❖

提高 IELTS 閱讀成績的四大要素是:字彙量、句子結構分析、閱讀方法與解題技巧。

1. 字彙量

字彙量是閱讀的基礎,沒有足夠的字彙,閱讀是沒有希望的。試想,一句話 10 個單字,其中一半以上你不認識,要想理解整句話的意思,是很困難的。

IELTS 考試不像其他考試,它沒有專門的字彙大綱。字彙當然是越多越好,但是背字彙很費時間。相信同學們都有背單字的痛苦經歷,有那麼多時間,可以做些別的更重要的事。

如果你不愛背單字,那就需要在其他三個方面,即句子結構分析、閱讀方法、解題技巧上下更大的功夫,掌握得更加熟練。

2. 句子結構分析

　　學會句子分析是提升閱讀水準的關鍵之一。閱讀理解文章難的原因之一在於句子結構的複雜。從近年 IELTS 考試的閱讀理解文章方面來看，可以看出句子的兩個特點：句子較長，句子結構複雜。

　　很多句子結構在 IELTS 閱讀的文章中比較普遍，因此考前熟悉它們非常必要。作者根據多年的教學經驗，從考題中挑選了一些較難的句子，進行結構分析，提供中文翻譯。同學們應認真閱讀這一部分。相信對提升閱讀水準會有幫助的。請詳見第五章。

3. 閱讀方法

　　IELTS 文章大都比較長，訊息量大。這樣一篇長文章帶着十多個題目擺在你面前，你怎麼閱讀和答題呢？是先讀文章後看問題，還是先看問題後讀文章？先讀文章，讀到什麼程度？請詳見第二章。

4. 解題技巧

　　IELTS 考試最大的特點是題型眾多，大多數題型可能是大家從未見過的。每種題型都有相關的答題要求、解題方法和注意事項。按照題型的解題技巧答題是 IELTS 閱讀的核心。請詳見第三章。

✦❖✦ 三、如何準備 IELTS 閱讀 ✦❖✦

有一定基礎的、在短期內要考 IELTS 的同學,應該:

1. 熟悉題型、掌握解題技巧

任何考試都是有規律可循的。任何人不能否認解題方法和技巧在應付考試中的重要性。筆者有一個學生,是英文系四年級學生,他在參加筆者任閱讀主講的一個培訓班之前做了一套閱讀題,60 分鐘只做了 35 道題,還有 5 道題沒有做完,35 道題中對了 26 題。參加完培訓班之後,基本能保證 50 分鐘做完一套題,平均做對 35 題,可見解題技巧的重要性。

2. 做大量的習題

通過答題,熟悉解題技巧。答題時,要注意選用與目前 IELTS 考試風格一致的模擬試題。本書的例題都選自劍橋大學出版社、澳洲考試中心等 IELTS 主辦單位出版的書籍,有的例題選自英國使館文化處發布的 IELTS 考試樣題。做這些題目,對同學們實際參加 IELTS 考試的幫助是最大的。

同學們千萬不能做某些作者自編的所謂"模擬試題"。這些題目與實際的考試題目從思路到解題方法上都大相徑庭。做這些題目,不僅無益反而有害。

除了選用適合的題目以外,還要講究科學地答題。有的同學在做完一套題後,一對答案,發現錯了很多,大罵一聲,然後就不了了之,這是很不好的。做完一套題並不算萬事 OK,重點工作應放在試題分析上。也就是將答案核對後,還要看某些題為什麼錯,為什麼沒有找到答案。要對照我們講的解題方法和規律,仔細分析這些題目。即使是做對的題目,也有必要了解為什麼做對了。總之,對於每一道已做的題目,要分析自己為什麼對或為什麼錯,對是對在那裏,錯是錯在何處,並按照解題方法進行驗證。同學們只要堅持這樣做,一定會逐步提高自己的閱讀和解題能力。

基礎較差的同學如果還想得到 6 分以上的理想分數,除了必須掌握一定的閱讀和答題技巧之外,還要在基本功上狠下功夫,包括擴大字彙量和做一些廣泛的閱讀。

在準備考試期間,保持信心是很重要的。只要你掌握了正確的方法,再付出一些努力,你一定會搬掉"閱讀"這個 IELTS 考試的"大石頭"。

CHAPTER II

IELTS 文章
閱讀方法

READING

❖ 一、閱讀方法 ❖

前面講過,除了 G 類第一部分的小文章外,IELTS 文章大都比較長,訊息量大。這樣一篇長文章帶着十多個題目擺在你面前,你該怎麼閱讀和答題呢?

一般來講,有三種閱讀和答題方法:

> 方法一:先將文章從頭到尾細讀一遍,然後做題目。有拿不準的再回頭讀文章,往往讀大半部分,然後再答題,並且也可能重複下去。

這種方法準確率較高,因為讀文章的時間較長。但這種方法很費時間,效率不高,通常要讀好幾遍文章。

這種方法只適用於閱讀程度很高的同學,他們字彙量大,而且閱讀速度快。他們先將文章從頭到尾細讀一遍,只需七、八分鐘,而且理解能力強,記憶力好,做題目時,不需要頻繁地回到原文中再去閱讀找答案。

> 方法二:不看文章,先看題目,然後到原文中去找答案。

這種方法雖然速度快(因為省掉了先讀文章的時間),但是準確率很低,在做題目之前,還不知道文章的大致內容。而且常常因為這個原因,在找答案時由於不知道到原文何處中去找更適合,往往速度也不快。所以我們不建議大家採用這種方法。

採用這種方法的唯一情況是:時間不夠。比如,由於某種原因,前面的文章和題目佔用了很多時間,最後一篇文章,只剩下十分鐘,這時候可能只好採用這種方法了。

> 方法三:先將文章大致瀏覽一下,掌握文章的大意。然後開始答題,邊做題邊回到原文中找答案。一邊做題目,一邊讀文章,將題目做完,也將文章讀完。

這種方法是前兩種方法的結合。既考慮到速度,又考慮到準確率,應該是適合大多數同學的閱讀方法。我們稱之為"雙向式閱讀法"。

下面,我們詳細介紹一下這種方法。"雙向式閱讀法"的閱讀步驟如下:

1. 先讀一下文章的標題。

文章的標題肯定說出了文章的主要意思。

2. 如果文章中有圖或圖表,應該先看一下。

IELTS 閱讀文章中,有很多圖及圖表,這些都比較直觀,也比較好理解。所以,先看一下這些內容,不僅費不了多少時間,有時還會有意想不到的收穫。

例如面對一篇題目為 "YOUR MOULEX IRON" 的文章,IRON 有 "鐵"、"熨斗" 的意思,這篇文章中有一個熨斗的圖,你一眼就會知道這是一篇關於熨斗的文章。

3. 如果文章中有小標題,應先看小標題。

有的文章中各段落還有一個小標題,小標題會說出該段落的主要意思,所以先將小標題看一下,有助於了解各段落的內容。

4. 如果文章後面的問題中有 Headings 題,則不必讀文章了,可以直接答題,先做 Headings 這一題。

Headings 題型及其解題步驟,在第三章會有詳細講解。

5. 如果文章中沒有小標題,文章後面的問題中也沒有 Headings 題,則需要讀一下原文每一段話的第一句。

每一段話的第一句,常常說出這一段話的中心意思。為什麼文章後面有 Headings 題,就不需要先讀原文每段話的第一句了呢? 實際上做 Headings 題時,就需要讀原文各段話的第一句,也就是說在做 Headings 題時,就把這一步做了。

在讀原文時,可以在重要的訊息下面畫線,以便加強印象。在考試時,你可以在試題卷上隨便畫,但答案紙上不能隨便畫。

6. 開始答題,嚴格按照解題技巧去做。

邊答題邊把文章讀完,由於在答題前已掌握了文章的大意和各個段落的主要內容,所以很多題目可以直接先定位到原文的一個段落。這時,再仔細閱讀該段落,確定正確答案。

IELTS 閱讀最大的特點是題型眾多,解題技巧是 IELTS 閱讀的核心。關於各題型的解題方法,在第三章有詳細的講解。

下面我們透過兩篇文章,詳細介紹一下這種閱讀方法以及這種方法的好處。

LIVING EXPENSES —
A GUIDE FOR OVERSEAS STUDENTS

In the mid-1990s it is estimated that a student living alone requires on average A $ 12,000 in living expenses for each year of study. Of course, these costs increase with time.

Upon arrival, students should have funds in excess of the average to cover the cost of textbooks and establishment expenses such as rental bond payment and basic furniture items. The amount spent on food, recreation, and entertainment expenses will vary according to requirements, budget, and location.

Those who are prepared to live in shared accommodation, which may not be suitable for all, might manage on A $ 10,000 per year. It is preferable for overseas students whose English is in need of practice to take advantage of live-in situations with native-speakers whenever possible. However, sharing with friends who are easy to communicate with is probably more sensible at first.

The above figures do not include the cost of large non-essential items such as household equipment or a car. Owning and maintaining a motor vehicle is expensive in Australia. Insurance is compulsory and costly, and parking both on and off campus can be a problem requiring additional expense. It is not advisable for a student to own a car unless it is absolutely necessary. A reasonable second-hand car can cost in excess of A $ 4000.

Educational institutions are almost always serviced by reliable public transport. The university and college campuses within the major cities are well served by public buses. In addition, the larger cities have extensive train systems. For example, in Sydney, most college and university campuses are only 10 or 20 minutes from a rail station.

The summer vacation requires special financial planning. Expenses for this period must be carefully estimated and added to costs for the academic year in order to give a realistic total figure for the calendar year. They are not included in the estimated A $ 10,000 – A $ 12,000 previously quoted. University eating facilities, and some university and college housing facilities, close during this time. As a general rule, international students should expect to spend at least as much on monthly living expenses during the summer as they do during the academic year.

Under present immigration regulations, international students are allowed to work up to 20 hours during term time and full-time during vacation. It is impossible for students to expect to earn sufficient funds by working part-time to pay for tuition fees and living costs. While some students are able to supplement their funds with money from part-time and/or vacation work, such work is not always regular even when available, and this can contribute to anxiety and study problems. In general, it is unrealistic to start a course with insufficient funds in the hope that "something will turn up". Students should be aware that vacation work has become more difficult to find over the last few years, but those interested can contact the Commonwealth Employment Service or the Students' Union on campus.

Warm clothes are necessary in the southern States during winter months, as night temperatures can drop to less than 10 degrees Celsius. Students should bring as much clothing from home as possible, especially if funds are limited. Information on where to buy inexpensive clothes can be obtained from the International Student Centre of most colleges and universities.

Do not rush into buying expensive textbooks. It is advisable to wait until your first lectures and tutorials, and then ask academic staff which are the essential purchases. There is usually a second-hand bookshop on campus, and used texts are also advertised on faculty notice boards.

The Students' Union coordinates a number of outlets on the various university campuses that provide stationery items and other essential study equipment at reasonable prices. Some courses require specialised equipment which can be quite costly, and it is wise to check any additional costs involved with the course of your choice.

In general, those practically orientated courses tend to incur higher additional costs. Expenses for books, stationery, and equipment vary greatly, but you should allow approximately A $ 500 – A $ 1000 a year.

Most university campuses have banks and/or credit unions. The banks issue drafts, traveller's cheques or foreign currency notes, and accept telex or airmail transactions. In some colleges and universities the credit union is the institution's own credit union. In addition to normal banking and financial services (with on transaction charges), credit unions usually provide special services for international students.

Money may be deposited or withdrawn from branches of the credit unions and banks during business hours from Monday to Friday (but not on public holidays) or 24 hours a day from the many on-campus automatic teller machines. Business hours for financial institutions vary, but credit unions are usually open from 9 am to 5 pm weekdays, and, generally, banks are open from 9.30 am to 4 pm (5 pm on Fridays). Some services are available on Saturday mornings in selected areas. While prices often compare favourably with prices overseas, because Australia is a large and exciting country, it is very easy to overspend, especially if on a tight budget.

先讀一下文章的標題"生活費用——對留學生的指南",知道這是一篇關於留學生的生活費用的文章。文章中沒有小標題,文章後面的題目中也沒有 Headings 題,則需要讀一下原文每一段話的第一句。

第一段是說二十世紀九十年代中,獨自住宿的學生的花費。

第二段是說到達以後,學生們就需要在書本和各項安置方面支付費用了。

第三段是說想與人合住的花費如何。

第四段是說上述花費沒有包括非重要的項目,如買車。

第五段是說公共交通很方便。

第六段是說暑假時的需要。

第七段是說對留學生兼職工作的要求和限制。

第八段是說衣服的問題。

第九段是說不用着急買昂貴的書。

第十段是說學生會能提供一些價格合適的文具等用品。

第十一段是面對實際的課程會引起更高的附加費用。

第十二段是大多數的大學都有銀行或信用聯盟。

第十三段是說存取錢的問題。

文章雖然不太難,但訊息量非常大。先用三至五分鐘將每一段話的第一句讀一下,然後再答題。請看以下題目:

Questions 1–6

You are advised to spend about 10 minutes on Questions 1–6.

Refer to the Reading Passage headed "Living Expenses —— A Guide for Overseas Students", and decide which of the answers best completes the following sentences. Write your answers in boxes 1~6 on your Answer Sheet. The first one has been done for you as an example.

Example: The annual living expense for a student in Australia living alone in the 1990s is estimated to be:

a) A $10,000　　　　　c) A $12,000

b) A $80,000　　　　　d) A $20,000

Answer: C

Q1. Sharing accommodation is:

   a) approximately A $10,000 per year cheaper than living alone

   b) more expensive than living alone

   c) not always suitable for students

   d) suitable for most students

Q2. Students buying a car should take the following costs into account:

   a) the purchase price of the car

   b) insurance costs

   c) parking costs

   d) all of the above

Q3. During summer vacation:

   a) all institutional housing facilities close down

   b) additional living costs are involved

   c) university canteens remain open

   d) monthly living expenses decrease

Q4. Regular part-time work is:

   a) always available

   b) not always available

c) sufficient to pay for tuition fees

d) 20 hours during full-time vacation

Q5. Courses that are more practical：

a) can require specialised equipment

b) are usually cheaper

c) cost A＄500 – A＄1000 a year

d) are usually more difficult

Q6. Credit unions on campus：

a) are open 24 hours a day

b) provide the usual financial services offered by banks

c) deduct fees for normal transactions

d) are sometimes open on public holidays

答案及詳解：

由於我們已對文章的內容有所了解，所以很多題目一下子就可以直接定位到一個段落。

1. 題目中的關鍵詞 Sharing accommodation 和第三段的第一句相對應，這時仔細閱讀原文第三段，確定此題的答案。

2. 題目中的關鍵詞 buying a car 和第四段的第一句相對應，這時仔細閱讀原文第四段，確定此題的答案。

3. 題目中的關鍵詞 summer vacation，對應第六段。

4. 題目中的關鍵詞 Regular part-time work，對應第七段。

5. 題目中的關鍵詞 practical courses，對應第十一段。

6. 題目中的關鍵詞 Credit unions，對應第十二段。

答案： 1. c 2. d 3. b 4. b 5. a 6. b

詳解請參見第三章。

AUTOMOBILES VS. PUBLIC TRANSPORT

Public transport plays a central role in any efficient urban transport system. In developing countries, where at least 16 cities are expected to have more than 12 million people each by the end of this decade, failing to give priority to public transport would be disastrous.

The term "public transport" covers many different types of vehicles, but most commonly refers to buses and trains. Rail services fall into four major categories: rapid rail (also called the underground, tube, metro, or subway), which operates on exclusive rights-of-way in tunnels or on elevated tracks; trams, which move with other traffic on regular streets; light rail, which is a quieter, more modern version of trams that can run either on exclusive rights-of-way or with other traffic; and suburban or regional trains, which connect a city with surrounding areas.

The recent trend in many cities is toward light rail over "heavy" rapid-rail systems. Whereas metros require exclusive rights-of-way, which often means building costly elevated or underground lines and stations, light rail can be built on regular city streets.

The concept of public transport also includes organised car pools, in which several people share the cost of riding together in the same private automobile. For U. S. commuters in areas with inadequate bus and train services, this is the only "public" transport option. But even where other systems are comprehensive, there is vast potential for car pooling; recent research shows that in cities the world over, private cars during commuting hours on average carry just 1.2-1.3 persons per vehicle.

Public transport modes vary in fuel use and emissions and in the space they require, but if carrying reasonable numbers of passengers, they all perform better than single-occupant private cars on each of these counts.

Although energy requirements vary according to the size and design of the vehicle and how many people are on board, buses and trains require far less fuel per passenger for each kilometre of travel. In the United States, for example, a light-rail vehicle needs an estimated 640 BTUs* of energy per passenger per kilometre; a city bus would use some 690 BTUs* per passenger-kilometre; and a car pool with four occupants 1,140 BTUs*. A single-occupant automobile, by contrast, burns nearly 4,580 BTUs* per passenger-kilometre.

The pollution savings from public transport are even more dramatic. Since both rapid and light rail have electric engines, pollution is measured not from the motor exhaust, but from the power plant generating electricity, which is usually located outside the city, where air quality problems are less serious. For typical U. S. commuter routes, rapid rail emits 30 grams of nitrogen oxides for every 100 kilometres each rail passenger travels, compared with 43 grams for light rail, 95 grams for transit buses, and 128 grams for single-occupant automobiles. Public transport's potential for reducing hydrocarbon and carbon monoxide emissions is even greater.

Although diesel buses —— especially in developing countries —— can be heavy polluters, existing technologies, such as filters, can control their exhaust. Buses can also run on less polluting fuels such as propane (used in parts of Europe) and natural gas (used in Brazil and China). Test buses in the Netherlands that run on natural gas are estimated to emit 90 percent less nitrogen oxide and 25 percent less carbon monoxide than diesel engines do.

In addition to reducing fuel consumption and pollution, public transport saves valuable city space. Buses and trains carry more people in each vehicle and, if they operate on their own rights-of-way, can safely run at much higher speeds. In other words, they not only take up less space but also occupy it for a shorter time. Thus, comparing ideal conditions for each mode in one lane of traffic, an underground metro can carry 70,000 passengers past a certain point in one hour, light rail can carry up to 35,000 people, and a bus, just over 30,000. By contrast, a lane of private cars with four occupants each can move only about 8,000 people an hour, and without such car-pooling the figure is, of course, far lower.

The availability and use of public transport vary widely in cities around the globe. Since variations in distances and city densities affect the total kilometres of travel, the annual number of trips each person takes by public transport provides a better standard for comparing its importance in various cities. The range of frequency of public transport use is shown in Table 1.

Urban public transport has long been a government priority in Western Europe. All major cities there have high car ownership, but well-developed bus and rail systems are available, and overall public transport typically accounts for between 20 and 30 percent of passenger-kilometres. In recent years, several large cities have stepped up their commitment to public transportation, combining further investments with complementary policies to restrict auto use.

Public transport also plays an important role in urban areas of the Third World. In many cities in Asia, Latin America, and Africa, buses make 50-80 percent of all motorised trips. Buses are sometimes hopelessly overcrowded; it is not uncommon to see several riders clinging to the outside. Yet most Third World cities have lower public transport use per person than those in Western Europe, reflecting the inability of small bus fleets to keep up with population growth.

Among the world's major cities, those in Australia and the United States make the least use of alternatives to the private car. Indeed, less than 5 percent of U. S. trips are by public transport, but in some cities such as New York City and Chicago, where service is provided extensively, it is used heavily. Indeed, nearly one quarter of the entire country's public transport trips are in New York City.

* BTUs: British Thermal Units(Treasure of energy consumed)

Table 1. Dependence on Public Transport in Selected Cities, 1989

City	Population	Mode	Trips *
Tokyo	11.6m	bus, tram, metro, rail	650
Buenos Aires	9.0m	bus, metro	248
Beijing	8.7m	bus, metro	107
Seoul	8.7m	bus, metro	457
Moscow	8.0m	bus, tram, metro	713
Chicago	6.8m	bus, metro, rail	101
Berlin	3.1m	bus, tram, metro, rail	356
Toronto	2.8m	bus, tram, metro	200
Melbourne	2.7m	bus, tram, rail	95
Abidjan	1.8m	bus, boat	132
Dallas	1.4m	bus	22

* trips: per person per year

先讀一下標題"小汽車與公共交通",知道這是一篇關於比較小汽車與公共交通的文章。文章中沒有小標題,文章後面的問題中也沒有 Headings,所以需要讀一下原文每一段話的第一句。

第一段是說公共交通在任何城市交通系統中都佔了最重要的角色。

第二段是說"公共交通"這個術語包含很多不同類型的車輛,但主要是指公共汽車和火車。

第三段是說在很多城市,最近的趨勢是傾向於輕軌而不是地鐵。

第四段是說公共交通的概念還包括幾個人乘坐在一輛小汽車裏。

第五段是說各種公共交通方式在燃料使用、廢氣排放和佔用的空間上不一樣,但如果裝載合理數目的乘客,它們在這三方面都比一個人佔用的小汽車表現要好。

第六段是說燃料使用(關鍵詞 energy requirements)。

第七段是說廢氣排放(關鍵詞 pollution)。

第八段還是說污染(關鍵詞 polluter)。

第九段是說佔用的空間。

第十段是說公共交通的可用性和使用在世界上各城市中變化很大。

第十一段是說城市公共交通在西歐一直是政府優先考慮的事。

第十二段是說公共交通在第三世界國家的城市區域也起了重要的作用。

第十三段是說在美國和澳洲的一些城市,小汽車以外的交通工具用得很少。

同樣是十三段,同樣是訊息量非常大,難度比上一篇文章有所增加。先用三至五分鐘將每一段文章的第一句讀一下,然後再答題。請看以下題目:

Questions 1 – 7

Questions 1 – 5

Answer the following questions using NO MORE THAN THREE WORDS and according to the information in Reading Passage 2. Write your answers in boxes 1 ~ 5 on your answer sheet.

1. What is one factor that makes light rail preferable to rapid rail?

2. What is one way in which rapid rail outperforms light rail?

3. Where is pollution from rail transport measured?

4. What is the average number of people you would expect to find in automobiles during commuting hours?

5. What proportion of passenger kilometres is undertaken by private automobile in Western Europe?

Questions 6 – 7

The table below ranks different forms of transport according to their fuel efficiency and the amount of pollution they produce. One ranking has been given in each case.

Complete the sequence of numbers (1, 2, 3, 4) for each column and write the two sequences of num-

bers（from top to bottom）in boxes 6 and 7 on your answer sheet.

transport type	fuel efficiency ranking[1]	nitrogen oxides emissions[2]
	(6)	(7)
citybuses	– – – –	– – – –
light rail	– – – –	– – – –
single occupant car	4	– – – –
rapid rail	n/a[a]	1
car pooling	– – – –	n/a[a]

[1] Ranked from 1（ ＝highest fuel efficiency）down to 4

[2] Ranked from 1（ ＝lowest nitrogen oxides）down to 4

[a] Information not available from the passage.

答案及詳解：

1. 根據題目中的關鍵詞 light rail preferable to rapid rail，對應到原文第三段。
2. 不太好直接定位到一個段落。
3. 根據題目中的關鍵詞 pollution，對應到原文第七段或第八段。
4. 對應到原文第四段，此題比較難對應。題目中有兩個關鍵詞：in automobiles 和 commuting hours（上下班時間）。而原文大多數段落都在說公共交通，只有這一段說：如果幾個人共乘一輛小汽車，也算公共交通。
5. 根據題目中的關鍵詞 in Western Europe，對應到原文第十一段（倒數第三段）。
6. 根據題目中的關鍵詞 fuel efficiency，對應到原文第六段。
7. 根據題目中的關鍵詞 emissions，對應到原文第七段或第八段。

答案：

1. less costly　　2. less pollution/more passengers　　3. power plant

4. 1.2－1.3　　5. 70－80%　　6. 213　　7. 324

　　從以上兩個例子可以看出"雙向式閱讀"的優點。由於在答題前已掌握了文章的大意和各個段落的主要內容（通過讀標題和每段話的第一句），所以在答題時，很多題目可以直接先定位到原文的一個段落。這時，再仔細閱讀該段落，確定正確答案。這樣做，既提高了速度，又提高了準確率。

二、時間分配

IELTS 閱讀的考試時間是 60 分鐘,大多數同學都感覺很緊張,很多同學答不完題。如何分配時間呢? 對不同程度及不同要求的同學,有不同的分配方法。

1. 對於程度較好、想拿 7 分及 7 分以上的同學

應嚴格按照每部分 20 分鐘的分配方法。對於中長文章,應根據不同情況,先用 2 – 5 分鐘瀏覽全文,再開始答題。

2. 對於程度普通、要拿 6 分的同學

可以採用每部分 20 分鐘的方法。但由於閱讀速度普通,這樣可能會有每部分都沒做痛快的感覺。這時候,可以採用 25,25,10 的分配方法,即前兩部分各用 25 分鐘,最後一部分用 10 分鐘。

對於 G 類閱讀,最後一部分肯定是最難的。對於 A 類閱讀,有兩種出題模式。一種是三篇文章難度均等,一種是三篇文章難度遞增。不管怎麼樣,一般來講最後一篇文章,不是很長,就是很難。

這種方法的核心是將重點放在前兩個部分。每部分增加 5 分鐘,爭取答對大多數題目(如共 26 – 27 題,爭取答對 20 題左右)。最後一部分,用 10 分鐘,一般是沒有時間先瀏覽文章,只能直接答題,根據解題方法和技巧,爭取答對 5 題,這樣共答對 25 題左右,能穩得 6 分。

實際上,想得 7 分的同學也可採用這種方法,這時應爭取前兩部分答對 23 – 24 題,第三部分答對 6 – 7 題,這樣可答對 30 題左右。

三、看清題目要求

在 IELTS 閱讀的試卷上,在每種題型前面都有一個題目要求,我們稱之為 instruction。在答題之前,一定要認真閱讀 instruction。在讀 instruction 時,要注意以下幾點:

1. 確定題型

IELTS 閱讀的題型很多,有時還會有新的題型出現,透過閱讀 instruction,確定題型,以便用相關的解題方法去答題。

2. 確定特殊要求

很多題目有特殊的答題要求,必須按照規定去答題。

(1)字數要求

如：Complete the table below. Choose NO MORE THAN THREE WORDS from the passage for each answer.

答案必須在三個字之內,否則不管答成什麼,肯定是錯誤的。

(2)答案寫什麼

如：Do the following statements reflect the claims of the writer in Reading Passage 3. In boxes 36 − 42 write：

YES   if the statement reflects the writer's claims

NO   if the statement contradicts the writer

NOT GIVEN   if there is no information about this in the passage

這種題型是 T/F/NG,同是這種題型,有時題目要求考生答 True/False/Not Given,有時要求答 T/F/NG,有時又要求考生答 Yes/No/Not Given(如本題),必須按照要求去做。否則,本來判斷正確,因為不符合要求而失分,很可惜。

(3)是寫選項本身,還是寫代表字母

有時題目要求答選項本身,如 vary。有時題目要求答選項前面的代表字母,如 A。這時也必須滿足要求。選項前有代表字母的,肯定是要求答代表字母。最近的考試中,選項前大部分都是有代表字母。

(4)答案是否必須為原文中的詞

如果題目要求中有 Choose words from the Reading Passage 的字樣,則答案一般應是原文中的原詞,而且不能做任何變動。

3. 有利訊息

有時題目要求中會給出一些有利訊息,如答案來自原文的某個段落等等,如果沒有注意到,則很可惜,不利於快速準確地找到答案。

如：Complete the summary below of the first two paragraphs of the Reading Passage. Choose **ONE OR TWO WORDS** from the Reading Passage for each answer. Write your answers in boxes 30 − 36 on your answer sheet.

答案應該在文章的前兩段中去找。另外注意,此題就有字數的要求:一個或兩個字。

4. 注意看例子

很多題目都會給出一個例子,經由例子,也能很快地掌握題目要求。

國際IELTS應考叢書

閱　讀

CHAPTER III

IELTS 閱讀
各題型技巧

READING

學習指導

　　IELTS 考試的一大特點是題型眾多。本章將分題型詳細介紹各種題型的解題方法。按照題型的解題技巧答題,是 IELTS 閱讀的核心。所以本章是本書最重要的部分,希望同學們仔細閱讀。

　　每種題型的講解都分為四個部分:

1. 題型要求

　　相當於回答一個"what"的問題,介紹這種題型的答題要求,並介紹這種題型在考試中出現的頻率。

2. 解題步驟

　　相當於回答一個"how"的問題,分步驟詳細介紹該題型的解題方法,是最重要的部分。筆者試圖達到的效果是使同學們能夠照着一步一步做。但請同學們不要太死記,要靈活運用。

3. 注意事項(NOTICE)

　　介紹做該題型時要注意的地方,都是一些容易出錯的地方,同時還介紹一些規律和經驗。

4. 例題講解

　　結合試題,詳細介紹解題方法。同學們應在閱讀完前三個部分之後再答題。答題時,先按照解題步驟自己做,然後再對照答案看講解,這樣收穫會更大。

❖ 一、Headings（找小標題）❖

1. 題型要求

　　文章由若干段話組成，要求給每段話找一個小標題。小標題即指該段話的段落大意、中心思想、主旨。

　　本題型不是讓你寫出每段話的小標題，這樣不好評判對錯。而是要求從選項列表（list of headings）中選擇。在現在的考試中，選項的數目往往遠多於文章中段落的數目，假如文章有五段話，選項的數目很可能是十個，甚至十二個。也就是說，有很多干擾選項。

　　題目形式通常是將文章中的一段話標出小標題作為例子，要求選餘下段落的小標題。提供小標題的段落通常是原文的第一段。

　　在考試中，該題型 A 類每次必考一組，共五題左右。有時會考兩組，共十題左右。G 類不是每次必考，考的時候，一般只考一組，共五題左右。

2. 解題步驟

（1）先將例子所在的選項從選項列表中畫去，同時，不讀例子所在的段落。

　　每個選項最多只能用一次，也就是說，兩個段落的小標題不可能是一個選項。這是因為不同段落的主旨肯定是不同的，原文將它們分為不同的段落，就是要分別說不同的內容。如果兩段的主旨相同，即表達的中心思想一致，應該將它們合為一段，是沒有必要分為兩段的。

　　有時這類題目的要求中有這樣一句話：You may use any heading more than once（你可以使用任何小標題超過一次）。這句話純屬誤導，也就是說，即使題目的要求中有這句話或類似的話，任何選項也不可能被使用兩次以上。

　　既然每個選項最多只能用一次，所以例子所在的段落已經使用的選項是不會被其他段落使用的,將其畫去,以免被其他的段落誤導。而且在選其他段落的答案時,可以不看該選項,以節省時間。

　　例子所在的段落已經提供了小標題,所以不必閱讀該段落了,以免浪費時間,直接從下一段讀起。

(2) 不要先看選項,而要從文章入手,讀一段話,做一道題。

　　大家先想一下,下面的答題方法好嗎?

　　先看第一個選項,讀懂它的意思。然後讀原文的各個段落,判斷該選項是原文哪個段落的小標題。然後按照同樣的方法處理其餘的各選項。

　　這樣的做法不好。因爲選項的數目遠多於原文段落的數目。所以這樣做,不僅花費的時間很多,而且極易受到干擾選項的誤導。很可能第一個選項就是干擾選項,你花費了很多時間將這個選項與原文的各段落相對照,結果發現它是一個干擾選項,這已經浪費了很多時間。

　　正確的方法是:

　　先不要看選項,而要先讀文章。讀文章的時候,不要一下把文章全讀完,而是讀一段話,做一道題。假如原文的第一段已作爲例子給出,那麼先讀第二段,然後到選項列表中找該段話的小標題。然後再讀第三段,以同樣方式處理,直至完成。這樣做,不僅速度快,而且準確率高。

(3) 讀每段話時,要抓住該段話的主題句和核心字彙。正確答案常常是主題句的改寫。

　　讀每段話時,並不是該段話全要仔細閱讀。這樣,既浪費時間,也不容易抓住重點。應該抓住該段話的主題句。

　　先讀該段話的第一句,然後,與選項列表中的各選項一一對應,確定正確答案,正確選項一般是該句話的改寫。如果答案不能確定,應再讀該段話的第二句,然後,與選項列表中的各選項一一對應。如果答案還是不能確定,應再讀該段話的最後一句,再與選項列表中的各選項一一對應。如果還是找不到正確的答案,則就需要閱讀整段話了。

　　根據作者的統計數據,段落的主題句在第一句的可能性超過50%,段落的主題句在第二句的可能性爲20%,段落的主題句在最後一句的可能性超過20%。也就是說,按照上述方法做這種題型,讀完該段話的第一句,就能在選項列表中找出該段話的 Heading,這種可能性超過 50% 。整段話都需要閱讀的可能性不到 10% 。

這個答題方法不僅有統計數據的依據,還有理論的基礎。英文的段落展開方法比較簡單,主要有兩種:演繹法(Deductive Method)及歸納法(Inductive Method)。演繹法指的是由觀點到例子及論據,所以主題句在該段話的第一句,但有時第一句是個過渡性或描述性的句子,主題句有可能放在該段話的第二句。總之,主題句在第一句或第二句都是演繹法。歸納法是指由例子及論據到觀點,所以主題句在該段話的最後一句。70% 左右的段落是用演繹法寫的,而且其中絕大部分主題句在第一句。20% 左右的段落是用歸納法寫的。

有的同學會說,我怎麼知道某段話是用演繹法寫的,還是用歸納法寫的? 是的,不讀完整段話,是不知道的。但讀完整段話很浪費時間,而且由於文章句子結構複雜,再加上有一些不熟悉的單字,很可能你也讀得不太懂。所以,若讀完整段話再來選擇該段話的 Heading,不僅時間不夠用,而且往往正確率也不高。

我們介紹的這種抓主題句的方法,就是按照概率,首先認為段落是用演繹法寫的,而且主題句在第一句,按照第一句的意思,在選項列表中確定正確答案。如果選項列表中有一項與這句話的意思相同,即可認為是正確答案。如果不能確定,再依次讀該段話的第二句和最後一句,再與選項列表中的各選項一一對應,確定正確答案。實踐證明,這種方法不僅節省時間,而且正確率也很高。

(4) 某段話的答案確定後,將它的選項從選項列表中畫去。

我們在前面講過,每個選項最多只能用一次,也就是說,不可能兩個段落的小標題是一個選項。所以,一段話的答案確定後,將它的選項從選項列表中畫去,以免被誤選為其他段落的小標題。而且在選其他段落的答案時,可以不看該選項以節省時間。但如果某段話的答案不太確定,如第三段可能是 C,也可能不是 C,這時不能將 C 從選項列表中畫去。

NOTICE

(1) 如果答案不確定,先將可能正確的選項全部選出。

　　如果一個段落的答案不確定,應將它們先都選出來,寫在題目的旁邊,再往下做。這樣做的好處是,下面某一段的答案確定後,便能推斷出上面段落的答案來。因為我們在前面講過,每個選項最多只能用一次,也就是說,不可能兩個段落的小標題是一個選項。例如:第二段的答案可能是 B 或 D,但你能夠確定第四段的答案是 D,所以第二段的答案就是 B 了。即使第二段後面各段落的 Heading 都不是 B 或 D,最後在確定第二段的 Heading 時,也是從 B 和 D 中選擇一個。

(2) 干擾選項的特點是:段落中未展開說明的細節。

　　作為干擾選項出現的常常是段落中提到的細節,但我們要找的是段落的主旨。這更說明做這種題要抓住段落的主題句,而不是整個段落全看。否則,特別容易受到干擾選項的誤導。

(3) 如果主題句比較複雜(如複合句),應着重在主要子句部分。

　　有時主題句是比較複雜的複合句,如果理解有困難,應集中精力看主要子句部分,正確答案應來自主要子句。
　　主題句中,常常有如下的句式:
　　Although/While/Despite/Despite the fact . . . , . . . 中文意思是:"雖然……,但是……"。前面是個讓步副詞子句,後面是主要子句,要說明的觀點在主要子句中。

例 某段話的主題句為:

　　However, despite the importance of the recruitment decision and the range of sophisticated and more objective selection techniques available, including the use of psychometric tests, assessment centres etc. , many organisations are still prepared to make this decision on the basis of a single 30 to 45 minutes unstructured interview.

譯文:雖然招收新人的決定很重要而且有很多成熟的和更客觀的選擇技巧,很多單位仍然準備基於 30 到 45 分鐘的無組織的面試來做出決定。

講解:這句比較複雜,不好理解。應着重在主要子句部分 many organisations are still prepared to make this decision on the basis of a single 30 to 45 minutes unstructured interview。正確答案爲:The unstructured interview and its validity。

(4) 如果主題句中有 show 和 suggest 等詞,應着重在其後的賓語從句。

show、suggest 是"表明"、"說明"的意思,其後的賓語從句往往是要說明的觀點,是該段話的主旨。

例 某段話的主題句爲:

Despite the significant increase in the number of women with dependent children who are in the paid workforce, Australian research studies over the last 15 years are consistent in showing that divisions of labour for family work are very rigid indeed (Watson 1991).

譯文:雖然有孩子的婦女參加工作的數目顯著上升,但過去 15 年澳洲的研究一致表明,家庭工作的勞動分工實際上是非常固定的。

講解:這句話比較複雜,不好理解。按照前面的注意事項 3,應着重在主要子句部分。主要子句部分中,有 show 的類似結構:showing that,所以其後的賓語從句是要說明的觀點,是該段話的主旨。正確答案應是 divisions of labour for family work are very rigid indeed 的改寫。其中,關鍵詞是 rigid,在本句中的意思是固定不變的。正確答案爲: The unchanged role of the female parent。

請注意:正確選項中的 unchanged 是原文主題句中關鍵詞 rigid 的同義詞。

(5) 如果主題句是 not only … but also 句型,應着重在 but also 後面的部分。

not only … but also 的意思是"不僅……而且……",常用來承上啓下。not only 後面的部分是"承上",即上一段的主旨,but also 後面的部分是"啓下",即本段話的主旨。所以着重在 but also 後面的部分。

例 某段話的主題句爲:

Diversity exists not only between cultures, but also within a single culture.

譯文: 多樣性不僅存在於不同的文化之間,而且還存在於同一文化之中。

講解: 本句用來承上啓下。not only 後面的部分是"承上",即上一段的主旨是:多樣性存在於不同的文化之間,but also 後面的部分是"啓下",即本段話的主旨是:多樣性存在於同一文化之中。正確答案爲: Variation within cultures。

請注意:正確答案中的 Variation 是原文主題句中 Diversity 的同義詞。這也說明,正確答案常常是主題句的改寫。

(6) 問句不會是主題句

問句通常作爲引題,是過渡性的句子。所以,在做 Headings 題時,如果某個段落的第一句、第二句或最後一句是問句,應該忽略,不用閱讀,肯定不是主題句。

例 某段話的第一句爲:

Should police assume all the responsibility for ensuring a rapid response?

譯文: 警察應該承擔保證快速反應的全部責任嗎?

講解: 此句雖然是該段話的第一句,但因爲是問句,所以不用看,肯定不是主題句,直接看該段話的第二句即可。

(7) 舉例子的句子不會是主題句

英文文章講究以理服人,經常用例證法,即舉個例子來論述自己的觀點。所以,在閱讀文章中,經常有以 For example 開始的句子。請同學們注意,舉例子的句子是用來解釋說明觀點的,它不會是段落的主題句。所以,在做 Headings 題時,如果某個段落的第一句、第二句或最後一句是舉例子的句子,應該忽略,不用閱讀,肯定不是主題句。

例 For example, it has been demonstrated that rapid response leads to a greater likelihood of arrest only if responses are in the order of 1 −2 minutes after a call is received by the police.

譯文:例如,只有在警察接到電話 1 −2 分鐘之後做出的快速反應才會提供抓住罪犯的更大可能性。

講解:這是一個以 For example 開始的舉例的句子,所以不用看,肯定不是主題句。

(8) 正確答案應是主題句的改寫,與主題句特別一致的選項應引起懷疑。

正確答案應是主題句的改寫,所以與主題句中的某些詞特別一致的選項應不是正確答案。

例 某段話的第一句(主題句)為:

Overall, female students outnumbered male students in the survey.

有一個選項為:

L. Female Students

原句的意思是:在調查中,女學生的數目超過男學生的數目。

上述選項只提到了女學生,所以不對。應用本條規律,你會發現它與主題句中的詞 female students 一模一樣,所以也應該懷疑它不是正確選項。

正確選項為:Gender

Gender 的意思是"性別"。在主題句中並沒有這個詞,可見正確答案應是主題句的改寫。

例 某段話的第一句(主題句)為:

While student visa holders took either 10 − 29 week or 40 week courses, most students on working holiday and tourist visas took courses of less than 10 weeks, or from 10 to 19 weeks in length.

容易誤選的選項為:

H. Visas

正確選項為:

B. Length of Courses

(9) 如果需要閱讀整個段落，應着重在閱讀該段落中的重點詞句

並不是每個段落都有主題句，有 10% 左右的 Headings 是必須閱讀整段才能找出的。受英文程度的限制，如果閱讀整個段落有困難，應着重在閱讀段落中的如下內容：

(1)反復出現的詞

(2)括號裏的詞

(3)引號裏的詞

(4)黑體字

(5)斜體字

3. 例題講解

Questions 1 – 5

Reading Passage 1, "The Nature of Disputes" has 6 sections.

Choose the most suitable heading for each section from the list of headings (i-xii) below.

Write the appropriate numbers (i-xii) in boxes 1 – 5 on your answer sheet.

N. B. There are more headings than sections so you will not use all of them.

List of Headings

i	The cost of adjudication
ii	Handling rights-based disputes
iii	Punishing acts of aggression
iv	The role of dependence in disputes
v	The role of arbitrators
vi	Methods of settling conflicting interests
vii	Ensuring choice for consumers

viii	Fulfilling employee's needs
ix	The use of negotiation for different dispute types
x	Advantages of negotiation over mediation
xi	The role of power in settling disagreements
xii	Disagreement of interests

1. Section A
2. Section B

| *Example* | *Answer* |
| Section C | ix |

3. Section D
4. Section E
5. Section F

THE NATURE OF DISPUTES

To resolve a dispute means to turn opposing positions into a single outcome. The two parties may choose to focus their attention on one or more of three basic factors. They may seek to (1) reconcile their interests, (2) determine who is right, and/or (3) determine who is more powerful.

Section A

Interests are needs, desires, concerns, fears —— the things one cares about or wants. They provide the foundation for a person's or an organisation's position in a dispute. In a dispute, not only do the interests of one party not coincide with those of the other party, but they are in conflict. For example, the director of sales for an electronics company gets into a dispute with the director of manufacturing over the number of TV models to produce. The director of sales wants to produce more models because her interest is in selling TV sets; more models mean more choice for consumers and hence increased sales. The director of manufacturing, however, wants to produce fewer models. His interest is in decreasing manufacturing costs and more models mean higher costs.

Section B

Reconciling such interests is not easy. It involves probing for deeply rooted concerns, devising creative solutions, and making trade-offs and compromises where interests are opposed. The most common procedure for doing this is negotiation, the act of communication intended to reach agreement. Another interests-based procedure is mediation, in which a third party assists the disputants, the two sides in the dispute, in reaching agreement.

Section C

By no means do all negotiations (or mediations) focus on reconciling interests. Some negotiations focus on determining who is right, such as when two lawyers argue about whose case has the greater merit. Other negotiations focus on determining who is more powerful, such as when quarrelling neighbours or nations exchange threats and counter threats. Often negotiations involve a mix of all three —— some attempts to satisfy interests, some discussion of rights, and some references to relative power.

Section D

It is often complicated to attempt to determine who is right in a dispute. Although it is usually straightforward where rights are formalized in law, other rights take the form of unwritten but socially accepted standards of behaviour, such as reciprocity, precedent, equality, and seniority.

There are often different —— and sometimes contradictory —— standards that apply to rights. Reaching agreement on rights, where the outcome will determine who gets what, can often be so difficult that the parties frequently turn to a third party to determine who is right. The most typical rights procedure is adjudication, in which disputants present evidence and arguments to a neutral third party who has the power to make a decision that must be followed by both disputants. (In mediation, by contrast, the third party does not have the power to decide the dispute.) Public adjudication is provided by courts and administrative agencies. Private adjudication is provided by arbitrators.

Section E

A third way to resolve a dispute is on the basis of power. We define power, somewhat narrowly, as the ability to pressure someone to do something he would not otherwise do. Exercising power typically means imposing costs on the other side or threatening to do so. The exercise of power takes two common forms: acts of aggression, such as physical attack, and withholding the benefits that derive from a relationship, as when employees stop working in a strike.

Section F

In relationships of mutual dependence, such as between labour and management or within an organisation or a family, the question of who is more powerful turns on who is less dependent on the other. If a company needs the employees' work more than employees need the company's pay, the company is more dependent and hence less powerful. How dependent one is turns on how satisfactory the alternatives are for satisfying one's interests. The better the alternative, the less dependent one is. If it is easier for the company to replace striking employees than it is for striking employees to find new jobs, the company is less dependent and thereby more powerful. Determining who is the more powerful party without a decisive and potentially destructive power contest is difficult because power is ultimately a matter of perceptions.

答案及詳解:

1. Section A,先讀該段話的第一句:

Interests are needs, desires, concerns, fears —— the things one cares about or wants.

譯文:利益是需要、渴望、關注、恐懼 —— 一個人關心或想要的東西。

講解:這句話相當於為 interests 下了一個定義,所以,關鍵詞為 interests。與選項一一對應,發現只有(vi) Methods of settling conflicting interests 和(xii) Disagreement of interests 中有 interests。哪一個是呢? 不能確定,先全都選上,本段話的 Heading 是 vi 或 xii。

2. Section B,先讀該段話的第一句:

Reconciling such interests is not easy.

譯文:使利益一致是不容易的。

講解:關鍵詞還是 interests。所以,本段話的 Heading 也是 vi 或 xii。經過分析,一般應先說利益不一致,再說解決的方法。所以,上一段的 Heading 是(xii) Disagreement of interests(利益的不一致)。本段的 Heading 是(vi) Methods of settling conflicting interests(解決利益衝突的方法)。

3. Section D, 先讀該段話的第一句:

It is often complicated to attempt to determine who is right in a dispute.

譯文: 試圖決定誰在衝突中是對的通常很複雜。

講解: 關鍵詞是 who is right。與選項一一對應, 正確答案爲: (ii) Handling rights-based disputes (處理基於對錯的衝突)。

4. Section E, 先讀該段話的第一句:

A third way to resolve a dispute is on the basis of power.

譯文: 解決衝突的第三種方法是基於力量。

講解: 關鍵詞是 power。與選項一一對應, 正確答案爲 (xi) The role of power in settling disagreements (力量在解決衝突中的作用)。

5. Section F, 先讀該段話的第一句:

In relationships of mutual dependence, such as between labour and management or within an organisation or a family, the question of who is more powerful turns on who is less dependent on the other.

譯文: 在相互依賴的關係中, 例如在勞資關係或在一個家庭、一個組織中, 誰更有力量的問題就轉換成誰更少依賴於另一方。

講解: 本句比較複雜, 中間有一個較長的插入語, 可先略去不讀 (處理插入語的方法, 請詳見第五章)。關鍵詞是 dependence 和 dependent。與選項一一對應, 正確答案爲 (iv) The role of dependence in disputes (依賴性在衝突中的作用)。

上述各段話的主題句均爲該段話的第一句。

Questions 6 – 10

Choose the most suitable heading for each section from the list of headings (i-xi) below. Write the appropriate numbers (i-xi) in boxes 6 – 10 on your answer sheet.

N. B. There are more headings than sections so you will not use all of them.

List of Headings

i	The presumptions of policy makers
ii	Need for more equitable parenting policies
iii	The impact of dual employment
iv	Comparison of employed and non-employed mothers
v	The benefits of balanced responsibility
vi	The unchanged role of the female parent
vii	The effect of stress on the female parent
viii	Disadvantages of parental equality
ix	The experts' view of the male parent's role
x	Commitment of mothers to their paid jobs
xi	Origins of anxiety in working mothers

Example	*Answer*
Section A	ii

6. Section B
7. Section C
8. Section D
9. Section E
10. Section F

PARENTING AND RESPONSIBILITY

Section A

There are still significant gaps between women and men in terms of their involvement in family life, the tasks they perform and the responsibilities they take. Yet, at least in developed Western countries, both women and men express a desire for greater equality in family life. It is evident that in terms of attitudes and beliefs, the problem cannot simply be thought of in terms of women wanting men to share more equally and men being reluctant to do so. The challenge now is to develop policies and practices bases on a presumption of shared responsibility between men and women, and a presumption that there are potential benefits for men and women, as well as for families and the community, if there is greater gender equality in the responsibilities and pleasures of family life. These are becoming key concerns of researchers, policy makers, community workers and, more importantly, family members themselves.

Section B

Despite the significant increase in the number of women with dependent children who are in the paid workforce, Australian research studies over the last 15 years are consistent in showing that divisions of labour for family work are very rigid indeed (Watson 1991). In terms of time, women perform approximately 90 per cent of child care tasks and 70 per cent of all family work, and only 14 per cent of fathers are highly participant in terms of time spent on family work (Russell 1983). Demo and Acock (1993), in a recent US study, also found that women continue to perform a constant and major proportion of household labour (68 per cent to 95 per cent) across all family types (first marriage, divorced, step-family or never married), regardless of whether they are employed or non-employed in paid work.

Section C

Divisions of labour for family work are particularly problematic in families in which both parents are employed outside the home (dual-worker families). Employed mothers adjust their jobs and personal lives to accommodate family commitments more than employed fathers do. Mothers are less likely to work overtime and are more likely to take time off work to attend to children's needs (VandenHeuvel 1993). Mothers spend less time on personal leisure activities than their partners, a factor that often leads to resentment (Demo and Acock 1993).

Section D

The parental role is central to the stress-related anxiety reported by employed mothers, and a major contributor to such stress is their taking a greater role in child care (VandenHeuvel 1993). Edgar and Glezer (1992) found that close to 90 per cent of both husbands and wives agreed that the man should share equally in child care, yet 55 per cent of husbands and wives claimed that the men actually did this. (These claims are despite the findings mentioned earlier that point to a much lower participation rate by fathers.) A mother's wanting her partner to do more housework and child care is a better predictor of poor family adjustment than is actual time spent by fathers in these tasks (Demo and Acock 1993). It is this desire, together with its lack of fulfillment in most families, that bring about stress in the female parent.

Section E

Family therapists and social work researchers are increasingly defining family problems in terms of a lack of involvement and support from fathers and are concerned with difficulties involved in having fathers take responsibility for the solution of family and child behaviour problems(Edgar and Glezer 1986). Yet, a father accepting responsibility for behaviour problems is linked with positive outcomes.

Section F

Research studies lend strong support to the argument that there are benefits for families considering a change to a fairer or more equitable division of the pleasures and pains of family life. Greater equality in the performance of family work is associated with lower levels of family stress and higher self esteem, better health, and higher marital satisfaction for mothers. There is also higher marital satisfaction for fathers, specially when they take more responsibility for the needs of their children —— fathers are happier when they are more involved (Russell 1984).

答案及詳解:

6. Section B, 先讀該段話的第一句:

   Despite the significant increase in the number of women with dependent children who are in the paid workforce, Australian research studies over the last 15 years are consistent in showing that divisions of labour for family work are very rigid indeed(Watson 1991).

   譯文:雖然有孩子的婦女參加工作的數目顯著上升,過去 15 年澳洲的研究一致表明,家庭工作的勞動分工實際上是非常固定的。

   講解:這句比較複雜,不好理解。應着重在主要子句部分中 showing that 其後的賓語從句 divisions of labour for family work are very rigid indeed 。正確答案爲:(vi) The unchanged role of the female parent(母親的作用沒有改變)。

7. Section C, 先讀該段話的第一句:

   Divisions of labour for family work are particularly problematic in families in which both parents are employed outside the home(dual-worker families).

   譯文:家庭工作的勞務分工在父母都在外工作的家庭(雙薪家庭)中尤其成問題。

講解:關鍵詞是 dual-worker families。所以,本段話的 Heading 是(iii) The impact of dual employment(雙薪員工的影響)。

8. Section D,先讀該段話的第一句:

The parental role is central to the stress-related anxiety reported by employed mothers, and a major contributor to such stress is their taking a greater role in child care(VandenHeuvel 1993).

譯文:在職母親有和壓力相關的焦慮,這種壓力的主要原因是孩子主要由她們照顧。

講解:此題是這五道題中最難的。如果搞不懂意思的話,很容易誤選(vii) The effect of stress on the female parent(母親壓力的影響)。而實際上本段說的是壓力的原因,正確答案爲(xi) Origins of anxiety in working mothers(在職母親焦慮的原因)。

9. Section E,先讀該段話的第一句:

Family therapists and social work researchers are increasingly defining family problems in terms of a lack of involvement and support from fathers and are concerned with difficulties involved in having fathers take responsibility for the solution of family and child behaviour problems(Edgar and Glezer 1986).

譯文:家庭學家和社會工作研究者認爲家庭問題與缺乏父親的參與有關,而且他們關注讓父親們負責家庭和照顧孩子的困難性。

講解:本句特別複雜,不好理解。但如果抓住句首的 Family therapists and social work researchers 並總結出後面談的都是有關父親的事,不難選出正確答案爲:(ix) The experts' view of the male parent's role(專家們關於父親們角色的觀點)。

10. Section F,先讀該段話的第一句:

Research studies lend strong support to the argument that there are benefits for families considering a change to a fairer or more equitable division of the pleasures and pains of family life.

譯文:研究表明,能夠平等分擔快樂和痛苦的家庭會受益。

講解:本句比較複雜,是一個同位語從句(請詳見第五章)。關鍵詞是 benefits、fairer 和 equitable。與選項一一對應,正確答案爲:(v) The benefits of balanced responsibility(平衡責任的益處)。

上述各段話的主題句均爲該段話的第一句。

Questions 11 – 15

Choose the most suitable headings for paragraphs B-F from the list of headings below, write the appropriate numbers (i-ix) in boxes 11 – 15 on your answer sheet.

N. B. : There are more headings than paragraphs so you will not use all of them. You may use any of the headings more than once.

List of headings

i Responsibilities of responding police officers

ii Perceived advantages of rapid response

iii Police response to public satisfaction

iv Communicating response time to people requesting help

v When rapid response is and is not necessary

vi Role of technology in improving police response

vii Response time and success of response

viii Public demand for catching criminals

ix Obstacles to quickly contacting the police

Example	*Answer*
Paragraph A	vi

11. Paragraph B
12. Paragraph C
13. Paragraph D
14. Paragraph E
15. Paragraph F

RAPID POLICE RESPONSE

A. Police departments in the United States and Canada see it as central to their role that they respond to calls for help as quickly as possible. This ability to react fast has been greatly improved with the aid of technology. The telephone and police radio, already long in use, assist greatly in the reduction of police response time. In more recent times there has been the introduction of the '911' emergency system. Which allows the public easier and faster contact with police, and the use of police computer systems, which allows the public easier and faster contact with police, and the use of police computer systems, which assist police in planning patrols and assigning emergency requests to the police officers nearest to the scene of the emergency.

B. An important part of police strategy, rapid police response is seen by police officers and the public alike as offering tremendous benefits. The more obvious ones are the ability of police to apply first-aid life-saving techniques quickly and the greater likelihood of arresting people who may have participated in a crime. It aids in identifying those who witnessed an emergency or crime. As well as in collecting evidence. The overall reputation of a police department, too, is enhanced if rapid response is consistent, and this in itself promotes the prevention of crime. Needless to say, rapid response offers the public some degree of satisfaction in its police force.

C. While these may be the desired consequences of rapid police response. Actual research has not shown it to be quite so beneficial. For example, it has been demonstrated that rapid response leads to a greater likelihood of arrest only if responses are in the order of 1 – 2 minutes after a call is received by the police. When response times increase to 3 – 4 minutes —— still quite a rapid response —— the likelihood of an arrest is substantially reduced. Similarly, in identifying witnesses to emergencies or crimes, police are far more likely to be successful if they arrive at the scene no more than four minutes on average, after receiving a call for help. Yet both police officers and the public define "rapid response" as responding up to 10 – 12 minutes after calling the police for help.

D. Should police assume all the responsibility for ensuring a rapid response? Studies have

45

shown that people tend to delay after an incident occurs before contacting the police. A crime victim may be injured and thus unable to call for help, for example, or no telephone may be available at the scene of the incident. Often, however, there is no such physical barrier to calling the police. Indeed. It is very common for crime victims to call their parents. Their minister, or even their insurance company first. When the police are finally called in such cases. The effectiveness of even the most rapid of responses is greatly diminished.

E. The effectiveness of rapid response also needs to be seen in light of the nature of the crime. For example, when someone rings the police after discovering their television set has been stolen from their home, there is little point, in terms of identifying those responsible for the crime, in ensuring a very rapid response. It is common in such burglary or theft cases that the victim discovers the crime hours, days, even weeks after it has occurred. When the victim is directly involved in the crime, however, as in the case of a robbery, rapid response, provided the victim was quickly able to contact the police, is more likely to be advantageous. Based on statistics comparing crimes that are discovered and those in which the victim is directly involved. Spelman and Brown(1981) suggest that three in four calls to police need not be met with rapid response.

F. It becomes clear that the importance of response time in collecting evidence of catching criminals after a crime must be weighed against a variety of factors. Yet because police department officials assume the public strongly demands rapid response, they believe that every call to the police should be met with it. Studies have shown, however, that while the public wants quick response, more important is the information given by the police to the person asking for help. If a caller is told the police will arrive in five minutes but in fact it takes ten minutes or more, waiting the extra time can be extremely frustrating. But if a caller is told he or she will have to wait 10 minutes and the police indeed arrive within that time. The caller is normally satisfied. Thus, rather than emphasising rapid response, the focus of energies should be on establishing realistic expectations in the caller and making every attempt to meet them.

答案及詳解:

11. Paragraph B,先讀該段話的第一句:

An important part of police strategy, rapid police response is seen by police officers and the public alike as offering tremendous benefits.

譯文：作爲警察策略重要的一部分,快速警察反應被警官和公眾一致認爲提供了大量的好處。

講解：正確答案爲:

（ii）Perceived advantages of rapid response（快速警察反應可以看到的好處）,主題句是該段話的第一句。

12. Paragraph C,先讀該段話的第一句:

While these may be the desired consequences of rapid police response. Actual research has not shown it to be quite so beneficial.

譯文：雖然這些是快速警察反應想得到的結果,實際的研究表明它並不是那麼的好。

講解：這句不太複雜,但也應着重在主要子句,即快速警察反應並不是那麼的好。只依據此句,並不好確定答案。再看第二句,第二句是個舉例子的句子,不用看。看最後一句:

Yet both police officers and the public define 'rapid response' as responding up to 10 – 12 minutes after calling the police for help.

譯文：警察官員和公眾都將快速反應定義爲打求助電話之後最多 10 – 12 分鐘。

講解：結合第一句和最後一句,正確答案爲:

（vii）Response time and success of response（反應時間和反應的成功性）,主題句是該段話的第一句和最後一句。

13. Paragraph D,該段話的第一句是一個問句,不用看。看該段的第二句:

Studies have shown that people tend to delay after an incident occurs before contacting the police.

譯文：研究表明人們在事件發生後和警察聯繫之前,傾向於延遲一段時間。

講解：正確答案爲:（ix）Obstacles to quickly contacting the police（快速和警察聯繫的障礙）,主題句是該段話的第二句。

14. Paragraph E,先讀該段話的第一句:

The effectiveness of rapid response also needs to be seen in light of the nature of the crime.

譯文：快速反應的有效性還和罪行的性質有關。

講解：只依據此句,並不好確定答案。再看第二句,第二句是個舉例子的句子,不用看。看最後一句:Spelman and Brown（1981）suggest that three in four calls to police need not be met with rapid response.

譯文：Spelman 和 Brown 指出四分之三打到警察局的電話並不需要快速反應。

講解：結合第一句和最後一句，正確答案為：（v.）When rapid response is and is not necessary（什麼時候快速反應是需要的和不需要的）。主題句是該段話的第一句和最後一句。

15. Paragraph F，需要閱讀全段。

講解：正確答案為：（iv.）Communicating response time to people requesting help.（把快速反應的概念傳遞給要求幫助的人）。沒有明顯的主題句。

❖ 二、Summary（摘要填空）❖

1. 題型要求

　　該類題目是一小段文字，是原文或原文中幾個段落主要內容的縮寫或改寫，我們稱之為摘要。摘要中有幾個空白部分要求考生填空。

　　按照範圍，摘要可分為兩種：全文摘要和部分段落摘要。全文摘要的訊息來自全文，題目空格的數目較多。部分段落摘要的訊息來自原文某幾個連續的段落，題目空格的數目較少。最近考試中出現的大部分是部分段落摘要，訊息來自原文連續的兩到三段，題目空格的數量在 5 題左右。對於部分段落摘要，有的在題目要求中會指出它來自原文的哪些段落，如 Complete the summary below of the first two paragraphs of the Reading Passage。但大部分的部分段落摘要只是在題目要求中說它是原文的一個摘要或部分段落摘要，並不指出它來自原文的哪些段落。

　　按照填空內容，摘要也可分為三種：. 原文原詞、從多個選項中選詞和自己寫詞。原文原詞的題目要求中常有 from the Reading Passage 的字樣。從多個選項中選詞，選項的數目常常超過題目空格的數目。從多個選項中選詞或自己寫詞的題目要求中沒有 from the Reading Passage 的字樣，有時會有 using the information in the passage 的字樣。最近考試中，絕大部分是原文原詞或從多個選項中選詞，很少有自己寫詞的。

　　這類題目在 A 類和 G 類考試中出現的頻率一般都是每兩次考一次,每次考一組,共五題左右。

2 解題步驟

(1) 仔細讀摘要的第一句話,找出它在原文中的出處,通常是和原文某段話的第一句相對應。

　　如果題目要求中已經指出了摘要的出處,則此步可以略去不做。

(2) 注意空格前後的詞,到原文中去找這些詞的對應詞。

　　對應詞的特點如下:
　　a. 原詞;
　　b. 詞性變化;如空格前的詞為 threatening,是形容詞,原文中的詞為 threat,是名詞。
　　c. 語態變化;一個是主動語態,一個是被動語態。
　　d. 同義詞;如空格前的詞為 throw away,原文中的詞為 discard,它們是同義詞。

(3) 仔細閱讀對應詞所在的句子,確定正確答案。
(4) 注意文法,所填答案必須符合文法規定。
(5) 注意順序性,即題目的順序和原文的順序基本上要一致。

NOTICE

1. 注意題目要求中是否有字數限制。

　　若要求從原文選詞或自己寫詞,會有字數要求,如 Use ONE OR TWO WORDS 等,答案必須滿足這個要求。

2. **若從原文選詞，只能選原文中連續的幾個詞，不能改變它們的順序。**

　　如原文為 virgin fibre，答案不可能是 fibre virgin。原文為 advances in the technology，答案不可能是 technology advances。

3. **若要求從原文選詞，越是生詞，越可能是答案。**

　　下列比較生僻的詞如 sustainable（可持續的）、biodegradable（可生物降解的）、contaminants（廢物，雜物）、nostrils（鼻孔）都是一些題目的答案。

4. **從選項中選詞，要注意看題目要求是寫答案本身，還是寫選項前的代表字母。**

　　選項前有代表字母的，肯定是要求答代表字母。最近的考試中，選項前大部分都有代表字母。
　　有代表字母的選項的例子如下：

A. passengers	H. single-occupant automobiles
B. Moscow	I. energy policies
C. fuel efficiency	J. economic development
D. availability of transport	K. fuel consumption
E. vehicles per hour	L. decentralisation
F. Tokyo	M. frequency of use
G. passengers per hour	N. Third World cities

這時，在答案紙上肯定是要求答 ABCD 等。

5. **從選項中選詞，答案與原文的六大對應關係。**

（1）原文原詞：與原文完全相同的詞或片語。
（2）詞性變化：原文為 necessary，是形容詞，選項為 necessity，是名詞。
（3）語態變化：原文為 Governments have encouraged waste paper collection and sorting schemes，是主動語態。摘要中的句子為 people have also been encouraged

by governments to collect their waste on a regular basis,是被動語態。

(4) 圖表:如果原文中有圖表,一般會有一題的答案來自圖表。

(5) 同義詞:原文爲 tight,選項爲 restricted,是同義詞。

(6) 歸納:有時文中沒有直接提及,須從幾句話中歸納出答案。一般比較難,目前考試中,至多有一個空格是歸納出來的。

6. 從選項中選詞,如果時間不夠,可以直接從選項中選擇,不看原文。

　　這時,要特別注意文法。這樣做的準確率在 50% 左右(視題目的難易及考生的程度而定)。所以,除非時間不夠,否則不建議大家這樣做。

7. 如果要求自己寫詞,答案絕大部分是原文原詞,少部分是對原文原詞做形式上的修改。

　　要求自己寫詞的機率很小,筆者只遇過一次。在這一次的 5 個題目中有 4 個答案是原文原詞,剩下一個原文原詞是 de-inked,答案根據文法的需要改爲 de-ink。

3. 例題講解

Questions 1 – 12

You should spend about 20 minutes on Questions 1 – 12 which are based on the Reading Passage below.

PAPER RECYCLING

A. Paper is different from other waste produce because it comes from a sustainable resource : trees. Unlike the minerals and oil used to make plastics and metals, trees are replaceable. Paper is also biodegradable, so it does not pose as much threat to the environment when it is discarded. While 45 out of every 100 tonnes of wood fibre used to make paper in Australia comes from waste paper, the rest comes directly from virgin fibre from forests and plantations. By world standard this is a good performance since the world-wide average is 33 per cent waste paper. Governments have encouraged waste paper collection and sorting schemes and at the same time, the paper industry has responded by developing new recycling technologies that have paved the way for even greater utilisation of used fibre. As a result, industry's use of recycled fibres is expected to increase at twice the rate of virgin fibre over the coming years.

B. Already, waste paper constitutes 70% of paper used for packaging and advances in the technology required to remove ink from the paper have allowed a higher recycled content in newsprint and writing paper. To achieve the benefits of recycling, the community must also contribute. We need to accept a change in the quality of paper products; for example, stationery may be less white and of a rougher texture. There also needs to be support from the community for waste paper collection programs. Not only do we need to make the paper available to collectors but it also needs to be separated into different types and sorted from contaminants such as staples, paperclips, string and other miscellaneous items.

C. There are technical limitations to the amount of paper which can be recycled and some paper products cannot be collected for reuse. These include paper in the form of books and permanent records, photographic paper and paper which is badly contaminated. The four most common sources of paper for recycling are factories and retail stores which gather large amounts of packaging material in which goods are delivered, also offices which have unwanted business documents and computer output, paper converters and printers and lastly households which discard newspapers and packaging material. The paper manufacturer pays a price for the paper and may also incur the collection cost.

D. Once collected, the paper has to be sorted by hand by people trained to recognise various types of paper. This is necessary because some types of paper can only be made from particular kinds of recycled fibre. The sorted paper then has to be repulped or mixed with water and broken down into its individual fibres. This mixture is called stock and may contain a wide variety of contaminating materials, particularly if it is made from mixed waste paper which has had little sorting. Various machinery is used to remove other materials from the stock. After passing through the repulsing process, the fibres from printed waste paper are grey in colour because the printing ink has soaked into the individual fibres. This recycled material can only be used in products where the grey colour does not matter, such as cardboard boxes but if the grey colour is not acceptable, the fibres must be de-inked. This involves adding chemicals such as caustic soda or other alkalis, soaps and detergents, waterhardening agents such as calcium chloride, frothing agents and bleaching agents. Before the recycled fibres can be made into paper they must be refined or treated in such a way that they bond together.

E. Most paper products must contain some virgin fibre as well as recycled fibres and unlike glass, paper cannot be recycled indefinitely. Most paper is down-cycled which means that a product made from recycled paper is of an inferior quality to the original paper. Recycling paper is beneficial in that it saves some of the energy, labour and capital that goes into producing virgin pulp. However, recycling requires the use of fossil fuel, a non-renewable energy source, to collect the waste paper from the community and to process it to produce new paper. And the recycling process still creates emissions which require treatment before they can be disposed of safely.

Nevertheless, paper recycling is an important economical and environmental practice but one which must be carried out in a rational and viable manner for it to be useful to both industry and the community.

Questions 1 ~ 7

Complete the summary below of the first two paragraphs of the Reading Passage. Choose ONE OR TWO WORDS from the Reading Passage for each answer. Write your answers in boxes 1 ~ 7 on your answer sheet.

SUMMARY

From the point of view of recycling, paper has two advantages over minerals and oil in that firstly it comes from a resource which is ....(1).... and secondly it is less threatening to our environment when we throw it away because it is ....(2).... Although Australia's record in the re-use of waste paper is good, it is still necessary to use a combination of recycled fibre and ....(3).... to make new paper. The paper industry has contributed positively and people have also been encouraged by . . . . (4) . . . . to collect their waste on a regular basis. One major difficulty is the removal of ink from used paper but. . . . (5) . . . . are being made in this area. However, we need to learn to accept paper which is generally of a lower. . . . (6) . . . . than before and to sort our waste paper by removing. . . . (7) . . . . before discarding it for collection.

Questions 8 – 12
Look at paragraphs C, D, and E and, using the information in the passage, complete the flow chart below. Write your answers in boxes 37 – 41 on your answer sheet. Use ONE OR TWO WORDS for each answer.

1. Waste paper collected from：

    Factories

    Retail stores

    (8) . . . .

    Paper converters and printers households

    Households

2. The paper is then (9) . . . .

3. and (10) . . . . by adding water

4. Chemicals are added in order to (11) . . . . . .

5. The fibres is then (12) . . . .

答案及詳解：

Questions 1 – 7
　　先看題目的要求,主要有以下幾點:部分段落摘要、來自原文前兩段、原文原詞、每個答案爲一個或兩個字。

1. 題目要求中已經指出了摘要的出處是第一段和第二段,所以直接看 1. 題空格前後的內容:comes from a resource,原文中對應句爲:it comes from a sustainable resource：trees,答案有可能爲 sustainable 或 trees,是哪一個呢? trees 不合文法的要求,正確答案爲 sustainable。原文是形容詞做定語,題目中改成了定語從句。

2. 空格前的內容：it is less threatening to our environment when we throw it away because it is，原文中對應句爲：Paper is also biodegradable, so it does not pose as much threat to the environment when it is discarded。正確答案爲 biodegradable。

3. 空格前後的內容：use a combination of recycled fibre and .... (3).... to make new paper。原文中對應句爲：While 45 out of every 100 tonnes of wood fibre used to make paper in Australia comes from waste paper, the rest comes directly from virgin fibre from forests and plantations。正確答案爲 virgin fibre。注意不要答成 plantations，因爲 plantations 前面還有一個 forests，forests 和 plantations 是並列的關係，但如果答爲 forests and plantations 又不滿足字數的要求（ONE OR TWO WORDS）。

4. 是這幾道題中比較簡單的。空格前後的內容：people have also been encouraged by .... (4).... to collect their waste on a regular basis。原文中對應句爲：Governments have encouraged waste paper collection and sorting schemes, 正確答案爲 governments。注意不要答成 government，因爲答案要求是原文原詞，原文中只有 governments，沒有 government。而且 government 也不合乎文法，可數名詞前必須要有限定詞。

5. 是這幾道題中最難的，關鍵要找到空格前後的關鍵詞，這裏應是：removal of ink。原文中對應句爲：advances in the technology required to remove ink from the paper have allowed a higher recycled content in newsprint and writing paper。其中有 removal of ink 的對應詞 remove ink。正確答案爲 advances。注意不要答成 technology（文法不對，主謂不一致）、advances in the technology（字數不滿足）或 technology advances（不能改變原文的詞序）。

6. 空格前的內容：we need to learn to accept paper which is generally of a lower.... (6).... than before，原文中對應句爲：We need to accept a change in the quality of paper products; for example stationery may be less white and of a rougher texture, 正確答案爲 quality。注意不要答成 white，它只是一個形容詞，空格中應填一名詞。大家看完第五章會發現，閱讀文章中常出現 for example，這個詞前面的內容重要，可能會有考題對應，後面的內容不重要，一般不會有考題對應。

7. 正確答案爲 contaminants，是一個生僻的詞。

Questions 8 – 12

先看題目的要求，主要有以下幾點：部分段落摘要、來自原文 C、D、E 三段，自己寫詞，每個答案爲一個或兩個字。

8. 對應原文 C 段中：The four most common sources of paper for recycling are factories and retail stores which gather large amounts of packaging material in which goods are delivered, also offices which have unwanted business documents and computer output, paper converters and printers and lastly households which discard newspapers and packaging material。這句較複雜,其中有多個定語從句。句子主幹是：The four sources are factories and retail stores, offices, paper converters and printers and lastly households。正確答案爲 offices。

9. 正確答案爲 sorted,對應原文 D 段的第一句：Once collected, the paper has to be sorted。

10. 對應原文 D 段中：The sorted paper then has to be repulped or mixed with water。正確答案爲 repulped。注意不要答成 mixed,因爲 mixed with water 已經和題目中的 by adding water 對應上了,請注意：對應詞本身不是答案,答案是對應詞所在句子中的其他詞。

11. 對應原文 D 段中：the fibres must be de-inked,滿足文法要求,答案爲 de-ink。

12. 對應原文 D 段中：Before the recycled fibres can be made into paper they must be refined,答案爲 refined。

注意：原文的最後一段,一道題也沒有考到,這說明在答題之前將文章細讀一遍是沒有必要的。

AUTOMOBILES VS. PUBLIC TRANSPORT

Public transport plays a central role in any efficient urban transport system in developing countries, where at least 16 cities are expected to have more than 12 million people each by the end of this decade, failing to give priority to public transport would be disastrous.

The term "public transport" covers many different types of vehicles, but most commonly refers to buses and trains. Rail services fall into four major categories: rapid rail(also called the underground, tube, metro, or subway), which operates on exclusive rights-of-way in tunnels or on elevated tracks; trams, which move with other traffic on regular streets; light rail, which is a quieter, more modern version of trams that can run either on exclusive rights-of-way or with other traffic; and suburban or regional trains, which connect a city with surrounding areas.

The recent trend in many cities is toward light rail over "heavy" rapid-rail systems. Whereas metros require exclusive rights-of-way, which often means building costly elevated or underground lines and stations, light rail can be built on regular city streets.

The concept of public transport also includes organised car pools, in which several people share the cost of riding together in the same private automobile. For U. S. commuters in areas with inadequate bus and train services, this is the only "public" transport option. But even where other systems are comprehensive, there is vast potential for car pooling; recent research shows that in cities the world over, private cars during commuting hours on average carry just $1.2-1.3$ persons per vehicle.

Public transport modes vary in fuel use and emissions and in the space they require, but if carrying reasonable numbers of passengers, they all perform better than single-occupant private cars on each of these counts.

Although energy requirements vary according to the size and design of the vehicle and how many people are on board, buses and trains require far less fuel per passenger for each kilometre of travel. In the United States, for example, a light-rail vehicle needs an estimated 640 BTUs* of energy per passenger per kilometre; a city bus would use some 690 BTUs* per passenger-kilometre; and a car pool with four occupants $1,140$ BTUs*. A single-occupant automobile, by contrast, burns nearly $4,580$ BTUs* per passenger-kilometre.

The pollution savings from public transport are even more dramatic. Since both rapid and light rail have electric engines, pollution is measured not from the motor exhaust, but from the power plant generating electricity, which is usually located outside the city, where air quality problems are less serious. For typical U. S. commuter routes, rapid rail emits 30 grams of nitrogen oxides for every 100 kilometres each rail passenger travels, compared with 43 grams for light rail, 95 grams for transit buses, and 128 grams for single-occupant automobiles. Public transport's potential for reducing hydrocarbon and carbon monoxide emissions is even greater.

Although diesel buses —— especially in developing countries —— can be heavy polluters, existing technologies, such as filters, can control their exhaust. Buses can also run on less polluting fuels such as propane(used in parts of Europe)and natural gas(used in Brazil and China). Test buses in the Netherlands that run on natural gas are estimated to emit 90 percent less nitrogen oxide and 25 percent less carbon monoxide than diesel engines do.

In addition to reducing fuel consumption and pollution, public transport saves valuable city space. Buses and trains carry more people in each vehicle and , if they operate on their own rights-of-way, can safely run at much higher speeds. In other words, they not only take up less space but also occupy it for a shorter time. Thus, comparing ideal conditions for each mode in one lane of traffic, an underground metro can carry 70,000 passengers past a certain point in one hour, light rail can carry up to 35,000 people, and a bus, just over 30,000. By contrast, a lane of private cars with four occupants each can move only about 8,000 people an hour, and without such car-pooling the figure is, of course, far lower.

The availability and use of public transport vary widely in cities around the globe. Since variations in distances and city densities affect the total kilometres of travel, the annual number of trips each person takes by public transport provides a better standard for comparing its importance in various cities. The range of frequency of public transport use is shown in Table 1.

Urban public transport has long been a government priority in Western Europe. All major cities there have high car ownership, but well-developed bus and rail systems are available, and overall public transport typically accounts for between 20 and 30 percent of passenger-kilometres. In recent years, several large cities have stepped up their commitment to public transportation, combining further investments with complementary policies to restrict auto use.

Public transport also plays an important role in urban areas of the Third World. In many cities in Asia, Latin America, and Africa, buses make 50 – 80 percent of all motorised trips. Buses are sometimes hopelessly overcrowded; it is not uncommon to see several riders clinging to the outside. Yet most Third World cities have lower public transport use per person than those in Western Europe, reflecting the inability of small bus fleets to keep up with population growth.

Among the world's major cities, those in Australia and the United States make the least use of alternatives to the private car. Indeed, less than 5 percent of U. S. trips are by public transport, but in some cities such as New York City and Chicago, where service is provided extensively, it is used heavily. Indeed, nearly one quarter of the entire country's public transport trips are in New York City.

* BTUs: British Thermal Units(Treasure of energy consumed)

Table 1. Dependence on Public Transport in Selected Cities, 1989

City	Population	Mode	Trips ★
Tokyo	11.6m	bus, tram, metro, rail	650
Buenos Aires	9.0m	bus, metro	248
Beijing	8.7m	bus, metro	107
Seoul	8.7m	bus, metro	457
Moscow	8.0m	bus, tram, metro	713
Chicago	6.8m	bus, metro, rail	101
Berlin	3.1m	bus, tram, metro, rail	356
Toronto	2.8m	bus, tram, metro	200
Melbourne	2.7m	bus, tram, rail	95
Abidjan	1.8m	bus, boat	132
Dallas	1.4m	bus	22

★ trips: per person per year

Questions 1 ~ 5

Below is a summary of some of the main points of "Automobiles vs. Public Transport".

Read the summary and select a word or phrase from the box below to fill each gap according to the information in the Reading Passage.

Write the corresponding letter(A, B, ... N) in boxes 1 −5 on your answer sheet.

N. B. There are more words and phrases than you will need to fill the gaps. You may use a word or phrase more than once if you wish.

KEY POINTS : AUTOMOBILES VS. PUBLIC TRANSPORT

The obvious advantages of public transport include lowering ..... (1) ..... and reducing exhaust emissions. Another important benefit is the amount of space that is taken up. This is measured by determining the number of ..... (2) ..... that pass a particular point under ideal conditions. As would be expected, public transport vehicles perform very well under these criteria. However, the success of public transport depends more importantly on its ..... (3) .... A 1989 survey revealed that ..... (4) ..... was the city in which the greatest number of trips per person were made on an annual basis. Interestingly, there is no clear correlation between acceptance of public transport and the degree of ..... (5) ..... of a country or city.

A. passengers	H. single-occupant automobiles
B. Moscow	I. energy policies
C. fuel efficiency	J. economic development
D. availability of transport	K. fuel consumption
E. vehicles per hour	L. decentralisation
F. Tokyo	M. frequency of use
G. passengers per hour	N. Third World cities

答案及詳解:

　　先看題目的要求,主要有以下幾點:從選項中選詞,選項前有代表字母。仔細讀摘要的第一句話,與原文第九段話的第一句相對應:In addition to reducing fuel consumption and pollution,public transport saves valuable city space。各題的答案應從這裏開始找。

1. 對應原文第九段的第一句,答案爲 K。注意不要答成 C,公共交通降低的是燃料的消費,而不是燃料的效率,它提高了燃料的效率。

2. 空格前後的詞:pass a particular point under ideal conditions,對應原文中的句子:carry 70,000 passengers past a certain point in one hour,答案爲 G,注意不要答成 A,因爲原文中有 in one hour,此題有一定的難度,屬於陷阱題。

3. 是這幾題中最難的。對應原文第十段中:Since variations in distances and city densities affect the total kilometres of travel,the annual number of trips each person takes by public transport provides a better standard for comparing its importance in various cities. The

range of frequency of public transport use is shown in Table 1。中文意思是:因爲距離和城市密度的不同影響了旅行的總公里數,每年每人使用公共交通的旅行次數爲各城市中公共交通的重要性提供了更好標準。公共交通使用的頻率如表1所示。答案爲 M。

4. 是這幾題中最簡單的,答案來自圖表,爲 B。

5. 答案爲 J,是歸納出來的。原文倒數第三段的第一句: Urban public transport has long been a government priority in Western Europe,中文意思是:城市公共交通在西歐一直是政府優先考慮的事。原文倒數第二段的第一句: Public transport also plays an important role in urban areas of the Third World, 中文意思是:公共交通在第三世界國家的城市區域起了重要的作用。結合這兩句話,可以歸納出題目中的表述: Interestingly, there is no clear correlation between acceptance of public transport and the degree of economic development of a country or city。中文意思是:有趣的是,在公共交通的接受程度和一個國家及城市的經濟發展程度之間沒有一個清楚的聯繫。

OF DUCKS AND DUCK EGGS

For people who like to keep poultry, ducks offer certain advantages over hens. Ducks are immune to some common diseases found in hens and are less vulnerable to others. Some breeds of duck produce bigger eggs than hens. In addition, ducks lay eggs over a longer season than do hens.

Poultry keepers with gardens have less to worry about if they keep ducks rather than hens because the former are less apt to dig up plants and destroy roots. While both hens and ducks benefit the garden by eating pests, hens are known to damage herb and grass beds. Ducks, on the other hand, will search for insects and snails more carefully. Only very delicate plants are at risk from the broad, webbed feet of ducks.

Like all waterbirds, ducks need access to water, and duck keepers typically provide this by building a pond. Something this large is not absolutely necessary, however: ducks need only to be able to dip their heads in the water to keep their nostrils clean. If a pond is provided, though, it is important to keep ducklings away from it until they are old enough to withstand the cool temperature of the water —— about eight weeks.

When keeping ducks, one has to consider just how many the land will support. Generally the rule is 100 ducks per half hectare. If more than this proportion is introduced, there is a risk of compacting the soil, which can lead to muddy conditions for long periods as the rain is not easily absorbed into the ground.

While ducks offer many advantages over hens, they must be given a greater quantity of food, especially if regular eggs are desired. An adult duck will eat between 170 to 200 grams of food a day. If the ducks have access to grass and a pond, they will be able to find for themselves approximately 70% of their daily dietary requirements in warmer months but less than half that in colder times. Therefore, it is important that they be fed enough food, such as grain, every day.

Experienced duck keepers raise duckling every three years or so because it is after this period of time that ducks' egg-laying powers begin to seriously weaken. If the aim is to hatch ducklings, keepers should be aware that not all ducks make good mothers, and that certain breeds of duck appear to be worse than others. The poor mothers abandon their eggs a few days after laying them. A sure way of making sure the rejected eggs hatch is to place them next to chicken eggs under a hen.

The eggs of ducks as food for humans have a mixed reputation. This is because of a number of cases of salmonella food poisoning in Europe in the 1970s. Although it was never conclusively shown that duck eggs were to blame, the egg-eating public stopped buying and many duck egg producers went bankrupt. Indeed there is a risk of salmonella poisoning when ducks lay their eggs in damp conditions, such as on ground that is constantly wet, but the same can be said for the eggs of hens. And commercial duck egg production in France and England, where the out-breaks of salmonella poisoning took place, followed the same standards as those used in the hen egg industry, which experienced no salmonella problems. (Storage of eggs, whether those of hen or duck, can also be a factor in contamination. Studies have found that bacterial growth reaches potentially dangerous levels at storage temperatures of 5°C or greater.)

The salmonella scare was over by the early 1980s, but, at least in smaller markets like Australia and New Zealand, few producers wished to risk investment in ducks for fear of problems. No large-scale commercial duck egg production exists in these countries. It has thus been left to small producers, and more commonly, home duck keepers.

例 poultry: farm birds(e. g. chickens, geese, ducks)

Questions 1 – 4

Complete the partial summary below, Choose ONE or TWO words from the passage for each answer. Write your answers in boxes 1 – 4 on your answer sheet.

To prevent their...(1)... from getting dirty, ducks should have access to water. This may be provided by building a pond, but ducklings under...(2)... of age should be prevented from entering it because of the ...(3)... of the water. If too many ducks are kept on a plot of land, the soil may eventually become...(4)... as a result of compaction. For this reason, it is advised that limits the number of ducks per half hectare of land to 100.

答案及詳解:

先看題目的要求,主要有以下幾點:從原文中選詞,是部分段落摘要,但不知道是哪幾個段落,答案爲一個或兩個字。仔細讀摘要的第一句話,與原文第三段話的第一句相對應:Like all waterbirds,ducks need access to water, and duck keepers typically provide this by building a pond。各題的答案應從這裏開始找。

1. 對應原文第三段中:ducks need only to be able to dip their heads in the water to keep their nostrils clean。答案爲 nostrils。

2.3. 對應原文第三段中最後一句:it is important to keep ducklings away from it until they are old enough to withstand the cool temperature of the water-about eight weeks。第 2 題答案爲 eight weeks,第 3 題答案爲 cool temperature。

4. 對應原文第四段中:there is a risk of compacting the soil, which can lead to muddy conditions for long periods,答案爲 muddy。

三、True/False/Not Given（是非題）

1. 題型要求

題目是若干個陳述句（statement），要求根據原文所給的訊息,判斷每個陳述句是對（True）、錯（False），還是未提及（Not Given）。

這種題型的難度在於在對和錯之外還有第三種狀態:未提及。很多同學難以區分"錯"和"未提及"。

實際上,這種題型本身有一定的缺陷,即不嚴謹。有些題目很難自圓其說,比如6道題中,可能會有1-2題老師也解釋不清,在實際考試中,老師也可能將它們做錯。但大多數題目還是有規律可循的,同學們應認真閱讀下面老師講的方法和規律,爭取做對大多數的題目。

這種題型,A類考試每次考1-2組,共5-10題左右。G類考試一般考3組,20題左右,最多一次超過30題。所以G類考生更應重視此種題型。

2 解題步驟

STEP 1:定位,找出題目在原文中的出處。

1. 找出題目中的關鍵詞,最好先定位到原文中的一個段落。

將題目中的關鍵詞與原文各段落的小標題或每段話的第一句相對照。有些題目能先定位到原文中的一個段落,這必將大大加快解題時間,並提高準確率。但並不是每個題目都能先定位到原文中的一個段落的。

2. 從頭到尾快速閱讀該段落,根據題目中的其他關鍵詞,在原文中找出與題目相關的一句話或幾句話。

確定一個段落後,答案在該段落中的具體位置是未知的。所以,需要從頭到尾快速閱讀該段落,找出該段落中與題目相關的一句話或幾句話,通常是一句話。

3. 仔細閱讀這一句話或幾句話,根據第二步驟中的原則和規律,確定正確答案。

4. 要注意順序性,即題目的順序和原文的順序基本上要一致。

題目是有順序性的。第一題的答案應在文章的前部,第二題的答案應在第一題的答案之後。這個規律也有助於同學們確定答案的位置。

STEP 2:判斷,根據下列原則和規律,確定正確答案。

筆者儘可能將規律總結得詳細些,使同學們能夠對號入座,加快解題的速度和準確率。但請同學們不要太死記,要靈活運用。

1. True

第一種情況:題目是原文的同義表達。

通常用同義詞或同義結構。

例 1

原文:Few are more than five years old.

譯文:很少有超過五歲的。

題目:Most are less than five years old.

譯文:大多數都小於五歲。

解釋:題目與原文是同義結構,所以答案應為 True。

例 2

原文:Frogs are losing the ecological battle for survival, and biologists are at a loss to explain their demise.

譯文:青蛙失去了生存下來的生態競爭能力,生物學家不能解釋它們的死亡。

題目:Biologists are unable to explain why frogs are dying.

譯文:生物學家不能解釋為什麼青蛙死亡。

解釋:題目中的 are unable to 與原文中的 are at a loss to 是同義詞,題目中的 why frogs are dying 與原文中的 their demise 是同義詞,所以答案應為 True。

例 3

原文:Women could not take part and were forbidden, on pain of death, even to attend the Games.

譯文:婦女不能參加甚至被禁止出席這個運動會。

題目:The spectators, as well as the participants, of the ancient Olympics were male.

譯文:古代奧運會的觀眾和參加者都是男的。

解釋:題目中的 spectators 與原文中的 attend 是同義詞,題目中的 participants 與原文中的 take part 是同義詞,所以答案應為 True。

第二種情況:題目是根據原文中的幾句話推斷或歸納而成。

這種情況有一定的難度。需要根據原文中的幾句話做出推斷或歸納。不推斷不行,但有時有些同學會走入另一極端,即自行推理或過度推理。

例 1

原文:Compare our admission inclusive fares and see how much you save. Cheapest is not the best and value for money is guaranteed. If you compare our bargain Daybreak fares, beware —— most of our competitors do not offer an all inclusive fare.

譯文:比較我們包含的費用會看到你省了很多錢。最便宜的不是最好的。如果你比較我們的價格,會發現絕大多數的競爭對手不提供一大堆費用。

題目: Daybreak fares are more expensive than most of their competitors.

譯文: Daybreak 的費用比絕大多數的競爭對手都昂貴。

講解: 雖然文章沒有直接提到 Daybreak 的費用比絕大多數的競爭對手都昂貴。但從原文幾句話中可以推斷出 Daybreak 和絕大多數的競爭對手相比,收費更高,但服務的項目要更齊全。與題目的意思一致,所以答案應為 True。

例 2

原文: For example, it has been demonstrated that rapid response leads to a greater likelihood of arrest only if responses are in the order of 1 – 2 minutes after a call is received by the police. When response times increase to 3 – 4 minutes —— still quite a rapid response —— the likelihood of an arrest is substantially reduced.

譯文: 例如,只有反應時間在警察接到電話之後 1 – 2 分鐘,快速反應才會使抓住罪犯的可能性更大。當反應時間增加到 3 – 4 分鐘,仍然是非常快的反應,抓住罪犯的可能性就實質性地降低。

題目: A response delay of 1 – 2 minutes may have substantial influence on whether or not a suspected criminal is caught.

譯文: 1 – 2 分鐘的反應延遲會對罪犯是否被抓住產生實質性的影響。

解釋: 從原文的兩句話可以推斷出:1 – 2 分鐘,抓住罪犯的可能性很大,3 – 4 分鐘,可能性就實質性地降低。所以,1 – 2 分鐘的反應延遲會對罪犯是否被抓住產生實質性的影響,答案應為 True。

2. False

第一種情況:題目與原文直接相反。

通常用反義詞、not 加同義詞及反義結構。

例 1

原文: A species becomes extinct when the last individual dies.

譯文: 當最後一個個體死亡時,一個物種就滅亡了。

題目:A species is said to be extinct when only one individual exists.

譯文:當只有一個個體存活時,一個物種就被說是滅亡了。

解釋:可以看出題目與原文是反義結構。原文說一個物種死光方才叫滅絕,而題目說還有一個個體存活就叫滅絕,題目與原文直接相反,所以答案應為 False。

例 2

原文:It has been successfully used in the United States to provide input into resource exploitation decisions and assist wildlife managers and there is now enormous potential for using population viability to assist wildlife management in Australia's forests.

譯文:在美國它已經成功地用於支持資源開發和幫助野生生命研究管理者。現在,在使用它對澳洲的森林中的野生生物管理上有巨大的潛力。

題目:PVA has been used in Australia for many years.

譯文:PVA 已經在澳洲使用多年了。

解釋:原文說 PVA 在澳洲的研究中有巨大的潛力,即剛剛開始。題目說在澳洲已經使用多年,所以題目與原文是反義結構,答案應為 False。

例 3

原文:You may qualify for the Common Interest Group system, if you are one of at least ten adults who are traveling together.

譯文:如果你是至少 10 個一起旅行的成人中的一個,你可能會適合 Common Interest Group 模式。

題目:The Common Interest Group scheme does not apply if there are 11 adults in the group.

譯文:如果一個組裏有 11 個成人,Common Interest Group 模式就不適用。

解釋:可以看出,題目與原文直接相反,答案為 False。

第二種情況:原文是多個條件並列,題目是其中一個條件(出現 must 或 only)。

　　原文是兩個或多個情形(通常是兩種情形)都可以,常有 both...and、and、or、及 also 等詞。題目是"必須"或"只有"其中一個情況,常有 must 及 only 等詞。

例 1

原文: Booking in advance is strongly recommended as all Daybreak tours are subject to demand. Subject to availability, stand-by tickets can be purchased from the driver.

譯文:提前預定是強烈建議的,因爲所有的 Daybreak 旅行都是由需求決定的。如果還有票的話,可直接向司機購買。

題目: Tickets must be bought in advance from an authorized Daybreak agent.

譯文:票必須提前從一個認證的代理處購買。

解釋:原文是提前預定、直接向司機購買都可以,是多個條件的並列。題目是必須提前預定,是必須其中一個情況。所以答案應爲 False。

例 2

原文: Since the Winter Games began, 55 out of 56 gold medals in the men's Nordic skiing events have been won by competitors from Scandinavia or the former Soviet Union.

譯文:自從多季奧運開始,在男子越野滑雪項目中的 56 塊中的 55 塊金牌被來自北歐和前蘇聯的選手獲得。

題目: Only Scandinavians have won gold medals in the men's winter Olympics.

譯文:只有北歐人獲得了多季奧運男子越野滑雪項目中的金牌。

解釋:原文是北歐人和前蘇聯的選手獲得了金牌,而且是獲得了 56 塊中的 55 塊,還有 1 塊不知道被誰獲得。題目是只有北歐人獲得了金牌。所以答案應爲 False。

例 2

原文: Apart from the Second World War period the Winter Olympics were held every four years, a few months before the summer Olympics. But in 1986 the IOC changed the schedule so that the summer and winter games would be held in different years. Thus, for the only time in history, the Lillehammer (Norway) Games took place just two years after the previous Winter Olympics which were held in Alvertville, France.

譯文:除了第二次世界大戰期間,多季奧運每四年舉行一次,在夏季奧運之前的幾個月。但在 1986 年,國際奧委會改變了安排,使得多季奧運和夏季奧運能在不同的年份舉行。因此,歷史上第一次,在 Albertville 多季奧運之後兩年就舉行了 Lillehammer(挪威)運動會。

題目：One Winter Olympics has succeeded another every four years since 1924 with a break only for the Second World War.

譯文：自從 1924 年，冬季奧運每四年成功舉行一次，其中只有一次例外，是因為第二次世界大戰。

解釋：原文提到有兩次例外。一次是第二次世界大戰，一次是 1986 年國際奧委會做了一個改變。而題目說只有一次例外。所以答案應為 False。

第三種情況：原文為人們對於某樣事物的理論或感覺，題目則強調是客觀事實或已被證明。

　　原文強調是一種"理論"或"感覺"，常有 feel、consider 及 theory 等詞。題目強調是一種"事實"，常有 fact 及 prove 等詞。

例 1

原文：But generally winter sports were felt to be too specialized.

譯文：但一般來說，冬季運動被感覺是很專門化的。

題目：The Antwerp Games proved that winter sports were too specialized.

譯文：Antwerp 運動會證明冬季運動是很專門化的。

解釋：原文中有 feel，強調是"感覺"。題目中有 prove，強調是"事實"。所以答案應為 False。

例 2

原文：Another theory is that worldwide temperature increases are upsetting the breeding cycles of frogs.

譯文：另一種理論是世界性溫度的升高破壞了青蛙的生長循環。

題目：It is a fact that frogs' breeding cycles are upset by worldwide increases in temperature.

譯文：一個事實是青蛙的生長循環被世界性溫度的升高所破壞。

解釋：原文中有 theory，強調是"理論"。題目中有 fact，強調是"事實"。所以答案應為 False。

第四種情況：原文和題目中使用了表示不同範圍、頻率、可能性的詞。

原文中常用 many（很多）、sometimes（有時）及 unlikely（不太可能）等詞。題目中常用 all（全部）、usually（通常）、always（總是）及 impossible（完全不可能）等詞。

例 1

原文：Frogs are sometimes poisonous.

譯文：青蛙有時是有毒的。

題目：Frogs are usually poisonous.

譯文：青蛙通常是有毒的。

解釋：原文中有 sometimes，強調是"有時"。題目中有 usually，強調是"通常"。所以答案應爲 False。

例 2

原文：Without a qualification from a reputable school or university, it is unlikely to find a good job.

譯文：不是畢業於著名學校的人不太可能找到一個好的工作。

題目：It is impossible to get a good job without a qualification from a respected institution.

譯文：不是畢業於著名學校的人找到一個好的工作是完全不可能的。

解釋：原文中有 unlikely，強調是"不太可能"。題目中有 impossible ，強調是"完全不可能"。所以答案應爲 False。

第五種情況：原文中包含條件狀語，題目中去掉條件成分。

原文中包含條件副詞，如 if 、unless 或 if not，也可能是用介系詞片語表示條件副詞，如 in、with、but for 或 except for。題目中去掉了這些表示條件副詞的成分。這時，答案應爲 False。

例 1

原文：The Internet has often been criticized by the media as a hazardous tool in the hands of young computer users.

譯文：Internet 通常被媒體指責爲是年輕的電腦使用者手中的危險工具。

題目：The media has often criticized the Internet because it is dangerous.

譯文：媒體經常指責 Internet，因爲它是危險的。

解釋：原文中有表示條件副詞的介系詞片語 in the hands of young computer users，題目將其去掉了。所以答案應爲 False。

3. Not Given

第一種情況：題目中的某些內容在原文中沒有提及。

題目中的某些內容在原文中找不到依據。

第二種情況：題目中涉及的範圍小於原文涉及的範圍，也就是更具體。

原文涉及一個較大範圍的範疇，而題目是一個具體的概念。也就是說，題目中涉及的範圍比原文要小。

例 1

原文：Our computer club provides printer.

譯文：我們電腦俱樂部提供列表機。

題目：Our computer club provides color printer.

譯文：我們電腦俱樂部提供彩色列表機。

解釋：題目中涉及的概念"color printer"比原文中涉及的概念"printer"要小。換句話說，電腦俱樂部提供列表機，但是彩色的還是黑白的，不知道或都有可能，文章中沒有提供進一步的訊息。所以答案應爲 Not Given。

例 1

原文：Tourists in Cyprus come mainly from Europe.

譯文：到塞浦路斯旅遊的遊客主要來自歐洲。

題目：Tourists in Cyprus come mainly from the UK.

譯文:到塞浦路斯旅遊的遊客主要來自英國。

解釋:題目中涉及的概念"UK"比原文中涉及的概念"Europe"要小。原文只說到塞浦路斯旅遊的遊客主要來自歐洲,有可能主要來自英國,也可能主要來自歐洲的其他國家,文章中沒有提供進一步的訊息。所以答案應為 Not Given。

第三種情況:原文是某人的目標、目的、想法、願望、保證、發誓等,題目是事實。

原文中常用 aim(目的)、purpose(目的)、promise(保證)、swear(發誓)及 vow(發誓)等詞。題目中用實意動詞。

例 1

原文:He vowed he would never come back.

譯文:他發誓他將永不回來。

題目:He never came back.

譯文:他沒再回來。

解釋:原文中說他發誓將永不回來,但實際怎麼樣,不知道。也可能他違背了自己的誓言。所以答案應為 Not Given。

例 2

原文:His aim was to bring together, once every four years, athletes from all countries on the friendly fields of amateur sport.

譯文:他的目的是把各國的運動員每四年一次聚集到友好的業餘運動的賽場上。

題目:Only amateur athletes are allowed to compete in the modern Olympics.

譯文:只有業餘運動員被允許在現代奧運中競爭。

解釋:原文中用 aim 表示"目的",題目用實意動詞表示"事實"。把各國的運動員聚集到友好的業餘運動的賽場上,這只是創建者的目的,實際情況如何,文章中沒說,所以答案應為 Not Given。

第四種情況:題目中有比較級,原文中沒有比較。

例 1

原文:In Sydney, a vast array of ethnic and local restaurants can be found to suit all palates and pockets.

譯文:在雪梨,有各式各樣的餐館。

題目:There is now a greater variety of restaurants to choose from in Sydney than in the past.

譯文:在雪梨,現在有更多種類的餐館可供選擇。

解釋:原文中提到了雪梨有各式各樣的餐館,但並沒有與過去相比,所以答案應為 Not Given。

NOTICE

1. 一定要依據原文,不能憑藉自己的知識。

原文是判斷答案的唯一根據。所以,無論你對文章的內容或背景多麼的熟悉,或者你的知識是多麼的豐富,都不能憑藉自己的知識來確定答案。即使題目中說"地球是正方形的"。如果文章中沒說,你只能答 Not Given,不能答 False。

例 1

原文:His aim was to bring together, once every four years, athletes from all countries on the friendly fields of amateur sport.

譯文:他的目的是把各國的運動員每四年一次聚集到友好的業餘運動的賽場上。

題目:Only amateur athletes are allowed to compete in the modern Olympics.

譯文:只有業餘運動員被允許在現代奧運中競爭。

解釋:有的同學會認為,現在奧運中有很多職業運動員參賽,所以答 False。但很可惜,這是你自己的知識,文章中沒說,所以答案應為 Not Given。

2. 可以根據原文做適當的推斷,但不能做無根據的自行推理或過度推斷。

　　有些題目需要根據原文做適當的推斷,才能確定正確答案,但必須是根據原文來做推斷,不能做毫無根據的推理。而且一般來講,即使有推理,也只推一步,不要推得很深。有些閱讀程度較好的同學,如不掌握前面講的規律和方法,做這種題型反而錯得更多,主要原因就是想得太多,或推理得太多和太深。

3. 要注意題目要求答什麼。

　　同是是非題,有時題目要求考生答 True/False/Not Given,有時要求答 T/F/NG,有時又要求考生答 Yes/No/Not Given,必須按照要求去做,否則,本來判斷正確,因為不符合要求而失分,很可惜。避免答錯的一個方法是:在平常練習中就按照題目的要求去答,而不是隨心所欲。

4. 題目中若出現 must、only、all 及 always,答案一般不會是 True。

　　題目中出現這些字彙很常見,95% 的答案都不是 True。筆者只遇到過一次題目中出現了 must 而答案為 True 的情況。題目中出現上述這些字,答案是 False 還是 Not Given 就不一定,需要根據上面講的規律再做判斷,一般答案是 False 的比例更大一些。不看原文,下面幾個題目的答案都是 False。

i. Europeans learned **all** of what they knew of edible wild plants from Aborigines.

ii. Before the dry plate process short exposures could **only** be achieved with cameras held in the hand.

5. 答案選擇有一定的規律。

筆者經由實踐得出如下的規律:

A. 題目數目在 5 個(或 5 個)以上時,三種答案(True/False/Not Given)都要出現。題目數目在 5 個以下時,則不一定。

B. 可以連續三題答案都一樣,如都是 True,但還沒有過連續四題答案都一樣。連續三題答案都一樣的情況也不多見,筆者只遇到過兩次,一次都是 True,一次都是 Not Given。

6. 要相信自己的第一感覺,不要輕易改答案。

　　在考試中,除非有特別強的理由,否則不要輕易改答案,人的第一感覺往往是正確的。很多同學都將正確的答案改錯了。

7. 要注意上述規律和方法的運用,不要鑽牛角尖。

　　這種題型本身有一定的缺陷,即不嚴謹。所以,上述規律和方法若能理解是最好不過了,如不能理解,就記住它們,考試時,照着做就可以了,這些規律都經過實際的檢驗。

3. 例題講解

Questions 1 –9

Read the article on International Students House and look at the statements below. In boxes 1 –9 on your answer sheet write

TRUE　if the statement is true
FALSE　if the statement is false
NOT GIVEN　if the information is not given in the passage
The first one has been done for you as an example.

Example	*Answer*
1. *The club is for overseas students only.*	*FALSE*

2. The club has long-term dormitory accommodation.

3. Membership must be renewed monthly.

4. The club provides subsidised restaurant meals.

5. The club is open to non-members on Tuesday evenings.

6. STA Travel help finance the Students Adviser.

7. The services of the Students Adviser are free to all club members.

8. You must make an appointment to see the Students Adviser.
9. There will be a surcharge for accommodation over the Christmas period.

INTERNATIONAL STUDENTS HOUSE

International Students House is a unique club and accommodation centre for British and overseas students in London. It is located in the heart of London's West End and is close to all public transport facilities.

ACCOMMODATION

* comfortable accommodation for up to 450 people in single, twin, 3/4 bedded and multibedded rooms
* 44 self-contained flats for married students and families
* long and short stays welcomed

MEMBERSHIP

Club membership is open to all full-time students, professional trainees, student nurses and au pairs. Membership costs are kept to an absolute minimum to enable the widest possible access. You can join for as little as one month and for up to one year at a time. Membership entitles you to use the various facilities of the House. It has:
* restaurants
* student bars and coffee shop
* study rooms
* clubs and societies
* aerobics and fitness training
* discos, dance, jazz and cinema
* travel and excursions and much more!

The best way to check out all we have on offer is to drop in any Tuesday evening between 7.15 pm and 8.30 pm for Open House in the Club Room. This is an opportunity for you to meet the staff and other club members, enjoy a free cup of coffee and find out all about what's going on. You can take advantage of special membership offers. (Useful tip: bring along 3 passport size photographs if you wish to take out membership.)

ADVICE SERVICE

Thanks to the support of STA Travel and in association with LCOS (the London Conference on Overseas Students). International Students House now provides the service of an International Students Adviser. This new welfare service is open to all students at London's bona-fide academic institutions. It aims to provide welfare support to help students overcome any personal or practical difficulties they may be experiencing whilst studying in Britain. One of the key features of the Advice Service is that the Adviser can be seen during the evenings until about 8pm, Monday to Thursday.

CHRISTMAS & NEW YEAR

Unable to get home for Christmas? How about joining in the fun at International Students House! Check out our special programme of activity taking place over the Christmas period. Even come and stay —— the House will be offering reduced accommodation rates for students wishing to spend a few days in London over Christmas. We'll also have an exciting New Year's Eve party. So come and join us and ring in the new year in the spirit of internationalism.

答案及詳解：

2. 題目中的關鍵詞是 accomodation，快速閱讀原文小標題為 accomodation 的段落，其中有一句：long and short stays welcomed，是題目的同義表達，答案為 TRUE。請注意題目要求答大寫字母 TRUE/FALSE/NOT GIVEN，如果答 True/False/Not Given 很可能會算錯。

3. 題目中的關鍵詞是 membership，快速閱讀原文小標題為 membership 的段落，其中有一句：You can join for as little as one month and for up to one year at a time。原文是多項條件並列，題目出現 must，只是其中一個條件，答案為 FALSE。

4. 原文小標題為 membership 的段落中提到了有餐廳，但沒有說提供資助（subsidised）的飲食，答案為 NOT GIVEN。

5. 題目中的關鍵詞是 non-members，快速閱讀原文小標題為 membership 的段落，其中的句子：The best way to check out all we have on offer is to drop in any Tuesday evening between 7.15 pm and 8.30 pm for Open House in the Club Room. This is an opportunity for you to meet the staff and other club members, enjoy a free cup of coffee and find out all about what's going on，是題目的同義表達，答案為 TRUE。

6. 題目中的關鍵詞是 adviser，快速閱讀原文小標題為 advice service 的段落，其中的句子：

Thanks to the support of STA Travel and in association with LCOS (the London Conference on Overseas Students), International Students House now provides the service of an International Students Adviser, 是題目的同義表達, 答案爲 TRUE。

7. 題目中的關鍵詞是 adviser, 快速閱讀原文小標題爲 advice service 的段落, 段落中說這是一個 welfare service (福利性服務), 但這與 free (完全免費) 並不相同, 答案爲 NOT GIVEN。

8. 題目中的關鍵詞是 adviser, 快速閱讀原文小標題爲 advice service 的段落, 發現原文並沒有提及是否需要預約, 答案爲 NOT GIVEN。

9. 題目中的關鍵詞是 Christmas, 快速閱讀原文小標題爲 CHRISTMAS & NEW YEAR 的段落, 其中有一句: the House will be offering reduced accommodation rates for students wishing to spend a few days in London over Christmas。題目中的 surcharge (超收) 與原文中的 reduced (降價) 是反義詞, 答案爲 FALSE。

STUDYING IN SYDNEY, AUSTRALIA——AN OVERVIEW FOR INTERNATIONAL STUDENTS

Paragraph (i)

Australia has been a popular choice for thousands of international students over many years. Australia's universities and colleges have become increasingly recognised overseas for their exceptionally high standard. In addition, Asian is conveniently close to South-East Asia (Jakarta, the capital of Australia's closest Asian neighbour, Indonesia, is only 5506 kilometers from Sydney). Revised entry procedures for overseas students have made it possible for an increasing number to study in Australia. Sydney, the largest Australian city, is the principal port of call for international airlines with services operating to Australia.

Paragraph (ii)

Named after an ex-Governor of New South Wales, Sydney is the state's capital city. Located on the south-east of Australia in the temperate zone, it enjoys a mild climate, averaging 14.5 hours of sunshine pet day in summer and 10.25hours in winter. It is also the largest, oldest, and perhaps most beautifully situated city in Australia. First established by the British as a convict settlement in 1788, it is a modern cosmopolitan city that has developed into one of the nation's major industrial, business, and manufacturing centres.

Paragraph (iii)

Sydney is home to nearly 4. 4 million people (as of 1997). The suburbs reach out from the city centre and harbour some 55km to the north, 35km to the west and 30 km to the south, creating a metropolitan area of about 3000 square kilometres. The 57 square kilometer harbour is one of the largest in the world, and famous for the unmistakable 134 metre high arch of the Harbour Bridge and the graceful sails of the Opera House. It is a busy waterway with ferries, freighters, hydrofoils and pleasure craft.

Paragraph (iv)

Not far from the city centre are the attractive old residential suburbs of Balmain, Glebe, and Paddington, where many people live in smart terraced houses, Art galleries, pubs, and restaurants abound in the cosy streets that tend to be quite narrow, whereas the suburbs surrounding the city's colleges and universities consist mainly of family homes and multi-unit blocks —— an ideal situation for students looking for a homestay, or to rent. Sydney's newer suburbs now have a large multicultural population, and local shopping centres reflect the influences of many cultures.

Paragraph (v)

Sydney is home to the State Art Gallery of New South Wales, the state Conservatorium of Music, the Australian Opera, the Sydney Dance Company, and the Australian Ballet. The world-class Sydney symphony Orchestra offers superb classical music all year round. Local theatre is innovative and well supported, and large-scale overseas productions tour regularly.

Paragraph (vi)

As well as Scores of cinemas and theatres throughout the city and suburbs, there are numerous clubs which appeal to people of all ages, and cater for all tastes. Pubs are the venue for smaller modern bands, while the big-name popular music artists, both local and international, attract capacity audiences at the huge Entertainment Centre in the heart of the city.

Dining Out

In Sydney, a vast array of ethnic and local restaurants can be found to suit all palates and pockets. In summer, café patrons often sit outside at tables under umbrellas, and enjoy the passing parade of shoppers. Students who prefer to cook at home can choose from several large weekend markets, where fresh fruit, fish, and vegetables may be bought more cheaply than at the local supermarket. Sydney also has its own Chinatown.

Shopper's Delight

In the heart of the city are several big department stores linked by enclosed over-the-street crossings and underground walkways. Most noticeable are the towering Centrepoint complex and the Queen Victoria Building, both containing many shopping arcades, coffee shops and restaurants. Out of town, in the suburbs, there are huge regional shopping centres. At the weekend markets, bargains can be had when shopping for clothing as well as for a wide range of assorted goods.

Sporting Facilities

Australia is recognised as one of the most sports-conscious nations in the world. Sydney boasts an impressive number of facilities for all types of indoor and outdoor sporting activities. Wherever one goes, there are golf courses, cricket pitches, football ovals, tennis and squash courts, and, of course, indoor and outdoor swimming pools. Avid ice-skating and ten-pin bowling fans will find that these activities are also popular and inexpensive.

Conclusion

Whatever a student is interested in, it is certain to be available somewhere in Sydney. Outside the colleges and universities the scope for filling the leisure hours is enormous, while on campus the choice is equally varied.

Questions 1 – 7

You are advised to spend about 10 minutes on questions 1 – 7.

Refer to Reading Passage 1 headed "Studying in Sydney, Australia——An Overview for International Students", and look at the statements below. Write your answers in boxes 1 – 7 on your Answer sheet.

Write   T   if the statement is True

          F   if the statement is False

　　　　　　N　if the information is Not Given in the text

Q1. Sydney was first established as a settlement for convicted criminals.

Q2. Sydney Harbour is the largest in the world.

Q3. The streets of Paddington are not very wide and contain houses arranged in rows.

Q4. The Entertainment Centre is only for international popular music artists who attract large audiences.

Q5. There is now a greater variety of restaurants to choose from in Sydney than in the past.

Q6. Some department stores in Sydney are joined by walkways above and below the ground.

Q7. Australians are sports-minded people, but this is not realised by the rest of the world.

答案及詳解：

1. 題目中的關鍵詞是 was first，對應原文的第二段，其中有一句：First established by the British as a convict settlement in 1788，是題目的同義表達，答案爲 T。

2. 題目中的關鍵詞是 Harbour，對應原文的第三段，其中有一句：The 57 square kilometer harbour is one of the largest in the world。原文說雪梨港是世界最大的港口之一，題目講雪梨港是世界最大的港口。題目的範圍小於原文的範圍，答案爲 N。注意答此題不能憑藉自己的知識，事實上，世界最大的港口是荷蘭的鹿特丹，但文章當中沒說，所以不能答 F。

3. 題目中的關鍵詞是 Paddington，對應原文的第四段，其中有一句：Paddington, where many people live in smart terraced houses，Art galleries, pubs, and restaurants abound in the cosy streets that tend to be quite narrow。terraced 對應題目中的 arranged in rows，quite narrow 對應題目中的 not very wide，原文和題目是同義表達，答案爲 T。此題主要考 terraced 的意思，目前考試中，很少考對一個字的理解。

4. 題目中的關鍵詞是 entertainment，對應原文的第六段，其中有一句：the big-name popular music artists, both local and international, attract capacity audiences at the huge Entertainment Centre in the heart of the city。原文說 both local and international，題目說 only for international。原文是兩個條件並列，題目是 only 其中一個條件。答案爲 F。

5. 題目中的關鍵詞是 restaurants，快速閱讀原文小標題爲 Dining Out 的段落，原文中提到了雪梨有各式各樣的餐館，但並沒有與過去相比，答案爲 N。

6. 題目中的關鍵詞是 department stores，快速閱讀原文小標題爲 Shopper's Delight 的段落，該段落第一句爲：In the heart of the city are several big department stores linked by enclosed over-the-street crossings and underground walkways。linked by 對應題目中的 joined by，原文和題目是同義表達，答案爲 T。

7. 題目中的關鍵詞是 sports，快速閱讀原文小標題爲 Sporting Facilities 的段落，該段落第一句爲：Australia is recognised as one of the most sports-conscious nations in the world。原文說 recognised，題目說 not realised，是 not 加同義詞，答案爲 F。

✧ **四、Short Answer Questions（簡答題）** ✧

1. 題型要求

　　每個題目都是一個特殊疑問句，要求根據原文做出回答。

　　絕大部分的題目要求中有字數限制，一般有如下幾種表述方式：(1) NO MORE THAN TWO/THREE/FOUR WORDS（不超過 2/3/4 個字）；(2) ONE OR TWO WORDS（一個或兩個字），(3) Use a maximum of TWO words（最多兩個字）。有字數限制的，一定要嚴格按照題目要求去做。

　　少部分的題目要求中沒有字數限制，這時請注意，答案字數也不會很長，一般不會超過四個字。

　　總之，這種題型的答案都是單字或片語，很少是句子，所以又叫"短問答"。

　　考試中，A 類和 G 類一般都是每次必考，考一組，共三題左右。

2 解題步驟

1. 找出題目中的關鍵詞，最好先定位到原文中的一個段落。

　　將題目中的關鍵詞與原文各段落的小標題或每段話的第一句相對照。有些題目能先定位到原文中的一個段落，這必將大大加快解題時間，並提高準確率。但並不是每個題目都能先定位到原文中的一個段落的。

　　題目中如果包含年代、人名、地名、數字，這些詞肯定是關鍵詞，因爲原文中不會對這些詞做改變，而且這些詞特別好找，所以依據這些詞在原文中確定答案比較快。

2. 從頭到尾快速閱讀該段落,根據題目中的其他關鍵詞,確定正確答案。

　　確定一個段落後,答案在該段落中的具體位置是未知的。所以,需要從頭到尾快速閱讀該段落,確定正確答案。

3. 答案要對應題目中的特殊疑問詞。

　　答案必須要對應題目中的特殊疑問詞。絕大部分的答案是名詞或名詞片語,也有少部分是動詞或形容詞片語。詳見下表:

特殊疑問詞	答案詞性(有可能是片語)	答案例子	注意事項
When	名詞(時間)	8:00am	不需要時間名詞前面的介系詞及冠詞,鐘點後面要有 am 或 pm。
Where	名詞(地點)	classroom	不需要地點名詞前面的介系詞及冠詞。
What	名詞	calcium deposit	
Who	名詞(人或單位)	Australian taxpayer	
How many	數詞	6	最好寫阿拉伯數字。
What proportion	數詞(比例)	20－30%	最好寫阿拉伯數字。
What is the cost	數詞(錢幣)	$ 25 million	
What do	動詞	evacuate the building	
What happen	短的句子	The licence may be cancelled.	
How	介系詞片語	by bike	

4. 要注意順序性,即題目的順序和原文的順序基本上要一致。

題目是有順序性的。第一題的答案應在文章的前部,第二題的答案應在第一題的答案之後。這個規律也有助於同學們確定答案的位置。

1. 所有的答案都不用大寫,專有名詞除外。

一句話的第一個字母需要大寫,我們的答案大部分都是單字或片語,都不是一句話,所以不用大寫。但答案中的專有名詞,如人名和地名需要大寫。例如:Australian taxpayer,不能答為:australian taxpayer。

2. 絕大部分的答案來自原文原詞,極少一部分需要自己寫答案。

大部分的答案來自原文原詞,而且是原文中連續的幾個詞。只有極少一部分需要自己寫答案。所以,在考試中,如果發現有很多都需要自己寫答案,應首先懷疑自己找錯答案的位置。需要自己寫答案的例子:

原文:if your iron produces droplets of water instead of giving off steam, your temperature control is set too low.

題目:What should you do if your iron starts to drip water?

答案及解釋:原文說:如果你的熨斗產生水滴而不是放出蒸氣,是因為你把溫度設定得過低。題目問:如果你的熨斗開始滴水,你應該做什麼? 答案應該是提高溫度的意思,但原文中並沒有相應的原詞,需要自己寫出來。最好的答案是根據 your temperature control is set too low 改為 set temperature high/higher。同樣正確的答案為:increase the temperature 或 turn up temperature。

3. 答案涉及數字的,最好寫阿拉伯數字,以免發生拼寫錯誤。

　　題目問 How many/How much/What proportion 時,答案一般是數詞,這時最好寫阿拉伯數字,這樣最保險,不用拼寫成英文。

4. 答案涉及數字的,一般要有簡單的四則運算。

　　題目問 How many/How much/What proportion/What is the cost 時,答案一般不會直接是原文中出現的數字,而要涉及到簡單的四則運算,通常是加減法。

原文:All major cities there have high car ownership, but well-developed bus and rail systems are available, and overall public transport typically accounts for between 20 and 30 percent of passenger-kilometres.

題目:What proportion of passenger kilometres is undertaken by private automobile in Western Europe?

答案及解釋:很多同學誤答 20−30% 。原文說:公共交通占 20−30% 。題目問:私人小汽車所占的比例。答案應為:70−80% 。

5. 答案涉及錢幣的,在數字前一定要有貨幣符號,在數字後可能會有單位。

原文:There may have been some consolation in the fact that the bid came in $1 million below the revised budget and $5 million below the original budget of $29 million formulated in mid-1991.

題目:What was the cost of the revised budget for the Sydney bid?

答案及解釋:根據注意事項 4,會有簡單的四則運算,此題應該是考過的題目中運算最複雜的。費用比修改後的預算少 1 million,比最初的預算少 5 million,最初的預算是 29 million,所以,修改後的預算(revised budget)應為 $25 million。注意,這三個詞一個也不能少,25、$25、25 million 都是錯誤的答案。

6. 找到答案後,要向後看一、兩句,看有無重大的改變。

原文中常用轉折詞修改前面說過的話或作補充。因此,對有些陷阱性題目,找到答案後,要向後看一、兩句,看有沒有轉折詞。一般只向後看一、兩句即可,不用看得太遠。

原文:You iron is designed to function using tap water. However, it will last longer if you use distilled water.

題目:What sort of water are you advised to use?

答案及解釋:題目問:建議你使用什麼樣的水? 有的同學從原文的第一句中得出答案:tap water(自來水),但原文中馬上就有一個轉折詞 However,正確答案為:distilled water(蒸餾水)。

7. 滿足字數限制的方法

大多數簡答題有字數的限制,找到答案後,如果答案超過了字數要求,就需要去掉一些詞。基本原則是:保留核心詞,去掉修飾詞。可依次去掉:

① 冠詞;a/an/the
② 副詞:副詞用來修飾動詞,保留動詞,去掉副詞。
③ 形容詞或分詞:常用來修飾名詞,保留名詞,去掉形容詞或分詞。
④ 如果有必要,將 A of B 改為 BA:這裏 A 和 B 都是名詞,如 type of fabric,可改為 fabric type,省掉一個字。

大家注意,在去掉多餘的字的時候,不要去得太厲害。在滿足字數要求的前提下,應盡可能多保留一些原文中的詞句。有時去得太厲害,會造成錯誤。例如正確答案為:Australian taxpayer,如果答成 taxpayer 是不對的。

原文: the amount of steam being given off depending upon the type of fabric being ironed.

題目:What factor makes you decide on the quantity of steam to use?

答案及解釋:如果沒有字數限制,可以答為:the type of fabric 或 the type of fabric being ironed。現在,字數限制為 NO MORE THAN THREE WORDS,答案應先去掉冠詞 the,再去掉分詞片語 being ironed,正確答案為 type of fabric。

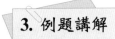

3. 例題講解

YOUR MOULEX IRON

A. Filling the reservoir

Your iron is designed to function using tap water. However, it will last longer if you use distilled water.

- Always unplug the iron before filling the reservoir.
- Always empty the reservoir after use.

B. Temperature and steam control

Your Moulex iron has two buttons which control the intensity of heat produced by the iron. You can, therefore, adjust the temperature of the iron and the amount of steam being given off depending upon the type of fabric being ironed.

- Turn the steam control to the desired intensity.
- Turn the thermostat control to the desired temperature.

Important: If your iron produces droplets of water instead of giving off steam, your temperature control is set too low.

C. Spray button

This button activates a jet of cold water which allows you to iron out any unintentional creases.

Press the button for one second.

D. Pressing button

This button activates a super shot of steam which momentarily gives you an additional 40g of steam, when needed.

Important: Do not use this more than five successive times.

E. Suits etc.

It is possible to use this iron in a vertical position so that you can remove creases from clothes on coathangers or from curtains. Turning the thermostat control and the steam button to maximum, hold the iron in a vertical position close to the fabric but without touching it. Hold down the pressing button for a maximum of one second. The steam produced is not always visible but is still able to remove creases.

Important: Hold the iron at a sufficient distance from silk and wool to avoid all risk of scorching. Do not attempt to remove creases from an item of clothing that is being worn, always use a coathanger.

F. Auto-clean

In order that your iron does not become furred up, Moulex have integrated an auto-clean system and we advise you to use it very regularly (1 −2 times per month).

- Turn the steam control to the off position.

- Fill the reservoir and turn the thermostat control to maximum.

- As soon as the indicator light goes out, unplug the iron and, holding it over the sink, turn the steam control to auto-clean. Any calcium deposits will be washed out by the steam. Continue the procedure until the reservoir is empty.

Questions 1 −4

Answer the following questions on the Moulex iron using NO MORE THAN THREE WORDS. Write your answers in boxes 1 −4 on your answer sheet.

1. What sort of water are you advised to use?

2. What factor makes you decide on the quantity of steam to use?

3. What should you do if your iron starts to drip water?

4. What could damage your iron if you do not clean it?

答案及詳解:

1. 題目中的關鍵詞是 water,對應原文 A 段,因爲 A 段的小標題爲 Filling the reservoir,reservoir 是水庫的意思,在這裏指熨斗的儲水箱。Reservoir 和 water 對應上了。根據 A 段中前兩句,答案爲 distilled water,只答 distilled 也對。

2. 題目中的關鍵詞是 steam,對應原文 B 段 Temperature and steam control,閱讀該段話,根據題目中的其他關鍵詞 decide on 、quantity ,找到 B 段中的句子:the amount of steam

being given off depending upon the type of fabric being ironed。decide on 對應 depending upon, quantity 對應 amount, 答案爲 type of fabric。

3. 題目中的關鍵詞是 drip water, 不太容易直接對應原文的一個段落, 根據順序性, 從第 2 題的答案位置向後找, 找到 B 段中的句子: if your iron produces droplets of water instead of giving off steam, your temperature control is set too low。原文中的 produces droplets of water 對應題目中的 drip water。答案爲 set temperature high/higher。也正確的答案 爲: increase the temperature 或 turn up temperature, 或其他表示升溫的答案。注意, 不能 答成 adjust/change the temperature, 因爲改變或調整溫度並不代表升溫, 也可能是降低 溫度。同樣不能答成 high/higher temperature, 因爲題目問 What should you do, 所以答 案的第一個字應是動詞。

4. 題目中的關鍵詞是 clean, 對應原文 F 段 Auto-clean, 閱讀該段話, 找到段落中的句子: Any calcium deposits will be washed out by the steam, 答案爲 any calcium deposits, 或 calcium deposits。

AUTOMOBILES VS. PUBLIC TRANSPORT

Public transport plays a central role in any efficient urban transport system in developing countries, where at least 16 cities are expected to have more than 12 million people each by the end of this decade, failing to give priority to public transport would be disastrous.

The term "public transport" covers many different types of vehicles, but most commonly refers to buses and trains. Rail services fall into four major categories: rapid rail(also called the underground, tube, metro, or subway), which operates on exclusive rights-of-way in tunnels or on elevated tracks; trams, which move with other traffic on regular streets; light rail, which is a quieter, more modern version of trams that can run either on exclusive rights-of-way or with other traffic; and suburban or regional trains, which connect a city with surrounding areas.

The recent trend in many cities is toward light rail over "heavy" rapid-rail systems. Whereas metros require exclusive rights-of-way, which often means building costly elevated or underground lines and stations, light rail can be built on regular city streets.

The concept of public transport also includes organised car pools, in which several people share the cost of riding together in the same private automobile. For U. S. commuters in areas with inadequate bus and train services, this is the only "public" transport option. But even where other systems are comprehensive, there is vast potential for car pooling; recent research shows that in cities the world over, private cars during commuting hours on average carry just 1. 2 - 1. 3 persons per vehicle.

Public transport modes vary in fuel use and emissions and in the space they require, but if carrying reasonable numbers of passengers, they all perform better than single-occupant private cars on each of these counts.

Although energy requirements vary according to the size and design of the vehicle and how many people are on board, buses and trains require far less fuel per passenger for each kilometre of travel. In the United States, for example, a light-rail vehicle needs an estimated 640 BTUs* of energy per passenger per kilometre; a city bus would use some 690 BTUs* per passenger-kilometre; and a car pool with four occupants 1,140 BTUs*. A single-occupant automobile, by contrast, burns nearly 4,580 BTUs per passenger-kilometre.

The pollution savings from public transport are even more dramatic. Since both rapid and light rail have electric engines, pollution is measured not from the motor exhaust, but from the power plant generating electricity, which is usually located outside the city, where air quality problems are less serious. For typical U. S. commuter routes, rapid rail emits 30 grams of nitrogen oxides for every 100 kilometres each rail passenger travels, compared with 43 grams for light rail, 95 grams for transit buses, and 128 grams for single-occupant automobiles. Public transport's potential for reducing hydrocarbon and carbon monoxide emissions is even greater.

Although diesel buses-especially in developing countries-can be heavy polluters, existing technologies, such as filters, can control their exhaust. Buses can also run on less polluting fuels such as propane(used in parts of Europe)and natural gas(used in Brazil and China). Test buses in the Netherlands that run on natural gas are estimated to emit 90 percent less nitrogen oxide and 25 percent less carbon monoxide than diesel engines do.

In addition to reducing fuel consumption and pollution, public transport saves valuable city space. Buses and trains carry more people in each vehicle and, if they operate on their own rights-of-way, can safely run at much higher speeds. In other words, they not only take up less space but also occupy it for a shorter time. Thus, comparing ideal conditions for each mode in one lane of traffic, an underground metro can carry 70,000 passengers past a certain point in one hour, light rail can carry up to 35,000 people, and a bus, just over 30,000. By contrast, a lane of private cars with four occupants each can move only about 8,000 people an hour, and without such car-pooling the figure is, of course, far lower.

The availability and use of public transport vary widely in cities around the globe. Since variations in distances and city densities affect the total kilometres of travel, the annual number of trips each person takes by public transport provides a better standard for comparing its importance in various cities. The range of frequency of public transport use is shown in Table 1.

Urban public transport has long been a government priority in Western Europe. All major cities there have high car ownership, but well-developed bus and rail systems are available, and overall public transport typically accounts for between 20 and 30 percent of passenger-kilometres. In recent years, several large cities have stepped up their commitment to public transportation, combining further investments with complementary policies to restrict auto use.

Public transport also plays an important role in urban areas of the Third World. In many cities in Asia, Latin America, and Africa, buses make 50-80 percent of all motorised trips. Buses are sometimes hopelessly overcrowded; it is not uncommon to see several riders clinging to the outside. Yet most Third World cities have lower public transport use per person than those in Western Europe, reflecting the inability of small bus fleets to keep up with population growth.

Among the world's major cities, those in Australia and the United States make the least use of alternatives to the private car. Indeed, less than 5 percent of U. S. trips are by public transport, but in some cities such as New York City and Chicago, where service is provided extensively, it is used heavily. Indeed, nearly one quarter of the entire country's public transport trips are in New York City.

＊BTUs：British Thermal Units（Treasure of energy consumed）

Table 1. Dependence on Public Transport in Selected Cities，1989

City	Population	Mode	Trips ＊
Tokyo	11.6m	bus，tram，metro，rail	650
Buenos Aires	9.0m	bus，metro	248
Beijing	8.7m	bus，metro	107
Seoul	8.7m	bus，metro	457
Moscow	8.0m	bus，tram，metro	713
Chicago	6.8m	bus，metro，rail	101
Berlin	3.1m	bus，tram，metro，rail	356
Toronto	2.8m	bus，tram，metro	200
Melbourne	2.7m	bus，tram，rail	95
Abidjan	1.8m	bus，boat	132
Dallas	1.4m	bus	22

＊trips：per person per year

Questions 1 – 5

Answer the following questions using *NO MORE THAN THREE WORDS* and according to the information in Reading Passage headed "Automobiles vs. Public Transport". Write your answers in boxes 1 – 5 on your answer sheet.

1. What is one factor that makes light rail preferable to rapid rail?

2. What is one way in which rapid rail outperforms light rail?

3. Where is pollution from rail transport measured?

4. What is the average number of people you would expect to find in automobiles during commuting hours?

5. What proportion of passenger kilometres is undertaken by private automobile in Western Europe?

答案及詳解:

1. 題目中的關鍵詞是 light rail preferable to rapid rail,對應原文第三段的第一句:The recent trend in many cities is toward light rail over "heavy" rapid-rail systems。第三段共兩句話,但不好確定答案。文中說,metros(即 "heavy" rapid-rail)要求建造花費很高的(costly)地上或地下的線路和車站,而 light rail 則不需要,所以,答案為 less costly。

2. 題目問 rapid-rail 超過 light rail 的方面。可從原文第七段得出答案 less pollution,也可從第九段得出答案 carrying more passengers 或 more passengers。

3. 題目中的關鍵詞是 "pollution",對應原文第七段的第一句:The pollution savings from public transport are even more dramatic。該段第二句中有 pollution is measured not from the motor exhaust, but from the power plant generating electricity,意思是:污染不是從廢氣中測量,而是從產生電力的發電廠測量。答案應為 power plant。

4. 題目問:在上下班時間(commuting hours),小汽車中人的平均數目。應對應到原文的第四段,答案在該段的最後一句,1.2 – 1.3。

5. 題目中的關鍵詞是 "Western Europe",對應原文倒數第三段的第一句:Urban public transport has long been a government priority in Western Europe,閱讀該段話,找到段落中的句子:overall public transport typically accounts for between 20 and 30 percent of passenger-kilometres,注意原文說的是公共交通占 20 – 30%,題目問的是私人小汽車所占的比例。答案為 70 –80%。

SYDNEY 2000 OLYMPICS

The cost of staging the year 2000 Olympics in Sydney is estimated to be a staggering $960 million, but the city is preparing to reap the financial benefits that ensue from holding such an international event by emulating the commercial success of Los Angeles, the only city yet to have made a demonstrable profit from the Games in 1984.

At precisely 4.20 am on Friday the 24th of September 1993, it was announced that Sydney had beaten five other competing cities around the world, and Australians everywhere. Not only Sydneysiders, were justifiably proud of the result. But, if Sydney had lost the bid, would the taxpayers of NSW and of Australia have approved of governments spending millions of dollars in a failed and costly exercise?

There may have been some consolation in the fact that the bid came in $1 million below the revised budget and $5 million below the original budget of $29 million formulated in mid-1991. However, the final cost was the considerable sum of $24 million, the bulk of which was paid for by corporate and community contributions, merchandising, licensing, and the proceeds of lotteries, with the NSW Government, which had originally been willing to spend up to $10 million, contributing some $2million. The Federal Government's grant of $5 million meant, in effect, that the Sydney bid was financed by every Australian taxpayer.

Prior to the announcement of the winning city, there was considerable debate about the wisdom of taking financial risks of this kind at a time of economic recession. Others argued that 70 per cent of the facilities were already in place, and all were on government-owned land, removing some potential areas of conflict which troubled previous Olympic bidders. The former NSW Premier, Mr. Nick Greiner, went on record as saying that the advantage of having the Games..... "is not that you are going to have $7.4 billion in extra gross domestic product over the next 14 years ... I think the real point of the Games is the psychological change, the catalyst of confidence ... apart from the other more obvious reasons, such as the building of sporting facilities, tourism, and things of that nature."

However, the dubiousness of the benefits that Melbourne, an unsuccessful bidder for the 1988 Olympic Games, received at a time when the State of Victoria was still in economic turmoil meant many corporate bodies were unenthusiastic.

There is no doubt that Sydney's seductive physical charms caused the world's media to compare the city favourably to its rivals Beijing, Berlin, Manchester, and Istanbul, Mr. Godfrey Santer, the Australian Tourist Commission's Manager of Corporate Planning Services, stated that soon after the bid was made, intense media focus was already having a beneficial effect on in-bound tourism.

Developers and those responsible for community development projects eagerly pointed to the improvements taking place to the existing infrastructure of the city, the creation of employment, and especially the building of sporting facilities, all of which meet the needs of the community and help to attract more tourists. At Homebush Bay $300 million was spent providing the twin athletic arenas and the "high-tech" Aquatic Centre.

However, perhaps the most impressive legacy was the new attitude shown towards both industrial relations and environmental problems. The high-profile nature of the bid, and the perception that it must proceed smoothly created a unique attitude of co-operation between the workforce and employers involved in the construction of the Olympic Village at Homebush Bay. The improvements included the lack of strikes, the breaking down of demarkation barriers, and the completion of projects within budget and ahead of time.

The Secretary of the NSW Labour Council, Mr. Michael Easson, was quoted as saying, . . . "what we've achieved should become the model for the rest of the building industry. . . great co-operation, good management, improvement in relations between employers and employees, and a feeling of optimism. . . "

The lasting benefits will be first-rate sporting facilities at Homebush Bay and an industrial relations model which should impact on the rest of the building industry.

Improved negotiations and co-operation over the bid between the Greenpeace environmental group and the State Government also saw a new respect develop on both sides, Suddenly, environmentalists were no longer regarded as being radically opposed to all development, and neither was the State Government perceived as inconsiderate towards environmental concerns.

The success of Sydney's bid laid to rest much of the opposition to the gamble, Nonetheless, most economists agree that it would be wise when considering future risks of this kind to bear well in mind the financial consequences of failure.

Questions 1 –6

You are advised to spend about 10 minutes on questions 1 –6.
Refer to Reading passage headed "Sydney 2000 Olympics", and answer the following questions. Write your answers in boxes 1 –6 on your Answer Sheet. The first one has been done

as an example.

Example	Answer
Which city profited from holding the Olympic Games in 1984?	Los Angeles

Q1. How many cities were competing in 1993 for the right to hold the 2000 Games?

Q2. What was the cost of the revised budget for the Sydney bid?

Q3. As a result of the Federal Government's $5 million grant, who also contributed towards the bid?

Q4. What phrase of three words in the text describes the State of Victoria when Melbourne bid for the Games?

Q5. What is the name given to the collection of buildings constructed for the 2000 Olympic Games at Homebush Bay?

Q6. How many achievements does the Secretary of the NSW Labour Council mention in his industrial relations model?

答案及詳解：

1. 題目中有年代，所以關鍵詞肯定是 in 1993，根據它找到原文第二段的第一句：At precisely 4.20 am on Friday the 24th of September 1993, it was announced that Sydney had beaten five other competing cities around the world，雪梨戰勝其他 5 個城市，根據簡單加法運算，答案應爲 6。這是最好的答案。同樣正確的答案可以是 6 cities/six/ six cities。

2. 題目中的關鍵詞是 revised budget 和 Sydney bid。對應原文第三段的第一句：the bid came in $1 million below the revised budget and $5 million below the original budget of $29 million。經過簡單四則運算，答案爲 $25 million。

3. 題目中有專有名詞和數字，所以關鍵詞是 Federal Government's $5 million grant，對應原文第三段的最後一句：The Federal Government's grant of $5 million meant, in effect, that the Sydney bid was financed by every Australian taxpayer。答案應爲 every Australian taxpayer 或 Australian taxpayer。

4. 題目中有專有名詞，所以關鍵詞是 the State of Victoria 和 Melbourne，對應第五段，答案爲 in economic turmoil。

5. 此題容易答錯。題目中的關鍵詞是 Homebush Bay，有的同學在第七段段尾找到答案 the twin athletic arenas and the "high-tech" Aquatic Centre。爲什麼不對呢？答案太長。我們說過，這種題目即使沒有限制，答案也不會很長，一般不超過 3 個字。所以，應首先懷疑自己找錯答案位置。正確答案應在第八段，原文中的句子爲 The high-profile na-

ture of the bid，and the perception that it must proceed smoothly created a unique attitude of co-operation between the workforce and employers involved in the construction of the Olympic Village at Homebush Bay。不僅有 Homebush Bay，而且文中的 construction 與題目中的 constructed 也對應得很好。答案為 the Olympic Village 或 Olympic Village。

6. 對應原文倒數第四段，答案為 4 或 four。

❖ 四、Multiple choice（選擇題）❖

1. 題型要求

　　這是一個傳統題型，大家都很熟悉。但就是這種大家都熟悉的題型，IELTS 考試也要弄出新花樣。其他考試中，如 TOEFL，只有單選題一種形式。IELTS 考試的選擇題分為單選題和複選題兩種。

　　單選題，選項肯定是四個。即要求從 A、B、C、D 四項中選擇一個最符合題意的選項。複選題，選項肯定是五個或五個以上，而正確答案的數目肯定在兩個以上。

　　哪個較難呢？很多同學會毫不猶豫地說是複選題。實際上，複選題很容易，是一種簡單題型。它具有以下幾個特點：

（1）正確答案的數目是已知的。在題目的要求中會告訴你要選出幾個選項。題目要求中常有 WHICH FOUR，WHICH THREE 等字樣。

（2）答案在原文中是集中出現的，對應原文中的列舉。找到一個答案，其餘幾個就在它的前後不遠處。

　　我們舉一個中文閱讀的例子來說明。文章如下：

　　帕金森症是一種頑症。它是由大腦中缺乏一種叫多巴胺的化學物質引起的。（以下刪減 100 字）。

　　很多名人深受其苦。比如，美國總統雷根、拳王阿里、音樂家李泰祥等等。（以下刪減 100 字）。

題目是:以下哪三個人得過帕金森症?

　　A. 雷根

　　B. 布希

　　C. 拳王阿里

　　D. 楊凡

　　E. 李泰祥

　　答案為:ACE

單選題在考試中,一般比較難。它的特點是:四個選項都很像。好像在原文中都提到了,但又都和原文的敘述不太一樣。很容易選錯。

選擇題和問答題的區別在於:問答題要求你自己從原文中找答案。而選擇題給你四個選項讓你選擇,在給你提示的同時,也給了你一個陷阱。有些選擇題如果改為問答題,你可能會答對,但給了你四個選項,反而選錯了。

考試中,單選題 A 類和 G 類一般都是每次必考,考一組,共 3 題左右。複選題不是每次必考。

2 解題步驟

1. 找出題目中的關鍵詞,最好先定位到原文中的一個段落。

將題目中的關鍵詞與原文各段落的小標題或每段話的第一句相對照。有些題目能先定位到原文中的一個段落,這必將大大減少解題時間,並提高準確率。但並不是每個題目都能先定位到原文中的一個段落的。

如果題目中的關鍵詞難以確定答案的位置,選項中的關鍵詞也可以作為定位的參考依據。

2. 從頭到尾快速閱讀該段落,根據題目中的其他關鍵詞及選項確定正確答案。正確選項常常是原文相關詞句的改寫。

確定一個段落後,答案在該段落中的具體位置是未知的。所以,需要從頭到尾快速閱讀該段落,確定正確答案。

短問答的答案常常是原文原詞,而選擇題的答案常常是原文相關詞句的改寫。

3. 有些題目比較簡單,可以直接選擇。對於難題,可以用刪除法確定正確答案。

有些題目比較簡單,可以從原文很快找到對應答案。這時可以直接選擇,不必看其他選項。這樣既可以節省時間,同時也避免受干擾選項的誤導。

有些題目比較難,看每個選項都有點像,但又都不太像。這時,可以用刪除法,先刪除掉肯定不對的選項,然後在剩下的選項中再做出選擇。通常,有兩個選項比較好刪除,另外兩個有一定的難度。請參見本題型的注意事項部分,其中分析了干擾選項的特點。

4. 要注意順序性,即題目的順序和原文的順序基本上要一致。

題目是有順序性的。第一題的答案應在文章的前部,第二題的答案應在第一題的答案之後。這個規律也有助於同學們確定答案的位置。

NOTICE

1. 如果一個選項合乎題意,還要看其他選項中是否有 both... and、all of the above 的字樣。

我們舉個中文閱讀的例子:
原文:如果你隨便停車,要被罰款,還要把你的車拖走。
題目:如果你隨便停車,將:
    A. 被罰款
    B. 你的車被拖走
    C. 沒事
    D. both 被罰款 and 你的車被拖走
答案:D

　　如果選項中有一個是 all of the above，它是正確選項的可能性很大。both...
and 是正確選項的可能性比 all of the above 小一些。總之，如果一個選項合乎題意，
不要馬上選。看一眼其餘選項中是否有 both... and、all of the above 的字樣。

2. 注意題目中是否有 not、except 的字樣。

　　題目中有這些字時，通常是將它們大寫並使用黑體，特別醒目。如果不注意看，
必然答錯題。

　　如前面的關於帕金森症的中文閱讀文章，可能出一道單選的題目：

題目：下面的人得過帕金森症 EXCEPT

　　　A. 雷根

　　　B. 布希

　　　C. 拳王阿里

　　　D. 李泰祥

答案：B

3. 干擾選項的特點

　　做選擇題的過程就是與干擾選項搏鬥的過程。清楚干擾選項的特點，就能做到
百戰百勝。干擾選項的特徵如下：

a. 無：選項中所講的內容在原文中根本不存在，或找不到語言依據。要注意，答題
　　的唯一依據是原文，不能憑藉自己的知識或主觀想像。

b. 反：與原文相矛盾的選項。這時要注意題目或原文中是否有 NOT 、EXCEPT 等
　　詞，也要注意反義詞。

c. 滿：含有"絕對意義"的字彙如 must、always、all、will 的選項，一般為錯誤選項。選
　　項中含有"相對意義"的字彙如 can、may、sometimes、some、not always，一般為正
　　確答案。也就是說，越是模稜兩可、含糊籠統，越可能是正確答案，因為它適用的
　　範圍更廣。這條規律的適用性很強，實踐證明它的準確率在 90% 以上。

我們看幾個試題的例子，不給大家原文，直接做下面幾題選擇題：

1. Your air tickets
    A. will be sent to your departure point.
    B. must be collected before leaving.
    C. will be enclosed with other documents.
    D. may be held by your coach driver.

2. Experimentation with wild plants. . .
    A. depended largely on botanical observation
    B. was unavoidable for early settlers in all parts of Australia.
    C. led Aborigines to adopt Leptospermum as a food plant.
    D. sometimes had unfortunate results for Aborigines.

3. Wild plant used by Aborigines. . .
    A. was limited to dry regions.
    B. was restricted to seed
    C. sometimes required the use of tools
    D. was more prevalent in the southern part of Australia

根據上面所講的規律，三道題的答案分別是 D、D、C。

d. 偏：似是而非，與原句部分相似的選項。這是不太容易排除的。

e. 混：即張冠李戴。有時題目是主語，選項是謂語，要留心題目的主語和選項的謂語構成的主謂結構是否張冠李戴。這種干擾選項規律也比較明顯，常常是這樣的：

原文：甲事物的特徵是 X。乙事物的特徵是 Y。

題目是甲事物，選項中肯定有特徵 Y，但肯定沒有特徵 X。為什麼呢？特徵 Y 就是讓你選的干擾選項，如果選項中有特徵 X，你肯定會選它，就不會選錯了。也就是出題者為了這個精心布置的陷阱成功，他會捨棄特徵 X，而在文章的其他地方談到甲事物的時候，出現一個正確答案。

例：

原文：Small parties are often based on one major current issue. Green party, which is a small party, is concerned with environmental issues.

題目：Small parties

其中選項 C：are concerned with environmental issues 就是一個很容易誤選的選項。注意,選項中肯定沒有 are often based on one major current issue。原因前面已經講過了。

4. 正確選項應是原文的改寫,與原文特別一致的選項應引起懷疑。

正確選項應是原文相關詞句的改寫,所以與原文特別一致的選項是正確選項的可能性不大。

3. 例題講解

CLASSIC TOURS —— COACH BREAK INFORMATION

Luggage

We ask you to keep luggage down to one medium-sized suitcase per person, but a small holdall can also be taken on board the coach.

Seat Allocation

Requests for particular seats can be made on most coach breaks when booking, but since allocations are made on a first come first served basis, early booking is advisable. When bookings are made with us you will be offered the best seats that are available on the coach at that time.

Travel Documents

When you have paid your deposit we will send to you all the necessary documents and labels, so that you receive them in good time before the coach break departure date. Certain documents, for example air or boat tickets, may have to be retained and your driver or courier will then issue them to you at the relevant point.

Special Diets

If you require a special diet you must inform us at the time of booking with a copy of the diet. This will be notified to the hotel or hotels on your coach break, but on certain coach breaks the hotels used are tourist class and whilst offering value for money within the price range, they may not have the full facilities to cope with special diets. Any extra costs incurred must be paid to the hotel by yourself before departure from the hotel.

Accommodation

Many of our coach breaks now include, within the price, accommodation with private facilites, and this will be indicated on the coach break page. Other coach breaks have a limited number of rooms with private facilities which, subject to availability, can be reserved and guaranteed at the time of booking-the supplementary charge shown in the price panel will be added to your account.

On any coach break there are only a limited number of single rooms. When a single room is available it may be subject to a supplementary charge and this be shown on the brochure page.

Entertainment

Some of our hotels arrange additional entertainment which could include music, dancing, film shows, etc. The nature and frequency of the entertainment presented is at the discretion of the hotel and therefore not guaranteed and could be withdrawn if there is a lack of demand or insufficient numbers in the hotel.

Questions 1 – 6

Choose the appropriate letters A-D and write them in boxes 1 – 6 on your answer sheet.

1. If you want to sit at the front of the coach
   A. ask when you get on the coach.
   B. arrive early on the departure date.
   C. book your seat well in advance.
   D. avoid travelling at peak times.

2. Your air tickets
   A. will be sent to your departure point.

B. must be collected before leaving.

C. will be enclosed with other documents.

D. may be held by your coach driver.

3. If you need a special diet you should

A. inform the hotel when you arrive.

B. pay extra with the booking.

C. tell the coach company.

D. book tourist class.

4. It may be necessary to pay extra for

A. a bathroom.

B. boat tickets.

C. additional luggage.

D. entertainment.

5. Entertainment is available

A. at all hotels.

B. if there is the demand.

C. upon request.

D. for an additional cost.

6. With every booking Classic Tours guarantee you will be able to

A. request high quality meals.

B. take hand luggage on the coach.

C. use your own personal bathroom.

D. see a film if you want to.

答案及詳解：

1. 題目中的關鍵詞是 sit，對應原文小標題為 Seat Allocation 的段落，該段的第一句為：
Requests for particular seats can be made on most coach breaks when booking，據此，答案
應為 C。

2. 題目中的關鍵詞是 air tickets，對應原文小標題為 Travel Documents 的段落，如果覺得對

應不明顯,可以先做第 3 題,再根據順序性確定此題的答案位置。該段的最後一句為：
air or boat tickets, may have to be retained and your driver or courier will then issue them
to you at the relevant point,意思是：飛機票或船票會被保留,司機會在相關地點把它們
交給你。據此,答案應為 D。實際上,選項 ABC 中都有說得很"滿"的詞 must 、will,所
以都不像正確選項。

3. 題目中的關鍵詞是 special diet,對應原文小標題為 Special Diets 的段落,該段的第一句
為：If you require a special diet you must inform us at the time of booking with a copy of
the diet,其中的 us 指的是這個 coach company。據此,答案應為 C。注意,有的同學會
根據該段話的最後一句：Any extra costs incurred must be paid to the hotel by yourself
before departure from the hotel 選擇 B：在預定時支付更多的錢。而原文的意思是：附加
的費用要由你自己在離開酒店前交給酒店。

4. 不好直接定位到原文的一個段落。可以先做第 5 題,再根據順序性確定此題答案在小
標題為 Accommodation 的段落,答案為 A,對應該段中反復提到的 private facilities。

5. 題目中的關鍵詞是 Entertainment,對應原文小標題為 Entertainment 的段落,選項 B 和 C
的區別很細微,選項 B 中的 demand 是指多數人的要求,選項 C 中的 request 是指個人
的請求,所以答案應為 B。此題對詞義的區別要求很細緻,不是目前 IELTS 考試的出
題方向。

6. 此題違背了順序性,答案在第一段,為 B。

NEW-AGE TRANSPORT

Computerised design, advanced materials and new technologies are being used to produce
machines of a type never seen before.

It looks as if it came straight from the set of Star Wars. It has four-wheel drive and rises
above rocky surfaces. It lowers and raises its nose when going up and down hills. And when
it comes to a river, it turns amphibious：two hydrojets power it along by blasting water under
its body. There is room for two passengers and a driver, who sit inside a glass bubble operating electronic, aircraft-type controls. A vehicle so daring on land and water needs windscreen wipers —— but it doesn't have any. Water molecules are disintegrated on the screen's
surface by ultrasonic sensors.

This unusual vehicle is the Racoon. It is an invention not of Hollywood but of Renault, a rather conservative French state-owned carmaker, better known for its family hatchbacks. Renault built the Racoon to explore new freedoms for designers and engineers created by advances in materials and manufacturing processes. Renault is thinking about startlingly different cars: other producers have radical new ideas for trains, boats and aeroplanes.

The first of the new freedoms is in design. Powerful computer-aided design (CAD) systems can replace with a click of a computer mouse hours of laborious work done on thousands of drawing boards. So new products, no matter how complicated, can be developed much faster. For the first time, Boeing will not have to build a giant replica of its new airliner, the 777, to make sure all the bits fit together. Its CAD system will take care of that.

But Renault is taking CAD further. It claims the Racoon is the world's first vehicle to be designed within the digitised world of virtual reality. Complex programs were used to simulate the vehicle and the terrain that it was expected to cross. This allowed a team led by Patrick Le Quement, Renault's industrial-design director, to "drive" it long before a prototype existed.

Renault is not alone in thinking that virtual reality will transform automotive design. In Detroit, Ford is also investigating its potential. Jack Telnac, the firm's head of design, would like designers in different parts of the world to work more closely together, linked by computers. They would do more than style cars. Virtual reality will allow engineers to peer inside the working parts of a vehicle. Designers will watch bearings move, oil flow, gears mesh and hydraulics pump. As these techniques catch on, even stranger vehicles are likely to come along.

Transforming these creations from virtual reality to actual reality will also become easier, especially with advances in materials. Firms that once bashed everything out of steel now find that new alloys of composite materials (which can be made from mixtures of plastic, resin, ceramics and metals, reinforced with fibres such as glass or carbon) are changing the rules of manufacturing. At the same time, old materials keep getting better, as their producers try to secure their place in the factory of the future. This competition is increasing the pace of development of all materials.

One company in this field is Scaled Composites. It was started in 1982 by Burt Rutan, an aviator who has devised many unusual aircraft. His company develops and tests prototypes that have ranged from business aircraft to air racers. It has also worked on composite sails for the America's Cup yacht race and on General Motors' Ultralite, a 100-miles-per-gallon experimental family car built from carbon fibre.

Again, the Racoon reflects this race between the old and the new. It uses conventional steel and what Renault describes as a new "high-limit elastic steel" in its chassis. This steel is 30% lighter than the usual kind. The Racoon also has parts made from composites. Renault plans to replace the petrol engine with a small gas turbine, which could be made from heat-resisting ceramics, and use it to run a generator that would provide power for electric motors at each wheel.

With composites, it is possible to build many different parts into a single component. Fiat, Italy's biggest car maker, has worked out that it could reduce the number of components needed in one of its car bodies from 150 to 16 by using a composite shell rather than one made of steel. Aircraft and cars may increasingly be assembled as if they were plastic kits.

Advances in engine technology also make cars lighter. The Ultralite, which Scaled Composites helped to design for General Motors, uses a two-stroke engine in a "power pod" at the rear of the vehicle. The engine has been developed from an East German design and weighs 40% less than a conventional engine but produces as much power. It is expected to run cleanly enough to qualify as an ultra-low emissions vehicle under California's tough new rules.

Questions 1 – 5

Choose the appropriate letters A-D for each question and write them in boxes 1 – 5 on your answer sheet.

1. How does the Racoon cross water?

    A. It swims.

    B. It raises its nose.

C. It uses hydrojets.

D. It uses its four-wheel drive.

2. What is Renault most famous for?

A. startlingly different cars

B. family cars

C. advances in design

D. boat and train design

3. Why will Boeing not need a replica of the 777?

A. It can use computers to check the design.

B. It already has enough experience with plans.

C. It will only need to upgrade the replica of the previous model.

D. It can make sure all the bits fit together.

4. How did Renault test drive the Racoon?

A. over rocky terrain

B. in actual reality

C. over French country roads

D. in virtual reality

5. Which of the following is NOT mentioned as an ingredient of a composite?

A. oil

B. resin

C. glass

D. steel

答案及詳解：

1. 題目中的關鍵詞是 Racoon，Racoon 在原文第二段的第一句第一次出現：This unusual vehicle is the Racoon，This 是代詞，代替前面出現的名詞，所以第一段描述的都是 Racoon 的特點。閱讀第一段，其中有一句：when it comes to a river, it turns amphibious：two hydrojets power it along by blasting water under its body。題目中的關鍵詞 cross water 和 comes to a river 對應，答案爲 two hydrojets power it along by blasting water under its body 的改寫，答案應爲 C。

2. 題目中的關鍵詞是 Renault，對應原文第二段中的一句：Renault, a rather conservative French state-owned carmaker, better known for its family hatchbacks, 題目中的關鍵詞 most famous for 和 better known for 對應，答案爲 family hatchbacks 的改寫，應爲 B。

3. 題目中的關鍵詞是 Boeing 及 777，對應原文第三段中的最後一句：Boeing will not have to build a giant replica of its new airliner, the 777, to make sure all the bits fit together. Its CAD system will take care of that。此題易誤選 D，原文中 to make sure all the bits fit together 實際上是表示目的的，而題目問的是原因。而且選項 D 與原文原詞特別一致，而正確選項一般是原文的改寫。正確答案應來自 Its CAD system will take care of that。CAD 解釋來自該段第二句，正確答案應爲 A。

4. 答案在第四段，正確答案應爲 D。

5. 答案在第六段，注意題目中有 NOT，B、C、D 在第六段中都提到了，正確答案爲 D。

LIVING EXPENSES —— A GUIDE FOR OVERSEAS STUDENTS

In the mid-1990s it is estimated that a student living alone requires on average A＄12,000 in living expenses for each year of study. Of course, these costs increase with time.

Upon arrival, students should have funds in excess of the average to cover the cost of text-books and establishment expenses such as rental bond payment and basic furniture items. The amount spent on food, recreation, and entertainment expenses will vary according to require-ments, budget, and location.

Those who are prepared to live in shared accommodation, which may not be suitable for all, might manage on A＄10,000 per year. It is preferable for overseas students whose English is in need of practice to take advantage of live-in situations with native-speakers whenever pos-sible. However, sharing with friends who are easy to communicate with is probably more sensible at first.

The above figures do not include the cost of large non-essential items such as household equipment or a car. Owning and maintaining a motor vehicle is expensive in Australia. In-surance is compulsory and costly, and parking both on and off campus can be a problem requiring additional expense. It is not advisable for a student to own a car unless it is absolutely necessary. A reasonable second-hand car can cost in excess of A $4000.

Educational institutions are almost always serviced by reliable public transport. The university and college campuses within the major cities are well served by public buses. In addition, the larger cities have extensive train systems. For example, in Sydney, most college and university campuses are only 10 or 20 minutes from a rail station.

The summer vacation requires special financial planning Expenses for this period must be carefully estimated and added to costs for the academic year in order to give a realistic total figure for the calendar year. They are not included in the estimated A $10,000 – A $12,000 previously quoted. University eating facilities, and some university and college housing facilities, close during this time. As a general rule, international students should expect to spend at least as much on monthly living expenses during the summer as they do during the academic year.

Under present immigration regulations, international students are allowed to work up to 20 hours during term time and full-time during vacation. It is impossible for students to expect to earn sufficient funds working part-time to pay for tuition fees and living costs. While some students are able to supplement their funds with money from part-time and / or vacation work, such work is not always regular even when available, and this can contribute to anxiety and study problems. In general, it is unrealistic to start a course with insufficient funds in the hope that "something will turn up". Students should be aware that vacation work has become more difficult to find over the last few years, but those interested can contact the Commonwealth Employment Service or the Students' Union on campus.

Warm clothes are necessary in the southern States during winter months, as night temperatures can drop to less than 10 degrees Celsius. Students should bring as much clothing from home as possible, especially if funds are limited. Information on where to buy inexpensive clothes can be obtained from the International Student Centre of most colleges and universities.

Do not rush into buying expensive textbooks. It is advisable to wait until your first lectures and tutorials, and then ask academic staff which are the essential purchases. There is usually a second-hand bookshop on campus, and used texts are also advertised on faculty notice boards.

The Students' Union coordinates a number of outlets on the various university campuses that provide stationery items and other essential study equipment at reasonable prices. Some courses require specialised equipment which can be quite costly, and it is wise to check any additional costs involved with the course of your choice.

In general, those practically orientated courses tend to incur higher additional costs. Expenses for books, stationery, and equipment vary greatly, but you should allow approximately $500 – $1000 a year.

Most university campuses have banks and/or credit unions. The banks issue drafts, traveller's cheques or foreign currency notes, and accept telex or airmail transactions. In some colleges and universities the credit union is the institution's own credit union. In addition to normal banking and financial services (with no transaction charges), credit unions usually provide special services for international students.

Money may be deposited or withdrawn from branches of the credit unions and banks during business hours from Monday to Friday (but not on public holidays) or 24 hours a day from the many on-campus automatic teller machines. Business hours for financial institutions vary, but credit unions are usually open from 9 am to 5 pm weekdays, and, generally, banks are open from 9.30 am to 4 pm (5 pm on Fridays). Some services are available on Saturday mornings in selected areas. While prices often compare favourably with prices overseas, because Australia is a large and exciting country it is very easy to overspend, especially if on a tight budget.

Questions 1 – 6

You are advised to spend about 10 minutes on Questions 1 – 6.
Refer to the Reading Passage headed "Living Expenses —— A Guide for Overseas Students", and decide which of the answers best completes the following sentences. Write your answers in boxes 1 – 6 on your Answer Sheet.

Q1. Sharing accommodation is：
    A. approximately ＄10,000 per year cheaper than living alone
    B. more expensive than living alone
    C. not always suitable for students
    D. suitable for most students

Q2. Students buying a car should take the following costs into account：
    A. the purchase price of the car
    B. insurance costs
    C. parking costs
    D. all of the above

Q3. During summer vacation：
    A. all institutional housing facilities close down
    B. additional living costs are involved
    C. university canteens remain open
    D. monthly living expenses decrease

Q4. Regular part-time work is：
    A. always available
    B. not always available
    C. sufficient to pay for tuition fees
    D. 20 hours during full-time vacation

Q5. Courses that are more practical：
    A. can require specialised equipment
    B. are usually cheaper
    C. cost ＄500- ＄1000 a year
    D. are usually more difficult

Q6. Credit unions on campus：
    A. are open 24 hours a day

B. provide the usual financial services offered by banks

C. deduct fees for normal transactions

D. are sometimes open on public holidays

答案及詳解：

1. 題目中的關鍵詞是 Sharing accommodation，對應原文第十二段的第一句。閱讀該段，與題目相關的句子是 may not be suitable for all（可能不是適合所有的人），有的同學可能會選 D（適合大多數的學生），正確答案應為 C（不總是適合學生），此選項中也含有不確定性的詞 not always。

2. 題目中的關鍵詞是 car，對應原文第四段的第一句。閱讀該段，發現 A、B、C 均提到了，所以正確答案應為 D。選項為 all of the above 一般都是正確選項。

3. 題目中的關鍵詞是 summer vacation，對應原文第六段的第一句。閱讀該段，正確答案應為 B，對應該段的最後一句。

4. 不好直接定位到某一段落，根據順序性，從第七段開始找 part-time work 或其同義詞，正確答案應為 B，此選項中也含有不確定性的詞 not always。

5. 是這幾題中最難的，很多同學誤選 C。根據是原文倒數第三段：In general, those practically orientated courses tend to incur higher additional costs. Expenses for books, stationery, and equipment vary greatly, but you should allow approximately $500-$1000 a year。此題是典型的張冠李戴，把前一句話的主語和後一句話的謂語拼湊到一起。原文說那些實用性的課程中，書本、文具和設備的費用大約是一年 500 到 1000 美元，並不是課程的費用。課程的費用是 expenses for courses 或 tuition。正確答案來自上面一段中的句子：Some courses require specialised equipment which can be quite costly，正確答案為 A。

6. 題目中的關鍵詞是 Credit unions，對應原文第十二段的第一句。閱讀該段，與題目相關的句子是 In addition to normal banking and financial services（with no transaction charges），credit unions usually provide special services for international students。直接從此句中對應到正確答案 B（提供銀行所能提供的通常的金融服務），正確選項中的 usual 和原文中的 normal 對應。這個選項與原文對應得很好，所以不必再看其他選項。A、C、D 都容易誤選，它們在原文中都部分提到了。A. 一天 24 小時開放的不是 Credit unions，而是 ATM。C. 交易費用不是減少（deduct），而是不需要（with no transaction charges）。D. 雖然有時在週六開放，但週六不算公眾假期（public holidays）。

六、Matching（從屬關係搭配題）

1. 題型要求

　　Matching（搭配題）是 IELTS 最常考的題型之一，每次考試至少有一組，很多時候達到兩組甚至更多，應該受到同學們的重視。

　　搭配題通常由三部分組成：題目要求、選項的集合、題目的集合。要求你根據某種關係將題目與選項配對。這種關係在題目要求中說明。

　　搭配題通常不具有順序性，也就是說，題目的順序和原文的順序是不一致的。所以做搭配題，讀過一遍原文一般是不可避免的。大多數同學會感覺這種題型不太難，但比較煩。如果有足夠的時間，肯定都能答對。

　　這種題型就是考大家的快速閱讀能力，即很快從文章中找到所需訊息的能力。大家在做搭配題的練習時，不僅要保證準確率，還要注意時間。一般每個題目 1－2 分鐘。例如一組 6 個題目的搭配題，應在 8－10 分鐘做完。

　　搭配題本身又分為三種類型：從屬關係搭配題、因果關係搭配題、作者及其觀點搭配題。不同類型的搭配題有不同的解題方法，所以我們分為三種題型分別介紹，希望這樣會更清楚。本節主要介紹從屬關係搭配題。

　　從屬關係搭配題是搭配題中最常考的類型。選項中的元素和題目中的元素是從屬的關係，要求根據原文，將每個題目與相應的選項搭配。請看下面中文閱讀的例子：

例

原文：介紹臺灣四個地區的情況。（略）
題目要求：將各地的著名小吃與相應的地區搭配。
選項：A. 宜蘭　B. 彰化　C. 臺南　D. 新竹

題目 : 1. 棺材板
　　　2. 肉圓
　　　3. 鴨賞
　　　4. 擔仔麵
答案 : 1. C　　2. B　　3. A　　4. C

　　考試中,A 類和 G 類一般都是每次必考,考兩組,共十題左右。有時也考一組或三組。

2 解題步驟

1. 仔細閱讀題目要求,搞清選項和題目之間的關係。

　　雖然都是從屬關係,但也有很大的不同。有的是汽車製造公司和它們的設計特點,有的是俱樂部和它們舉辦的活動等等。所以在答題前一定要仔細閱讀題目要求,搞清選項和題目之間的關係。

2. 先把題目從頭到尾看一遍,儘可能多記些關鍵詞。

　　做這種題,讀過一遍原文一般是不可避免的,但最好只讀一遍原文。能做到這點的前提是:在讀原文之前,先把題目從頭到尾看一遍,記住盡可能多的題目中的關鍵詞。這樣,在讀文章時,就知道要找什麼東西。例如,前面介紹的中文閱讀文章,在答題前應看一下 1－4 題,知道要找:棺材板、肉圓、鴨賞和擔仔麵。在讀文章時,就特別注意這些詞。這麼做的主要原因是因為這種題型沒有順序性,如果只看第 1 題:棺材板,就閱讀原文。棺材板的描述在原文任何位置都有可能,很有可能就在文章的結尾處。這樣,你讀完一遍文章,只做了第 1 題,做第 2 題時,你還需要從頭再閱讀原文,這樣很浪費時間。
　　這一步是做這種題型的關鍵,否則,就會造成反覆地讀原文,浪費時間。

3. 從頭到尾快速閱讀原文,遇到所記住的關鍵詞或其對應詞,當即解答該題。

　　從頭到尾依順序快速閱讀原文,在閱讀原文時,注意尋找所記住的題目中的關鍵詞,如果關鍵詞是專有名詞或者很生僻的詞,一般在原文中出現的就是該詞本身,否則會有同義詞或同義表述的對應。

　　選項常常是一些專有名詞,包含大寫字母。這時,在閱讀原文時,應特別注意包含大寫字母的地方,注意其前後的詞是否與所記住的關鍵詞相同或相對應。

　　在閱讀原文時,要特別注意原文中一些有特殊標記的詞,如反覆出現的詞、括號裏的詞、引號裏的詞、黑體字、斜體字,這些詞常常是題目中的關鍵詞或其改寫。

　　如果關鍵詞比較抽象,比如是專有名詞或者很生僻的詞,不好記憶,大家也不要害怕。這可能是件好事,在原文中出現的很可能就是該詞本身。所以即使記不住,在閱讀原文時,可以採用邊讀文章邊看選項的方法。

　　因為在讀原文之前,已把題目從頭到尾看了一遍,所以最好只讀一遍文章就能解決絕大部分的題目。比如一組 6 個題目,能解決 4－5 個。

4. 解答沒有匹配上的題目。

　　由於有的關鍵詞沒有記住,或者有的與原文沒有對應上。讀完一遍文章後,有的題目沒有找到答案。比如一組 6 個題目,1－2 個沒能找到。這已是很不錯的表現了。對於這 1－2 個題目,可以有如下的解決辦法:

a) 如果有印象在文章的某個部位,閱讀原文的該部分,確定答案。

b) 如果沒有一點感覺,但時間比較充裕,再快速讀一遍原文,尋找這幾道題的答案。

c) 如果沒有一點感覺,而且時間比較緊迫,可以選擇放棄。

NOTICE

1. 大多數情況下,每個題目只能選一個選項。

　　絕大部分的搭配題,每個題目只能選一個選項。筆者只遇到過一次,每個題目可以選多個選項。這時,題目要求中有如下的字樣:Note, for some questions you will need to write more than one letter.（注意，對一些問題你需要選多個選項）。如果題目沒有類似上述要求，應該是每個題目只能選一個選項。

2. 有些選項可能會用到兩次以上。

絕大部分的搭配題，有些選項可能會用到兩次以上。如前面舉的中文閱讀的例子，第 1 題和第 4 題的答案都是選項 C：臺南。在搭配題中，這是普遍存在的現象。

3. 有的選項可能用不上。

並不是所有的選項都會用上。如前面舉的中文閱讀的例子，雖然文章中也說了新竹的一些特點，但沒有出搭配題，所以選項 D 沒有被用上。在搭配題中，這也是普遍存在的現象。不要因為這樣而懷疑自己的答案。

4. 第一題的答案往往在文章的後部，最後一題的答案往往在文章的前部。

從屬關係的搭配題是沒有順序性的。而且，出題者為了顛倒黑白，混淆是非，讓考生產生障礙，往往將一個在文章的後部的訊息作為搭配題的第一題，在文章的前部的一個內容作為最後一題。這個規律的準確率在 80% 以上。

我們可以利用這個規律，在找第一題的答案時，着重在文章的後部。在找最後一題的答案時，着重在文章的前部。

5. 注意題目的答題要求。

要注意題目要求你在答案紙上寫什麼。如題目要求為：

Write the letters for the appropriate company in boxes 9 – 14 on your answer sheet.

SC   if it is Scaled Composites

R   if it is Renault

GM   if it is General Motors

F   if it is Fiat

B   if it is Boeing

那麼,你在答案紙上寫的答案只能是 SC、R、GM、F、B 中的一個。如果寫成 Scaled Composites 等就錯了。

3. 例題講解

NEW-AGE TRANSPORT

Computerised design, advanced materials and new technologies are being used to produce machines of a type never seen before.

It looks as if it came straight from the set of Star Wars. It has four-wheel drive and rises above rocky surfaces. It lowers and raises its nose when going up and down hills. And when it comes to a river, it turns amphibious: two hydrojets power it along by blasting water under its body. There is room for two passengers and a driver, who sit inside a glass bubble operating electronic, aircraft-type controls. A vehicle so daring on land and water needs windscreen wipers-but it doesn't have any. Water molecules are disintegrated on the screen's surface by ultrasonic sensors.

This unusual vehicle is the Racoon. It is an invention not of Hollywood but of Renault, a rather conservative French state-owned carmaker, better known for its family hatchbacks. Renault built the Racoon to explore new freedoms for designers and engineers created by advances in materials and manufacturing processes. Renault is thinking about startlingly different cars: other producers have radical new ideas for trains, boats and aeroplanes.

The first of the new freedoms is in design. Powerful computer-aided design (CAD) systems can replace with a click of a computer mouse hours of laborious work done on thousands of drawing boards. So new products, no matter how complicated, can be developed much faster. For the first time, Boeing will not have to build a giant replica of its new airliner, the 777, to make sure all the bits fit together. Its CAD system will take care of that.

But Renault is taking CAD further. It claims the Racoon is the world's first vehicle to be designed within the digitised world of virtual reality. Complex programs were used to simulate the vehicle and the terrain that it was expected to cross. This allowed a team led by Patrick Le Quement, Renault's industrial-design director, to "drive" it long before a prototype existed.

Renault is not alone in thinking that virtual reality will transform automotive design. In Detroit, Ford is also investigating its potential. Jack Telnac, the firm's head of design, would like designers in different parts of the world to work more closely together, linked by computers. They would do more than style cars. Virtual reality will allow engineers to peer inside the working parts of a vehicle. Designers will watch bearings move, oil flow, gears mesh and hydraulics pump. As these techniques catch on, even stranger vehicles are likely to come along.

Transforming these creations from virtual reality to actual reality will also become easier, especially with advances in materials. Firms that once bashed everything out of steel now find that new alloys of composite materials (which can be made from mixtures of plastic, resin, ceramics and metals, reinforced with fibres such as glass or carbon) are changing the rules of manufacturing. At the same time, old materials keep getting better, as their producers try to secure their place in the factory of the future. This competition is increasing the pace of development of all materials.

One company in this field is Scaled Composites. It was started in 1982 by Burt Rutan, an aviator who has devised many unusual aircraft. His company develops and tests prototypes that have ranged from business aircraft to air racers. It has also worked on composite sails for the America's Cup yacht race and on General Motors' Ultralite, a 100-miles-per-gallon experimental family car built from carbon fibre.

Again, the Racoon reflects this race between the old and the new. It uses conventional steel and what Renault describes as a new "high-limit elastic steel" in its chassis. This steel is 30% lighter than the usual kind. The Racoon also has parts made from composites. Renault plans to replace the petrol engine with a small gas turbine, which could be made from heat-resisting ceramics, and use it to run a generator that would provide power for electric motors at each wheel.

With composites, it is possible to build many different parts into a single component. Fiat, Italy's biggest car maker, has worked out that it could reduce the number of components needed in one of its car bodies from 150 to 16 by using a composite shell rather than one made of steel. Aircraft and cars may increasingly be assembled as if they were plastic kits.

Advances in engine technology also make cars lighter. The Ultralite, which Scaled Composites helped to design for General Motors, uses a two-stroke engine in a "power pod" at the rear of the vehicle. The engine has been developed from an East German design and weighs 40% less than a conventional engine but produces as much power. It is expected to run cleanly enough to qualify as an ultra-low emissions vehicle under California's tough new rules.

Questions 1 – 6

These five companies are mentioned in Reading Passage. Which company is each of the following design features associated with?
Write the letters for the appropriate company in boxes 1 – 6 on your answer sheet.
SC   if it is Scaled Composites
R   if it is Renault
GM   if it is General Motors
F   if it is Fiat
B   if it is Boeing

1. a power pod

2. electronic controls

3. a composite body

4. elastic steel

5. aircraft prototypes

6. ultrasonic sensors

答案及詳解：

　　先看題目的要求，選項是一些公司的名字，題目是一些設計特點。將題目從頭到尾看一遍，題目中的詞都比較專業，比較生僻。不用緊張，原文中出現的可能就是這些原詞,比較好找。另外,選項都是專有名詞,是大寫字母,在閱讀原文時,注意大寫字母。

1. GM,在最後一段,第一題的答案往往在文章的後部。注意,原文爲:Scaled Composites helped to design for General Motors, uses a two-stroke engine in a "power pod" at the rear of the vehicle, SC 幫助 GM 設計了 power pod,答案應爲 GM 而不是 SC。比如,原文說,高雄幫助臺南研製了棺材板。棺材板應該算是臺南的而不是高雄的。一般來講,在原文中離題目關鍵詞最近的選項是正確選項,GM 離 power pod 更近。

2. 答案爲 R,在第一段。

3. 答案爲 F,在倒數第二段。

4. 答案爲 R,在倒數第三段。

5. 答案爲 SC,在倒數第四段。

6. 答案爲 R,在第一段。最後一題的答案往往在文章的前部。

   選項 R 用了三次,選項 B 沒有用上,每個題目都只對應一個選項。

CLUBS FOR STUDENTS

There are a variety of Clubs which provide social and cultural activities for those wishing to meet others with similar interests from the same or from different national backgrounds.

A. Commonwealth Trust

Organised discussion meetings, learned talks, cultural events, excursions to places of interest and invitations to major British diary events. Open to overseas visitors and students.

B. Charles Peguy Centre

French youth centre providing advice, support and information to young Europeans aged between 18 – 30. Facilities include an information and advice service regarding education, work placement and general welfare rights. Moreover the centre holds a database of jobs, accommodation and au pair placements, specifically in London. Members may use a fax machine, a copier and computers for CVs.

Hours: Monday: 14.00 – 17.00

Tuesday-Friday: 10.00 – 17.00

Membership: £235 per year, plus £35 per month.

C. Kensington Committee of Friendship for Overseas Students

KCOF is the society for young people from all countries. Each month there are some 40 parties, discos, visits to theatres, concerts, walks and other gatherings where you will be able to meet lots of people. A new programme is sent each month directly to members (£5 to join in October, less later in the year). Events are free or at low, often reduced, prices. Office open 10.30 – 17.30 weekdays only.

D. Royal Overseas League

Open 365 days per year, this is a club with facilities in London and Edinburgh with restaurants, bars and accommodation. There are branches around the world and 57 reciprocal clubs world-wide. Quarterly magazine, literary lectures, annual music and art competitions, and summer and winter programme of events for members. Membership fees: overseas students aged 17 – 24 £47 per year finitial joining fee £235.50; others £70 per year-initial joining fee £35 (half price after July). Further information from the Membership Secretary.

E. YMCA London Central

Facilities include: photography, art, drama, pottery, language courses, badminton, squash exercise to music, circuit training, sports clinic, fitness testing and other activities.
Hours: weekdays 07.00 – 22.30, weekends 10.00 – 21.00. Membership fees: aged 16 – 17 £25 per year plus attendance charge of £1.30 per visit; aged 18 – 19 £213 per year; aged 20 – 25 £366 per year.

F. London Inter-Varsity Club (IVC)

IVC is an activities and social club with a varied range of events, from cycling and drama to windsurfing and yoga. Most members are young English professionals, but overseas visitors are welcome. The club arranges restaurant meals, dancing and parties, weekends away around Britain, plus a weekly club night in a Covent Garden bar. There are usually over 25 different events every week run by IVC members for IVC members. To find out more, telephone the club or write(Freepost) to the office.

G. Central Club

Provides accommodation and club facilities. No membership fee. Coffee shop open for all meals, swimming pool(open 06.00), multi-gym, hairdressing salon.

Questions 7 – 13

Look at the article "Clubs for Students". Which club would you contact for each of the requirements below? Write the appropriate letter A-G in boxes 7 – 13 on your answer sheet.

You may use each letter more than once.

The first one has been done for you as an example.

Example	Answer
You wish to go swimming at 7 am every morning.	*G*

7. You would like to take Spanish classes.

8. You want to join a club that has international branches.

9. You would like an opportunity to speak in public.

10. You would like to take part in amateur theatrical productions.

11. You want to visit some famous sites with a group of other students.

12. You are interested in finding out about part-time work.

13. You want to meet some English people who have started their careers.

答案及詳解:

先看題目的要求,實際上是俱樂部及其活動的搭配。注意,選項不是俱樂部的名稱,而是原文的段落。這在考試中也很常見,選項就是原文段落的集合。

把題目從頭到尾看一遍,記住盡可能多的關鍵詞。各題的關鍵詞分別是:7. Spanish; 8. has international branches; 9. speak in public; 10. theatrical productions; 11. visit some famous sites; 12. part-time work; 13. English people who have started their careers。

從頭到尾閱讀原文,通過先看題目發現題目都是關於一些活動內容的,與開放時間及費用沒有關係,而原文中有很多這些方面的內容,應略去不讀。

A 段中的 Organised discussion meetings, learned talks,與 9. speak in public 相對應,所以 9 題的答案為 A。

B 段中的 work placement 及 a database of jobs 與 12. part-time work 相對應,所以 12 題的答案為 B。

D 段中的 There are branches around the world 與 8. has international branches 相對應,所以 8 題的答案為 D。

E 段中的 drama 與 10. theatrical productions 相對應,所以 10 題的答案為 E。有的同學 10 題會誤選 C,C 段中有 visits to theatres,是參觀劇院的意思。10 題是要參與業餘戲劇演出,是不一樣的。

E 段中的 language courses 與 7. Spanish 相對應,所以 7 題的答案爲 E。

F 段中的 Most members are young English professionals 與 13. English people who have started their careers 相對應,所以 13 題的答案爲 F。

讀完全篇文章,7 個題找到 6 個,成績相當不錯。11 題比較難,它對應原文 A 段中的 excursions to places of interest (遠足到感興趣的地方),答案爲 A。

A、E 各用了兩次,C 沒有用上,每個題目都只對應一個選項。

WHY SOME WOMEN CROSS THE FINISH LINE AHEAD OF MEN —— RECRUITMENT

The course is tougher but women are staying the distance, reports **Andrew Crisp**.

A. Women who apply for jobs in middle or senior management have a higher success rate than men, according to an employment survey. But of course far fewer of them apply for these positions. The study, by recruitment consultants NB Selection, shows that while one in six men who appear on interview shortlists get jobs, the figure rises to one in four for women.

B. The study concentrated on applications for management positions in the $45,000 to $110,000 salary range and found that women are more successful than men in both the private and public sectors. Dr. Elisabeth Marx from London-based NB Selection described the findings as encouraging for women, in that they send a positive message to them to apply for interesting management positions. But she added, "We should not lose sight of the fact that significantly fewer women apply for senior positions in comparison with men."

C. Reasons for higher success rates among women are difficult to isolate. One explanation suggested is that if a woman candidate manages to get on a shortlist, then she has probably already proved herself to be an exceptional candidate. Dr. Marx said that when women apply for positions they tend to be better qualified than their male counterparts but are more selective and conservative in their job search. Women tend to research thoroughly before applying for positions or attending interviews. Men, on the other hand, seem to rely on their ability to sell themselves and to convince employers that any shortcomings they have will not prevent them from doing a good job.

D. Managerial and executive progress made by women is confirmed by the annual survey of boards of directors carried out by Korn/Ferry/Carre/Orban International. This year the survey shows a doubling of the number of women serving as non-executive directors compared with the previous year. However, progress remains painfully slow and there were still only 18 posts filled by women out of a total of 354 non-executive positions surveyed. Hilary Sears, a partner with Korn/Ferry, said, women have raised the level of grades we are employed in but we have still not broken through barriers to the top.

E. In Europe a recent feature of corporate life in the recession has been the de-layering of management structures. Sears said that this has halted progress for women in as much as de - layering has taken place either where women are working or in layers they aspire to. Sears also noted a positive trend from the recession, which has been the growing number of women who have started up on their own.

F. In business as a whole, there are a number of factors encouraging the prospect of greater e-quality in the workforce. Demographic trends suggest that the number of women going into employment is steadily increasing. In addition a far greater number of women are now passing through higher education, making them better qualified to move into management positions.

G. Organisations such as the European Women's Management Development Network provide a range of opportunities for women to enhance their skills and contacts. Through a series of both pan-European and national workshops and conferences the barriers to women in employment are being broken down. However, Ariane Berthoin Antal, director of the International Institute for Organisational Change of Archamps in France, said that there is only anecdotal evidence of changes in recruitment patterns. And she said , "It's still so hard for women to even get on to shortlists ,—— there are so many hurdles and barriers. " Antal agreed that there have been some positive signs but said "Until there is a belief among employers, until they value the difference, nothing will change. "

Questions 14 – 19

This passage has 7 paragraphs (A - G). State which paragraph discusses each of the points below. Write the appropriate Letter (A - G) in boxes 14 -19 on your answer sheet.

Example	*Answer*
The salary range studied in the NB Selection survey.	B

14. The drawbacks of current company restructuring patterns.

15. Associations that provide support for professional women.

16. The success rate of female job applicants for management positions.

17. Male and female approaches to job applications.

18. Reasons why more women are being employed in the business sector.

19. The improvement in female numbers on company management structures.

答案及詳解:

這是從屬關係搭配題常考的一種類型。選項就是原文的段落。題目是一些陳述句,要求與原文的段落搭配。也就是問,原文哪段話包含下列訊息。

把題目從頭到尾看一遍,記住盡可能多的關鍵詞。各題的關鍵詞分別是:

14. company, restructuring patterns

15. Associations, Support

16. female job applicants, management positions

17. approaches

18. business sector

19. numbers

從頭到尾閱讀原文,注意看每段話的第一句,因為每段話的第一句常常說出這段話的主要意思。

14. 對應 E 段的第一句,對應關係如下:

原　　　文	題　　　目
corporate life	company
Structures	restructuring patterns

答案為 E。

15. 對應 G 段的第一句,對應關係如下:

原　　　文	題　　　目
Organisations	Associations
a range of opportunities	Support

答案為 G。

16. 對應 A 段的第一句,對應關係如下:

原　　　文	題　　　目
Women who apply for jobs	female job applicants
middle or senior management	management positions

答案為 A。

17. 對應 C 段中的訊息,答案為 C。

18. 對應 F 段中的訊息,答案為 F。

19. 對應 D 段中的訊息,答案為 D。

注意,這種題型不同於 Headings。Headings 是找段落的主旨,適合從文章到選項的做法(請詳見本章第一部分)。而這種題型,題目中的訊息有的是段落的主旨,有的是段落的細節,所以應該採用先題目後文章的方法。即先把題目從頭到尾看一遍,記住儘可能多的關鍵詞,然後從頭到尾閱讀原文。讀文章時,既要注意每段話的主題句,又要快速閱讀每段的全部內容。

❖ 七、Matching(因果關係搭配題) ❖

1. 題型要求

　　和從屬關係搭配題一樣,因果關係搭配題也有一個選項的集合和一個題目的集合。題目是一些結果(effects)或問題(problems),選項是原因(causes)。所以這種題目實際上是找原因。

與從屬關係搭配題不同的是,這種題型有順序性,即題目的順序與原文的順序基本上一致。而且題目在原文中的出處常常集中於幾個連續的段落。所以一般這種題型比從屬關係搭配題要容易一些。

考試中,A 類和 G 類都不是每次必考。

2 解題步驟

1. 不必先把題目從頭到尾看一遍,而應該一道題一道題地做。

既然有順序性,就沒有必要先把題目從頭到尾看一遍,而是先從第一題做起,先找第一題的答案。找到後,再找第二題的答案,第二題的答案肯定在第一題的答案之後。

2. 先找出題目中的關鍵詞,再到原文中去找它的對應詞。

在做每題時,先找出題目中的關鍵詞,然後快速閱讀原文,尋找該關鍵詞的對應詞。

3. 仔細閱讀關鍵詞所在的句子,確定正確答案。

正確答案常常是原文詞句的改寫。因爲是因果關係搭配,在確定答案時,要對表示因果關係的詞特別敏感,搞清句子中描述的因果關係。

NOTICE

1. 答題時,要特別注意原文中表示因果關係的詞。

我們把考試中經常出現的表示因果關係的詞給大家總結一下:

a. 連接詞：because, since, as, for, therefore, so, thus, why；
b. 動詞：result in, result from, follow from, base...on..., be due to；
c. 名詞：basis, result, consequence, reason；
d. 介系詞：because of, thanks to；
e. 副詞：as a result, consequently

在閱讀原文尋找答案時，要特別注意上述表示因果關係的詞。同時，掌握這些詞，對大家寫作也有好處。

2. 要注意一因多果。

在因果關係搭配題中，有的選項也可能會用到兩次以上，即有兩個結果是同一個原因，我們稱之為一因多果。原文中的表述常常是這樣的：原因 A，結果 1；結果 2。在兩個結果之間沒有說出新的原因，這說明結果 1 和結果 2 的原因是一樣的，都是原因 A。

3. 例題講解

FINDING THE LOST FREEDOM

1. The private car is assumed to have widened our horizons and increased our mobility. When we consider our children's mobility, they can be driven to more places (and more distant places) than they could visit without access to a motor vehicle. However, allowing our cities to be dominated by cars has progressively eroded children's independent mobility. Children have lost much of their freedom to explore their own neighborhood or city without adult supervision. In recent surveys, when parents in some cities were asked about their own childhood experiences, the majority remembered having more, or far more, opportunities for going out on their own, compared with their own children today. They had more freedom to explore their own environment.

2. Children's independent access to their local streets may be important for their own personal, mental and psychological development. Allowing them to get to know their own neighborhood and community gives them a 'sense of place'. This depends on 'active exploration', which is not provided for when children are passengers in cars. (Such children may see more, but they learn less.) Not only is it important that children be able to get to local play areas by themselves, but walking and cycling journeys to school and to other destinations provide genuine play activities in themselves.

3. There are very significant time and money costs for parents associated with transporting their children to school, sport and to other locations. Research in the United Kingdom estimated that this cost, in 1990, was between 10 billion and 20 billion pounds.

4. The reduction in children's freedom may also contribute to a weakening of the sense of local community. As fewer children and adults use the streets as pedestrians, these streets become less sociable places. There is less opportunity for children and adults to have the spontaneous exchanges that help to engender a feeling of community. This in itself may exacerbate fears associated with assault and molestation of children, because there are fewer adults available who know their neighbors' children, and who can look out for their safety.

5. The extra traffic involved in transporting children results in increased traffic congestion, pollution and accident risk. As our roads become more dangerous, more parents drive their children to more places, thus contributing to increased levels of danger for the remaining pedestrians. Anyone who has experienced either the reduced volume of traffic jams near schools at the end of a school day, will not need convincing about these points. Thus, there are also important environmental implications of children's loss of freedom.

6. As individuals, parents strive to provide the best upbringing they can for their children. However, in doing so, (e. g. by driving their children to sport, school or recreation) parents may be contributing to a more dangerous environment for children generally. The idea that 'streets are for cars and back yards and playgrounds are for children' is a strongly held belief, and parents have little choice as individuals but to keep their children off the streets if they want to protect their safety.

7. In many parts of Dutch cities, and some traffic calmed precincts in Germany, residential streets are now places where cares must give way to pedestrians. In these areas, residents are accepting the view that the function of streets is not solely to provide mobility for cars. Streets may also be for social interaction, walking, cycling and playing. One of the most important aspects of these European cities, in terms of giving cities back to children, has been a range of 'traffic calming' initiatives, aimed at reducing the volume and speed of traffic. These initiatives have had complex interactive effects, leading to a sense that children have been able to 'recapture' their local neighborhood, and more importantly, that they have been able to do this in safety. Recent research has demonstrated that children in many German cities have significantly higher levels of freedom to travel to places in their own neighborhood or city than children in other cities in the world.

8. Modifying cities in order to enhance children's freedom will not only benefit children. Such cities will become more environmentally sustainable, as well as more sociable and more livable for all city residents. Perhaps it will be our concern for our children's welfare that convinces us that we need to challenge the dominance of the car in our cities.

Questions 1 – 4

In Paragraphs 4 and 5, there are FOUR problems stated. These problems, numbered as questions 1 – 4, are listed below. Each of these problems has a cause, listed A-G. Find the correct cause for each of the problems and write the corresponding letter A-G, in the spaces numbered 1 – 4 on the answer sheet. One has been done for you as an example. There are more causes than problems so you will not use all of them and you can use any cause more than once.

Problems	Causes
Example: Low sense of community feeling	*Answer* F

Q1. streets become less sociable ____

Q2. fewer chances for meeting friends ____

Q3. fears of danger for children ____

Q4. higher accident risk ____

A. few adults know local children

B. fewer people use the streets

C. increased pollution

D. streets are less friendly

E. less traffic in school holidays

F. reduced freedom for children

G. more children driven to school

答案及詳解:

　　題目的要求中告訴了答案來自原文的第四段和第五段,所以仔細看題目的要求很重要,有時它會告訴你很多有利的訊息。

1. 閱讀原文第四段,應該注意第一句就是一個表示因果關係的句子,其中有表示因果關係的動詞 contribute to,這一句是作爲本組題目的例子給出。該段的第二句:As fewer children and adults use the streets as pedestrians, these streets become less sociable places,其中 these streets become less sociable places 與題目中的 streets become less sociable 是對應的。仔細分析這句話,as 在這裏是表示原因的連接詞,答案應是 fewer children and adults use the streets as pedestrians 的改寫,所以爲 B。

2. 繼續向下閱讀,下一句 There is less opportunity for children and adults to have the spontaneous exchanges that help to engender a feeling of community 實際上與第 2 題就對應上了。less opportunity 即 fewer chances, have the spontaneous exchanges that help to engender a feeling of community 即 meeting friends。但在這句前沒有說出新的原因(沒有新的表示因果的詞句),所以是一因多果,答案爲 B。

3. 繼續向下閱讀,下一句 This in itself may exacerbate fear associated with assault and molestation of children, because there are fewer adults available who know their neighbors' children, and who can look out for their safety 與本題對應上。because 是表示原因的連接詞,答案應是 there are fewer adults available who know their neighbors' children 的改寫,所以爲 A。

4. 對應第五段的第一句 The extra traffic involved in transporting children results in increased traffic congestion, pollution and accident risk,注意 results in 表示導致,原因在前,結果在後。答案應是 The extra traffic involved in transporting children 的改寫,所以爲 G。

八、Mathing（作者及其觀點搭配題）

1. 題型要求

　　在原文中,就一個主題,若干人或組織提出了若干個觀點,題目要求將觀點與其提出者(作者)搭配。這種搭配題也有一個選項的集合和一個題目的集合。題目是觀點,選項是作者。

　　這種題型一般比較難,主要表現在:

（1）沒有順序性,即題目的順序與原文的順序是不一致的。

（2）文章題材多樣,有的比較偏。作者提出的觀點一般都比較抽象,不好理解。

（3）文章句式複雜。一般句子都比較長,有很多都是複合句、混合句、多重複合句,造成大家理解上的困難。

（4）題目中的觀點與原文中的對應觀點在句子形式上變化較大,造成對應困難。

　　與從屬關係搭配題一樣,作者及其觀點搭配題也沒有順序性。但不能用同樣的解題方法。

　　怎麼做從屬關係搭配題呢? 前面介紹的方法是:在閱讀文章前,先將題目從頭到尾看一遍,記住盡可能多的關鍵詞。

　　但不能用這種方法做作者及其觀點搭配題。主要是因為題目都是一些觀點,意思抽象,句式複雜。先將題目從頭到尾看一遍,不僅會花很多時間,而且很可能讀完題目之後,沒有什麼印象,也抓不住什麼關鍵詞。那麼應該怎麼做呢? 請看下面的解題步驟。

　　考試中,A 類一般考得比較多,考一組,共五題左右。G 類一般考得比較少。

2 解題步驟

1. 在原文中將作者及其觀點用線畫出。

作者都包含大寫字母，有的還有年代，表明是什麼時候提出來的觀點，所以一般都比較好找。他的觀點在他的名字之前或者之後。表述觀點一般有兩種方法：

a. 觀點在作者的名字之前；例如：

In terms of time, women perform approximately 90 per cent of child care tasks and 70 per cent of all family work, and only 14 per cent of fathers are highly participant in terms of time spent on family work (Russell 1983).

b. 觀點在作者的名字之後；例如：

Demo and Acock (1993), in a recent US study, also found that women continue to perform a constant and major proportion of household labour (68 per cent to 95 per cent) across all family types (first marriage, divorced, step-family or never married), regardless of whether they are employed or non-employed in paid work.

2. 看題目的第一個觀點，最好讀懂它的意思，或者找出其中幾個關鍵詞。

做這種題型，應該一道題一道題地做。先看題目的第一個觀點，最好能讀懂它的意思。否則，找出其中的幾個關鍵詞。

3. 將此觀點與原文畫線處一一對應。意思相同的或關鍵詞對應上的即為答案。

答案確定後，在原文觀點處寫上此題的題號。原文的每個觀點只能與一個題目相對應，所以將已經與某一題目對應的觀點做上標記，在做其他題目時，就不用再看這個觀點了。

4. 依此方法做其他題目。

NOTICE

1. 每個題目只能選一個選項。

　　每個題目只能和原文的一個觀點對應,而該觀點肯定是由一個人或組織提出來的。

2. 有些選項可能會用到兩次以上。

　　在原文中,可能會有作者提出兩個或更多的觀點,而這些觀點都出現在題目中。所以,有些選項可能會用到兩次以上。

3. 有些選項可能用不上。

　　有的作者雖然在原文中提出了觀點,但這些觀點沒有出現在題目中,所以有些選項可能會用不上。

4. 第一題往往對應文章的後幾個觀點,最後一題往往對應文章的前幾個觀點。

　　作者及其觀點的搭配題是沒有順序性的。而且,出題者為了顛倒黑白,混淆是非,讓考生產生障礙,第一題往往對應文章的後幾個觀點,最後一題往往對應文章的前幾個觀點。這個規律的準確率在 80% 以上。

　　我們可以利用這個規律,在找第一題的答案時,着重在文章的後幾個觀點。在找最後一題的答案時,着重在文章的前幾個觀點。

3. 例題講解

PARENTING AND RESPONSIBILITY

Section A

There are still significant gaps between women and men in terms of their involvement in family life, the tasks they perform and the responsibilities they take. Yet, at least in developed western countries, both women and men express a desire for greater equality in family life. It is evident that in terms of attitudes and beliefs, the problem cannot simply be thought of in terms of women wanting men to share more equally and men being reluctant to do so. The challenge now is to develop policies and practices based on a presumption of shared responsibility between men and women, and a presumption that there are potential benefits for men and women, as well as for families and the community, if there is greater gender equality in the responsibilities and pleasures of family life. These are becoming key concerns of researchers, policy makers, community workers and, more importantly, family members themselves.

Section B

Despite the significant increase in the number of women with dependent children who are in the paid workforce, Australian research studies over the last 15 years are consistent in showing that divisions of labour for family work are very rigid indeed(Watson 1991). In terms of time, women perform approximately 90 per cent of child care tasks and 70 per cent of all family work, and only 14 per cent of fathers are highly participant in terms of time spent on family work(Russell 1983). Demo and Acock(1993), in a recent US study, also found that women continue to perform a constant and major proportion of household labour(68 per cent to 95 per cent) across all family types(first marriage, divorced, step-family or never married), regardless of whether they are employed or non-employed in paid work.

Section C

Divisions of labour for family work are particularly problematic in families in which both parents are employed outside the home (dual -worker families). Employed mothers adjust their jobs and personal lives to accommodate family commitments more than employed fathers do. Mothers are less likely to work overtime and are more likely to take time off work to attend to children's needs (VandenHeuvel 1993). Mothers spend less time on personal leisure activities than their partners, a factor that often leads to resentment (Demo and Acock 1993).

Section D

The parental role is central to the stress -related anxiety reported by employed mothers, and a major contributor to such stress is their taking a greater role in child care (VandenHeuvel 1993). Edgar and Glezer (1992) found that close to 90 per cent of both husbands and wives agreed that the man should share equally in child care, yet 55 per cent of husbands and wives claimed that the men actually did this. (These claims are despite the findings mentioned earlier that point to a much lower participation rate by fathers.) A mother's wanting her partner to do more housework and child care is a better predictor of poor family adjustment than is actual time spent by fathers in these tasks (Demo and Acock 1993). It is this desire, together with its lack of fulfillment in most families, that brings about stress in the female parent.

Section E

Family therapists and social work researchers are increasingly defining family problems in terms of a lack of involvement and support from fathers and are concerned with difficulties involved in having fathers take responsibility for the solution of family and child behaviour problems (Edgar and Glezer 1986). Yet, a father accepting responsibilty for behaviour problems is linked with positive outcomes.

Section F

Research studies lend strong support to the argument that there are benefits for families considering a change to a fairer or more equitable division of the pleasures and pains of family life. Greater equality in the performance of family work is associated with lower levels of family stress and higher self esteem, better health, and higher marital satisfaction for mothers. There is also higher marital satisfaction for fathers, especially when they take more responsibility for the needs of their children —— fathers are happier when they are more involved (Russell 1984).

Questions 1 –9

Below is a list of research findings mentioned in Reading Passage "Parenting And Responsibility".

Indicate which researcher(s) are responsible for each research finding:

DA   Demo and Acock
EG   Edgar and Glezer
R   Russell
VH   VandenHeuvel
W   Watson

Write the appropriate letters(DA, EG, R, VH, or W)in boxes 1 –9 on your answer sheet.

Research Findings

Example	Fathers spend more time than mothers on personal leisure activities.
Answer	DA

1. The number of hours a father spends doing child care is not the best indicator of how well the family is adjusted.
2. The vast majority of fathers do not take part to any great extent in family work.
3. Women do the majority of housework whether they are married or not.
4. With regard to the issue of equal responsibility for child care, there is a discrepancy between the wishes and the claims of parent couples.
5. Both mothers and fathers are happier where the father assumes some responsibility for issues relating to the behaviour of the children.
6. Researchers now link family problems to fathers' lack of involvement in rearing children.
7. In terms of dealing with family issues, employed fathers make fewer sacrifices in their jobs than do working women.
8. Anxiety results from the mother being the primary care giver.
9. There has been little recent change in the housework and child care roles of mothers and

fathers.

答案及詳解:

先在原文中將作者及其觀點用線畫出,然後看題目,一道題一道題地做。

1. 答案:DA

題目的中文意思:父親們在照顧孩子上花費的時間不是家庭調整得如何的最好的表示者。

對應原文:Section D 的第三個觀點。

原文觀點的中文意思:一個母親希望她的丈夫做更多的家務和照顧孩子,這比丈夫們在這些工作上花費的實際時間更能表示家庭的調整。

對應關係:

原　　文	題　　目
predictor	indicator
family adjustment	family is adjusted

2. 答案:R

題目的中文意思:大多數的父親沒有很大程度地參與家庭工作。

對應原文:Section B 的第二個觀點。

原文觀點的中文意思:在時間方面,婦女做 90% 的照顧孩子的工作和 70% 的所有的家務。只有 14% 的父親很大程度地參與家務工作。

對應關係:

原　　文	題　　目
highly	great extent
participant	take part

3. 答案:DA

題目的中文意思:女人做大多數的家務工作,不管她們是否結婚。

對應原文:Section B 的第三個觀點。

原文觀點的中文意思:各種婚姻類型(首次結婚、離婚、再婚、未婚),婦女一直是承擔家務工作的主要部分。

對應關係:

原　　　文	題　　　目
Major proportion	Majority
Family type	Married or not

4. 答案:EG

題目的中文意思:在照顧孩子的平等責任的問題上,父母雙方在希望和聲稱之間是不一致的。

對應原文:Section D 的第二個觀點。

原文觀點的中文意思:接近 90% 的雙方都同意男人應該平等分擔照顧孩子的責任,但 55% 的雙方聲稱男人確實這麼做了。

5. 答案:R

題目的中文意思:如果父親承擔一些和孩子的行為有關的事情的責任,父親和母親都會更高興。

對應原文:Section F 中的觀點。

原文觀點的中文意思:特別是當父親們對孩子們的需要負更大責任時,他們有更高的婚姻滿意程度。當父親們參與更多時,他們更高興。

6. 答案:EG

題目的中文意思:研究者們現在把家庭問題和父親們缺乏參與照顧孩子聯繫起來。

對應原文:Section E 中的觀點。

原文觀點的中文意思:家庭學家和社會工作研究者認為家庭問題與缺乏父親的參與有關,而且他們關注讓父親們負責家庭和照顧孩子的困難性。

7. 答案:VH

題目的中文意思:考慮到處理家庭事務,在職的父親比在職的母親做出更少的犧牲。

對應原文:Section C 的第二個觀點。

原文觀點的中文意思:母親們更少可能超時工作,更可能早退來滿足孩子的需要。

8. 答案:VH

題目的中文意思:焦慮來自於母親是主要的照顧孩子提供者。

對應原文:Section D 的第一個觀點。

原文觀點的中文意思:在職母親有和壓力有關的焦慮,這種壓力的主要原因是她們在照顧孩子方面起到更大的作用。

對應關係:

原　　　文	題　　　目
contributor to	result from
greater role	primary

9. 答案:W

題目的中文意思:母親和父親在家務工作和照顧孩子上的作用幾乎沒有改變。

對應原文:Section B 的第一個觀點。

原文觀點的中文意思:雖然有孩子的婦女參加工作的數目顯著上升,過去 15 年澳洲的研究一致表明,家庭工作的勞動分工實際上是固定不變的。

對應關係:

原　　　文	題　　　目
rigid	little change

這篇文章的句子比較長,句式比較複雜,是很好的精讀材料。請大家結合第五章的難句分析,儘量把本文每句話的句子結構都搞懂。

WHY SOME WOMEN CROSS THE FINISH LINE AHEAD OF MEN —— RECRUITMENT

The course is tougher but women are staying the distance, reports **Andrew Crisp**.

A. Women who apply for jobs in middle or senior management have a higher success rate than men, according to an employment survey. But of course far fewer of them apply for these positions. The study, by recruitment consultants NB Selection, shows that while one in six men who appear on interview shortlists get jobs, the figure rises to one in four for women.

B. The study concentrated on applications for management positions in the ＄45,000 to

$110,000 salary range and found that women are more successful than men in both the private and public sectors. Dr. Elisabeth Marx from London-based NB Selection described the findings as encouraging for women, in that they send a positive message to them to apply for interesting management positions. But she added, "We should not lose sight of the fact that significantly fewer women apply for senior positions in comparison with men. "

C. Reasons for higher success rates among women are difficult to isolate. One explanation suggested is that if a woman candidate manages to get on a shortlist, then she has probably already proved herself to be an exceptional candidate. Dr. Marx said that when women apply for positions they tend to be better qualified than their male counterparts but are more selective and conservative in their job search. Women tend to research thoroughly before applying for positions or attending interviews. Men, on the other hand, seem to rely on their ability to sell themselves and to convince employers that any shortcomings they have will not prevent them from doing a good job.

D. Managerial and executive progress made by women is confirmed by the annual survey of boards of directors carried out by Korn/Ferry/Carre/Orban International. This year the survey shows a doubling of the number of women serving as non-executive directors compared with the previous year. However, progress remains painfully slow and there were still only 18 posts filled by women out of a total of 354 non-executive positions surveyed. Hilary Sears, a partner with Korn/Ferry, said, women have raised the level of grades we are employed in but we have still not broken through barriers to the top.

E. In Europe a recent feature of corporate life in the recession has been the de-layering of management structures. Sears said that this has halted progress for women in as much as de - layering has taken place either where women are working or in layers they aspire to. Sears also noted a positive trend from the recession, which has been the growing number of women who have started up on their own.

F. In business as a whole, there are a number of factors encouraging the prospect of greater equality in the workforce. Demographic trends suggest that the number of women going into employment is steadily increasing. In addition a far greater number of women are now passing through higher education, making them better qualified to move into management positions.

G . Organisations such as the European Women's Management Development Network provide a range of opportunities for women to enhance their skills and contacts. Through a series of both pan -European and national workshops and conferences the barriers to women in employment are being broken down. However, Ariane Berthoin Antal, director of the International Institute for Organisational Change of Archamps in France, said that there is only anecdotal evidence of changes in recruitment patterns. And she said, "It's still so hard for women to even get on to shortlists, —— there are so many hurdles and barriers. " Antal agreed that there have been some positive signs but said "Until there is a belief among employers, until they value the difference, nothing will change. "

Questions 10 –13

The author makes reference to three consultants in the Reading Passage. Which of the list of points below do these consultants make? In boxes 10 – 13 write

M   if the point is made by Dr. Marx

S   if the point is made by Hilary Sears

A   if the point is made by Ariane Berthoin Antal

10 . Selection procedures do not favour women.

11 . The number of female-run businesses is increasing.

12 . Male applicants exceed female applicants for top posts.

13 . Women hold higher positions now than they used to.

答案及詳解：

先在原文中將作者及其觀點用線畫出，然後看題目，一道題一道題地做。

10. 答案：A

題目的中文意思：選擇過程不利於女性。

對應原文：G 段中的句子：

However, Ariane Berthoin Antal, director of the International Institute for Organisational Change of Archamps in France, said that there is only anecdotal evidence of changes in recruitment patterns. And she said, "It's still so hard for women to even get on to shortlists ,—— there are so many hurdles and barriers. "

原文觀點的中文意思：法國 Archamps 機構改革國際研究所主管 Ariane Berthoin Antal 說，在招聘模式上只有改變的傳說的跡象，對女性來說，甚至上候選名單仍然是很困難的，有很多的障礙。

對應關係：

原　　　文	題　　　目
recruitment patterns	selection procedures
so hard for women	do not favour women

11. 答案：S

題目的中文意思：女性自己開辦企業的數目在增加。

對應原文：E 段中的句子：

Sears also noted a positive trend from the recession, which has been the growing number of women who have started up on their own.

原文觀點的中文意思：Sears 還指出了這種衰退的一個積極的傾向，那就是自己開辦企業的女性在增加。

對應關係：

原　　　文	題　　　目
growing	increasing
women who have started up on their own	female-run businesses

12. 答案：M

題目的中文意思：申請高級職位的男性數目超過女性。

對應原文：B 段中的句子：

But she added, "We should not lose sight of the fact that significantly fewer women apply for senior positions in comparison with men."

原文觀點的中文意思：但她又說到，"我們不應該忽視這個事實：與男性相比，申請高級職位的女性要少得多。"

對應關係：

原　　　文	題　　　目
significantly fewer women	male applicants exceed female
senior positions	top posts

13. 答案：S

題目的中文意思：女性現在比以前處於更高的職位。

對應原文：D 段中的句子：

Hilary Sears, a partner with Korn/Ferry, said, women have raised the level of grades we are employed in but we have still not broken through barriers to the top.

原文觀點的中文意思：Hilary Sears, Korn/Ferry 的一個合作者說女性已經提高了她們的級別水準，但我們仍然沒有突破直抵高層的障礙。

對應關係：

原　　　文	題　　　目
have raised the level of grades	hold higher positions

✣ 九、Sentence Completion（完成句子）✣

1. 題型要求

　　每個題目都是一個敘述句，但留有一個或兩個空格，要求根據原文填空。目前考試中，絕大部分都是一個空格，而且在句子的結尾。例如：

　　The international community has begun to demand.........

　　絕大部分的題目要求中有字數限制，一般有如下幾種表述方式：(1) NO MORE THAN TWO/THREE/FOUR WORDS（不超過 2/3/4 個字）；(2) ONE OR TWO WORDS（一個或兩個字）；(3) USE A MAXIMUM OF TWO WORDS（最多兩個字）。有字數限制的，一定要嚴格按照題目要求去做，必須滿足要求。

少部分的題目要求中沒有字數限制,這時請注意,答案字數也不會很長,一般不會超過四個字。

這種題型的解題方法和短問答類似,但一般比短問答要難。難度在於題目中的關鍵詞和原文中的相應詞對應不明顯。

考試中,A 類一般是每次必考,考一組,共三題左右。G 類一般是兩次考一次,考一組,共三題左右。

2 解題步驟

1. 找出題目中的關鍵詞,最好先定位到原文中的一個段落。

將題目中的關鍵詞與原文各段落的小標題或每段話的第一句相對照。有些題目能先定位到原文中的一個段落,這必將大大加快解題速度,並提高準確率。但也並非每個題目都能先定位到原文中的一個段落的。

2. 從頭到尾快速閱讀該段落,根據題目中的其他關鍵詞確定正確答案。

確定一個段落後,答案在該段落中的具體位置是未知的。所以需要從頭到尾仔細閱讀該段落,找出題目中的關鍵詞的對應詞。仔細閱讀對應詞所在的句子,確定正確答案。

3. 要注意順序性,即題目的順序和原文的順序基本上要一致。

這種題型是有順序性的。第二題的答案應在第一題的答案之後。這個規律也有助於同學們確定答案的位置。

NOTICE

1. 所填答案必須符合文法。

因爲是填空,所以所填答案必須符合文法規定。同樣有文法要求的題型是摘要填空(Summary),而短問答則不太要求文法。

2. 絕大部分的答案來自原文原詞。

大部分的答案來自原文原詞,而且是原文中連續的幾個詞。

3. 答案字數不會很長。

絕大部分的題目要求中有字數限制,這時必須滿足要求。即使題目要求中沒有字數限制,答案字數也不會很長,一般不會超過四個字。如果發現找到的答案字數很多,應首先懷疑自己找錯答案的位置。

例 原文:In addition to basic residence fees, most universities make minor additional charges for items such as registration fees, damage deposits, and power charges.

題目:As well as the basic college residence fees, additional charges are usually made, but are describes as ...

有的同學可能會答 registration fees, damage deposits, and power charges,因爲字數太多,所以應首先懷疑是錯誤的。正確答案應爲 minor。即附加費用被描述爲是少量的、微不足道的。

4. 答案絕大部分是名詞片語。

所填答案絕大部分是名詞片語,對應原文相應句子的受詞。也有少數題目的答案是形容詞片語或副詞片語。

5. 要特別注意順序性。

　　由於這種題型定位比較難,所以要特別注意順序性的運用。一道題若找了很長時間、很多段落也沒有找到答案,可能是因為題目中的關鍵詞和原文中的相應詞對應不明顯,答案位置已經過去了。可以先做下一道題。

　　這種題型比較難,所以通常出現為一篇文章的第二種或第三種題型。它與前面的題型也構成順序性,即這種題型第一題的答案位置絕大部分應在前一種題型的最後一題的答案位置之後。

3. 例題講解

THE NATURE OF DISPUTES

To resolve a dispute means to turn opposing positions into a single outcome. The two parties may choose to focus their attention on one or more of three basic factors. They may seek to (1) reconcile their interests, (2) determine who is right, and/or (3) determine who is more powerful.

Section A

Interests are needs, desires, concerns, fears - the things one cares about or wants. They provide the foundation for a person's or an organisation's position in a dispute. In a dispute, not only do the interests of one party not coincide with those of the other party, but they are in conflict. For example, the director of sales for an electronics company gets into a dispute with the director of manufacturing over the number of TV models to produce. The director of sales wants to produce more models because her interest is in selling TV sets; more models mean more choice for consumers and hence increased sales. The director of manufacturing, however, wants to produce fewer models. His interest is in decreasing manufacturing costs and more models mean higher costs.

Section B

Reconciling such interests is not easy. It involves probing for deeply rooted concerns, devising creative solutions, and making trade-offs and compromises where interests are opposed.

The most common procedure for doing this is negotiation, the act of communication intended to reach agreement. Another interests-based procedure is mediation, in which a third party assists the disputants, the two sides in the dispute, in reaching agreement.

Section C

By no means do all negotiations (or mediations) focus on reconciling interests. Some negotiations focus on determining who is right, such as when two lawyers argue about whose case has the greater merit. Other negotiations focus on determining who is more powerful, such as when quarrelling neighbours or nations exchange threats and counter threats. Often negotiations involve a mix of all three —— some attempts to satisfy interests, some discussion of rights, and some references to relative power.

Section D

It is often complicated to attempt to determine who is right in a dispute. Although it is usually straightforward where rights are formalised in law, other rights take the form of unwritten but socially accepted standards of behaviour, such as reciprocity, precedent, equality, and seniority.

There are often different —— and sometimes contradictory —— standards that apply to rights. Reaching agreement on rights, where the outcome will determine who gets what, can often be so difficult that the parties frequently turn to a third party to determine who is right. The most typical rights procedure is adjudication, in which disputants present evidence and arguments to a neutral third party who has the power to make a decision that must be followed by both disputants. (In mediation, by contrast, the third party does not have the power to decide the dispute.) Public adjudication is provided by courts and administrative agencies. Private adjudication is provided by arbitrators.

Section E

A third way to resolve a dispute is on the basis of power. We define power, somewhat narrowly, as the ability to pressure someone to do something he would not otherwise do. Exercising power typically means imposing costs on the other side or threatening to do so. The exercise of power takes two common forms: acts of aggression, such as physical attack, and withholding the benefits that derive from a relationship, as when employees stop working in a strike.

Section F

In relationships of mutual dependence, such as between labour and management or within an organisation or a family, the question of who is more powerful turns on who is less dependent on the other. If a company needs the employees' work more than employees need the company's pay, the company is more dependent and hence less powerful. How dependent one is turns on how satisfactory the alternatives are for satisfying one's interests. The better the alternative, the less dependent one is. If it is easier for the company to replace striking employees than it is for striking employees to find new jobs, the company is less dependent and thereby more powerful. Determining who is the more powerful party without a decisive and potentially destructive power contest is difficult because power is ultimately a matter of perceptions.

Glossary

disputant: one of the parties in a dispute

Questions 1 – 4

Complete the sentences below with words taken from Reading Passage.

Use NO MORE THAN THREE WORDS for each answer.

Write your answers in boxes 1 – 4 on your answer sheet.

1. Two common procedures used in the resolution of interest-based disputes are . . . . AND . . . .

2. When rights are . . . . , coming to a resolution is a relatively simple process.

3. Determining who is right becomes more complicated when behavioural issues such as . . . . and . . . . must be taken into consideration.

4. Arbitrators and adjudicators must receive . . . . and . . . . from the disputing parties before they can help resolve the dispute.

答案及詳解：

　　這篇文章我們做過 Headings 題型，請大家先再看一下原文各段的主題句。題目中有字數要求：NO MORE THAN THREE WORDS。

1. 題目中的關鍵詞是 resolution 和 interest-based，對應原文 Section B。閱讀該段，再根據題目中的其他關鍵詞 common procedures，確定答案為 negotiation mediation。此題有兩個空格，兩個詞算一個答案，必須都正確。目前考試中，絕大多數題目都只有一個空格。

2. 此題比較難。題目中的關鍵詞是 rights,對應原文 Section D。閱讀該段,再根據題目中的其他關鍵詞 relatively simple process,找到該段中的句子:it is usually straightforward where rights are formalised in law,確定答案爲 formalised in law。其中,原文中 straightforward(直截了當的)與題目中的關鍵詞 relatively simple process 相對應,此題反映了目前考試中這種題型的特點,即對應不明顯。

3. 此題比較容易。先根據題目中的關鍵詞 who is right,對應到原文 Section D。閱讀該段,再根據題目中的其他關鍵詞 behavioural 和 such as 找到 Section D 中第一段的最後一句:other rights take the form of unwritten but socially accepted standards of behaviour, such as reciprocity, precedent, equality, and seniority,答案爲 reciprocity, precedent, equality, seniority 中任選兩個。因爲題目中有字數要求:NO MORE THAN THREE WORDS,此題兩個空格算一個題目,所以四個詞都寫是不對的。

4. 此題是一道難題,首先不好定位到一個段落。只有根據順序性,從第 3 題的答案向後找。正確答案來自 Section D 中第二段的一句:The most typical rights procedure is adjudication, in which disputants present evidence and arguments to a neutral third party who has the power to make a decision that must be followed by both disputants,答案爲 evidence arguments。對應同樣不明顯。原文的意思是:最典型的判斷對錯的方法叫裁決,在裁決中,衝突雙方拿出證據和論據給一個中立的第三方,他有權做出一個決定,衝突雙方必須遵守。題目的意思是:仲裁人和裁決人在幫助解決衝突之前必須從衝突方那裏得到證據和論據。

NEW-AGE TRANSPORT

Computerised design, advanced materials and new technologies are being used to produce machines of a type never seen before.

It looks as if it came straight from the set of Star Wars. It has four-wheel drive and rises above rocky surfaces. It lowers and raises its nose when going up and down hills. And when it comes to a river, it turns amphibious: two hydrojets power it along by blasting water under its body. There is room for two passengers and a driver, who sit inside a glass bubble operating electronic, aircraft-type controls. A vehicle so daring on land and water needs windscreen wipers-but it doesn't have any. Water molecules are disintegrated on the screen's surface by ultrasonic sensors.

This unusual vehicle is the Racoon. It is an invention not of Hollywood but of Renault, a rather conservative French state-owned carmaker, better known for its family hatchbacks. Renault built the Racoon to explore new freedoms for designers and engineers created by advances in materials and manufacturing processes. Renault is thinking about startlingly different cars: other producers have radical new ideas for trains, boats and aeroplanes.

The first of the new freedoms is in design. Powerful computer-aided design (CAD) systems can replace with a click of a computer mouse hours of laborious work done on thousands of drawing boards. So new products, no matter how complicated, can be developed much faster. For the first time, Boeing will not have to build a giant replica of its new airliner, the 777, to make sure all the bits fit together. Its CAD system will take care of that.

But Renault is taking CAD further. It claims the Racoon is the world's first vehicle to be designed within the digitised world of virtual reality. Complex programs were used to simulate the vehicle and the terrain that it was expected to cross. This allowed a team led by Patrick Le Quement, Renault's industrial-design director, to "drive" it long before a prototype existed.

Renault is not alone in thinking that virtual reality will transform automotive design. In Detroit, Ford is also investigating its potential. Jack Telnac, the firm's head of design, would like designers in different parts of the world to work more closely together, linked by computers. They would do more than style cars. Virtual reality will allow engineers to peer inside the working parts of a vehicle. Designers will watch bearings move, oil flow, gears mesh and hydraulics pump. As these techniques catch on, even stranger vehicles are likely to come along.

Transforming these creations from virtual reality to actual reality will also become easier, especially with advances in materials. Firms that once bashed everything out of steel now find that new alloys of composite materials (which can be made from mixtures of plastic, resin, ceramics and metals, reinforced with fibres such as glass or carbon) are changing the rules of manufacturing. At the same time, old materials keep getting better, as their producers try to secure their place in the factory of the future. This competition is increasing the pace of development of all materials.

One company in this field is Scaled Composites. It was started in 1982 by Burt Rutan, an aviator who has devised many unusual aircraft. His company develops and tests prototypes that have ranged from business aircraft to air racers. It has also worked on composite sails for the America's Cup yacht race and on General Motors' Ultralite, a 100-miles-per-gallon experimental family car built from carbon fibre.

Again, the Racoon reflects this race between the old and the new. It uses conventional steel and what Renault describes as a new "high-limit elastic steel" in its chassis. This steel is 30% lighter than the usual kind. The Racoon also has parts made from composites. Renault plans to replace the petrol engine with a small gas turbine, which could be made from heat-resisting ceramics, and use it to run a generator that would provide power for electric motors at each wheel.

With composites, it is possible to build many different parts into a single component. Fiat, Italy's biggest car maker, has worked out that it could reduce the number of components needed in one of its car bodies from 150 to 16 by using a composite shell rather than one made of steel. Aircraft and cars may increasingly be assembled as if they were plastic kits.

Advances in engine technology also make cars lighter. The Ultralite, which Scaled Composites helped to design for General Motors, uses a two-stroke engine in a "power pod" at the rear of the vehicle. The engine has been developed from an East German design and weighs 40% less than a conventional engine but produces as much power. It is expected to run cleanly enough to qualify as an ultra-low emissions vehicle under California's tough new rules.

Questions 5 – 7

Using NO MORE THAN THREE WORDS, complete the following statements, write your answers in boxes 5 – 7 on your answer sheet.

5. One future design feature of the Racoon might be a. . . . .

6. In the future cars might be put together like. . . . .

7. The advantage of the Ultralite engine is that it is 40% . . . . than other car engines.

答案及詳解:

題目中有字數要求:NO MORE THAN THREE WORDS。

5. 此題最難,首先不好定位到一個段落。這時,可以考慮運用順序性,這種題型通常與前一種題型也構成順序性。這篇文章前一種題型是選擇題,我們在"五、選擇題"中做過,其中最後一題的答案在原文倒數第五段,所以首先考慮從倒數第四段開始找答案。從倒數第四段的第一句知道,這一段主要是關於 Scaled Composites 公司,而題目中的關鍵詞 Racoon 不是該公司的車型,而是 Renault 公司的(從做前面的選擇題可以得出),所以答案不應在這段。看下一段,下一段(倒數第三段)的第一句中有 Racoon,所以答案在此段的可能性很大。仔細讀這一段,有的同學可能會從第二句中找到 high-limit e-lastic steel,實際這一句與題目沒有任何對應關係。正確答案應來自該段的最後一句:Renault plans to replace the petrol engine with a small gas turbine,plans(計畫)對應題目中的 might be(可能),都是不確定的詞。答案是 small gas turbine。

6. 根據順序性向下找,答案來自倒數第二段的最後一句:Aircraft and cars may increasingly be assembled as if they were plastic kits,may 對應題目中的 might,assembled 對應題目中的 put together。答案是 plastic kits。

7. 通過 40%,比較容易定位到最後一段中的句子:The engine has been developed from an East German design and weighs 40% less than a conventional engine,但不太好確定答案,答案應符合文法規定。答案是 lighter。實際上這個詞出現在該段的第一句。

❖ 十、Diagram/Flowchart/Table Completion（填圖填表題） ❖

1. 題型要求

　　題目中有一個圖表或一個表格,其中有一些訊息,留出空格,要求根據文章填空。一般沒有選項可供選擇。

　　所填的內容一般分為以下幾類:

(1) 時間、事件及人物。圖表中是原文中的一些事件及其發生時間和涉及人物,給出一些已知訊息,要求填其餘的。有時也可能只考其中的一項或兩項。時間往往只涉及到年代,不會涉及到具體的日期。

(2) 數字及排位。這時要看清要求填的是具體的數字還是相應的排位。題目要求中一般用 rank 一詞表示排位,也可以看題目所給的例子。

（3）物體的構成及功能。文章的某一段提到了一個物體,講述了它的構造和各部分的功能。題目是該物體的簡圖,給出一些部件的名稱及功能,要求填其餘部件的名稱及功能。所填訊息常常集中於原文中的一個段落。

（4）流程圖。文章的某一段提到了做一件事情的過程,題目以流程圖的形式描述這個過程,要求填其中幾個環節的內容。

（5）抽象名詞:圖表中常常是文章中提到的一些事物,根據圖表中的關係填空,通常是分類關係。所填訊息常常集中於原文中的一個段落。

填空題類別較多,所填內容五花八門,但一般都比較容易。有的定位容易,有的集中於原文中的一個段落。

這種題型,A 類和 G 類一般都是每次必考,共五題左右。

2 解題步驟

1. 找出題目中的關鍵詞。

如果圖表中涉及時間或數字,它們肯定是關鍵詞,而且肯定是原詞對應,即原文中出現的也是這些詞本身。

如果圖表中沒有涉及時間或數字,往往要根據具體的意思,在已知的訊息中確定一個關鍵詞。

2. 到原文中去找關鍵詞的對應詞。

3. 仔細閱讀對應詞所在的句子,確定正確答案。

4. 要注意順序性,即題目的順序和原文的順序基本上要一致。

NOTICE

1. 注意題目要求中是否有字數限制。

大多數題目有字數要求,這時必須滿足題目要求。方法詳見短問答題型講解。

2. 絕大部分的答案是原文原詞,而且是原文中連續的幾個詞。

3. 一般比較簡單，注意快速答題。

　　填圖填表題一般都比較簡單。雖然有的題目看起來比較嚇人，如出現物體的構成及功能、流程圖、抽象名詞、圖表等，實際上都能明確地對應到原文，而且涉及訊息常常集中於原文中的一個段落。

3. 例題講解

"THE ROLLFILM REVOLUTION"

The introduction of the dry plate process brought with it many advantages. Not only was it much more convenient, so that the photographer no longer needed to prepare his material in advance, but its much greater sensitivity made possible a new generation of cameras. Instantaneous exposures had been possible before, but only with some difficulty and with special equipment and conditions. Now, exposures short enough to permit the camera to be held in the hand were easily achieved. As well as fitting shutters and viewfinders to their conventional stand cameras, manufacturers began to construct smaller cameras intended specifically for hand use.

One of the first designs to be published was Thomas Bolas's "Detective" camera of 1881. Externally a plain box, quite unlike the folding bellows camera typical of the period, it could be used unobtrusively. The name caught on, and for the next decade for so almost all hand cameras were called "Detectives". Many of the new designs in the 1880s were for magazine cameras, in which a number of dry plates could be pre-loaded and changed one after another following exposure. Although much more convenient than stand cameras, still used by most serious workers, magazine plate cameras were heavy, and required access to a darkroom for loading and processing the plates. This was all changed by a young American bank clerk turned photographic manufacturer, George Eastman, from Rochester, New York.

Eastman had begun to manufacture gelatine dry plates in 1880, being one of the first to do so in America. He soon looked for ways of simplifying photography, believing that many people were put off by the complication and messiness. His first step was to develop, with the camera manufacturer William H. Walker, a holder for a long roll of paper negative "film". This could be fitted to a standard plate camera and up to forty-eight exposures made before reloading. The combined weight of the paper roll and the holder was far less than the same number of glass plates in their light-tight wooden holders. Although roll-holders had been made as early as the 1850s, none had been very successful because of the limitations of the photographic materials then available. Eastman's rollable paper film was sensitive and gave negatives of good quality; the Eastman-Walker roll-holder was a great success.

The next step was to combine the roll-holder with a small hand camera: Eastman's first design was patented with an employee, F. M. Cossitt, in 1886. It was not a success. Only fifty Eastman detective cameras were made, and they were sold as a lot to a dealer in 1887; the cost was too high and the design too complicated. Eastman set about developing a new model, which was launched in June 1888. It was a small box, containing a roll of paper-based stripping film sufficient for 100 circular exposures 6cm in diameter. Its operation was simple: set the shutter by pulling a wire string; aim the camera using the V line impression in the camera top; press the release button to activate the exposure; and turn a special key to wind on the film. A hundred exposures had to be made, so it was important to record each picture in the memorandum book provided, since there was no exposure counter. Eastman gave his camera the invented name "Kodak"—— which was easily pronounceable in most languages, and had two Ks which Eastman felt was a firm, uncompromising kind of letter.

The importance of Eastman's new roll-film camera was not that it was the first. There had been several earlier cameras, Notably the Stirn "America", first demonstrated in the spring of 1887 and on sale from early 1888. This also used a roll of negative paper, and had such refinements as a reflecting viewfinder and an ingenious exposure marker. The real significance of the first Kodak camera was that it was backed up by a developing and printing service. Hitherto, virtually all photographers developed and printed their own pictures. This required the facilities of a darkroom and the time and inclination to handle the necessary chemicals, make the prints and so on. Eastman recognized that not everyone had the resources or the desire to do this. When a customer had made a hundred exposures in the Kodak camera, he sent it to Eastman's factory in Rochester (or later in Harrow in England) where the film was unloaded, processed and printed, the camera reloaded and returned to the owner. "You

Press the Button, We Do the Rest" ran Eastman's classic marketing slogan; photography had been brought to everyone. Everyone, that is, who could afford $25 or five guineas for the camera and $10 or two guineas for the developing and printing. A guinea ($5) was a week's wages for many at the time, so this simple camera cost the equivalent of hundreds of dollars today.

In 1889 an improved model with a new shutter design was introduced, and it was called the NO. 2 Kodak camera. The paper-based stripping film was complicated to manipulate, since the processed negative image had to be stripped from the paper base for printing. At the end of 1889 Eastman launched a new roll film on a celluloid base. Clear, tough, transparent and flexible, the new film not only made the roll-film camera fully practical, but provided the raw material for the introduction of cinematography a few years later. Other, larger models were introduced, including several folding versions, one of which took pictures 21.6 cm × 16.5 cm in size. Other manufacturers in America and Europe introduced cameras to take the Kodak roll-films, and other firms began to offer developing and printing services for the benefit of the new breed of photographers.

By September 1889, over 5,000 Kodak cameras had been sold in the USA, and the company was daily printing 6 – 7,000 negatives. Holidays and special events created enormous surges in demand for processing: 900 Kodak users returned their cameras for processing and reloading in the week after the New York centennial celebration.

Questions 1 – 4

Complete the table below. Choose NO MORE THAN THREE WORDS from the passage for each answer.

Write your answers in boxes 1 – 4 on your answer sheet.

Year	Developments	Name of person/people
1880	Manufacture of gelatine dry plates	...(1)...
1881	Release of "Detective" camera	Thomas Bolas
...(2)...	The roll-holder combined with...(3)...	Eastman and F. M. Cossitt
1889	Introduction of model with...(4)...	Eastman

答案及詳解：

　　這是時間、事件及人物的填圖填表題。注意，時間肯定是關鍵詞。答案要求在三個字之內。

1. 關鍵詞是 1880，快讀文章，從頭到尾找 1880。注意第二段中有 1880s 意思是 19 世紀 80 年代，與 1880 是不同的。應對應到第三段的第一句，答案爲 Eastman。

2. 3. 雖然要求填的是年代，也要按照年代去找答案。從文章中向下閱讀，尋找年代。第三段偏後位置有 1850s，但根據邏輯，第 2 題的答案應該大於 1881，所以不用看，肯定不對。第四段第一句中有一個 1886，在 1881 之後。仔細讀該句話，與題目中已知的訊息相對照，確定是正確答案。第 3 題的答案爲 small hand camera，原文爲 a small hand camera，不滿足字數要求，根據規律去掉冠詞 a。

4. 關鍵詞是 1889，向下快讀原文，在倒數第二段的第一句找到 1889，仔細讀該句話，與題目中已知的訊息相對照，確定是正確答案。第 4 題的答案爲 new shutter design，原文爲 a new shutter design，不滿足字數要求，根據規律去掉冠詞 a。

PEOPLE AND ORGANISATIONS：
THE SELECTION ISSUE

A. In 1991 according to the Department of Trade and Industry, a record 48,000 British companies went out of business. When businesses fail, the post-mortem analysis is traditionally undertaken by accountants and market strategists. Unarguably organisations do fail because of undercapitalisation, poor financial management, adverse market conditions etc. Yet, conversely, organisations with sound financial backing, good product ideas and market acumen often underperform and fail to meet shareholders' expectations. The complexity, degree and sustainment of organisational performance requires an explanation which goes beyond the balance sheet and the "paper conversion" of financial inputs into profit making outputs. A more complete explanation of "what went wrong" necessarily must consider the essence of what an organisation actually is and that one of the financial inputs, the most important and often the most expensive, is people.

B. An organisation is only as good as the people it employs. Selecting the right person for the job involves more than identifying the essential or desirable range of skills, educational and professional qualifications necessary to perform the job and then recruiting the candidate who is most likely to possess these skills or at least is perceived to have the ability and predisposition to acquire them. This is a purely person/skills match approach to selection.

C. Work invariably takes place in the presence and/or under the direction of others, in a particular organisational setting. The individual has to "fit" in with the work environment, with other employees, with the organisational climate, style of work, organisation and culture of the organisation. Different organisations have different cultures (Cartwrigha & Cooper, 1991; 1992). Working as an engineer at British Aerospace will not necessarily be a similar experience to working in the same capacity at GEC or Plessey.

D. Poor selection decisions are expensive. For example, the costs of training a policeman are about £ 20,000 (approx. US $ 30,000). The costs of employing an unsuitable technician on an oil rig or in a nuclear plant could, in an emergency, result in millions of pounds of damage or loss of life. The disharmony of a poor person-environment fit (PE-fit) is likely to result in low job satisfaction, lack of organisational commitment and employee stress, which affect organisational outcomes i. e. productivity, high labour turnover and absenteeism, and individual outcomes i. e. physical, psychological and mental well-being.

E. However, despite the importance of the recruitment decision and the range of sophisticated and more objective selection techniques available, including the use of psychometric tests, assessment centres etc. , many organisations are still prepared to make this decision on the basis of a single 30 to 45 minute unstructured interview. Indeed, research has demonstrated that a selection decision is often made within the first four minutes of the interview. In the remaining time, the interviewer then attends exclusively to information that reinforces the initial 'accept' or 'reject' decision. Research into the validity of selection methods has consistently demonstrated that the unstructured interview, where the interviewer asks any questions he or she likes, is a poor predictor of future job performance and fares little better than more controversial methods like graphology and astrology. In times of high unemployment, recruitment becomes a "buyer's market" and this was the case in Britain during the 1980s.

F. The future, we are told, is likely to be different. Detailed surveys of social and economic trends in the European Community show that Europe's population is falling and getting older. The birth rate in the Community is now only three-quarters of the level needed to ensure replacement of the existing population. By the year 2020, it is predicted that more than one in four Europeans will be aged 60 or more and barely one in five will be under 20. In five-year period between 1983 and 1988 the Community's female workforce grew by almost six million. As a result, 51% of all women aged 14 to 64 are now economically active in the labour market compared with 78% of men.

G. The changing demographics will not only affect selection ratios. They will also make it increasingly important for organisations wishing to maintain their competitive edge to be more responsive and accommodating to the changing needs of their workforce if they are to retain and develop their human resources. More flexible working hours, the opportunity to work from home or job share, the provision of childcare facilities etc, will play a major role in attracting and retaining staff in the future.

Questions 5 – 7

Complete the notes below with words taken from Reading Passage 2 Use NO MORE THAN ONE or TWO WORDS for each answer.

Write your answers in boxes 5 – 7 on your answer sheet.

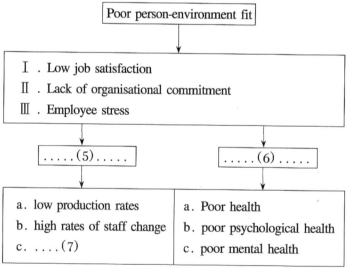

答案及詳解：

此題要求填抽象名詞,看起來好像很難,實際上是一個簡單題型。涉及訊息常常集中於原文的一個段落。

根據已知的關鍵詞 poor person-environment fit 對應到原文的 D 段中的句子：The disharmony of a poor person-environment fit（PE-fit）is likely to result in low job satisfaction, lack of organisational commitment and employee stress, which affect organisational outcomes i. e. productivity, high labour turnover and absenteeism, and individual outcomes i. e. physical, psychological and mental well-being。原文與題目的對應詞為：

原　　　文	題　　　目
productivity	low production rates
high labour turnover	high rates of staff change
physical	poor health

5. 答案為：organisational outcomes

6. 答案為：individual outcomes

7. 答案為：absenteeism

❖ 十一、其他題型 ❖

前面介紹的是 IELTS 考試中必考或常考的十種題型。下面介紹的幾種題型也曾經考過，但出現的頻率不是很高。

（一）直接填空

與從選項中選詞的摘要填空（Summary）類似。題目是一小段文字，其中有幾個空格，要求你從選項中選詞填空。選項的數目常常比空格的數目要多。

與摘要填空不同的是，這種題型沒有原文，所以我們稱之為直接填空。

A 類和 G 類都考過這種題型。G 類通常是一段單獨的小文章，A 類是一篇長文章的一段（通常是最後一段）。

這種題型一般不難。由於沒有原文可以對應，所以文法在解題過程中佔有很大的重要性。具體解題步驟如下：

　　1. 根據空格前後的詞，判斷空格中應填詞的詞性。

　　2. 在選項中找出滿足詞性要求的詞。

　　3. 結合句意，在選出的幾個詞中確定正確答案。

請看下面的例子：

Questions 1 – 6

Read the passage below, then fill in each gap with ONE word from the box below the passage. You may use a word more than once if you wish. Write your answers in the spaces following the passage. The first one has been done as an example.

USE ELECTRICITY SAFELY

Most electrical accidents in the home (*example*) because people fail to observe basic safety procedures. Always switch off at the powerpoint before you remove the plug. Always remove the plug by grasping it —— not by ....(1).... the cord. Check to see that the power is ....(2).... off when changing lightbulbs. Do not use electrical appliances ....(3).... a swimming pool. A shock could cause paralysis, resulting in drowning. Check the ....(4).... of leads and extension cords regularly to ensure that they are functioning properly. Switch off appliances if the power ....(5).... . Fires have been caused when power returns unexpectedly. Teach children that electrical appliances, cords and switches are not toys. Insert safety plugs in powerpoints to ....(6).... young children.

Your answers

Example: occur

1. . . . .
2. . . . .
3. . . . .
4. . . . .
5. . . . .
6. . . . .

avoid	accident	warning
condition	near	switched
removed	protect	touch
fails	pulling	
occur	tested	

答案及詳解：

1. 根據上下文，空格中應填動名詞，選項中有兩個詞候選：pulling 和 warning。結合句義，正確答案應為：pulling。

2. 正確答案為：switched。

3. 正確答案為：near。

4. 根據上下文，空格中應填名詞，選項中有三個詞候選：condition、accident、touch。結合句意，正確答案應為：condition。

5. 根據上下文，空格中應填動詞，而且是一般現在式第三人稱單數。選項中只有一個詞候選：fails，當然就是正確答案。

6. 根據上下文，空格中應填動詞原形，選項中有四個詞候選：avoid、protect、touch、occur。結合句意，正確答案應為：protect。

（二）複選＋排序

　　與選擇題中的複選類似，只是在題目的要求中有 in the correct order 的字樣，即需要將選出的選項以正確的順序排序，順序非常重要。例如正確答案是 1、4、3、5、2，如果你的答案是 1、3、4、5、2，則五道題中你答對了三道題，如果你的答案是 3、4、5、2、1，則五道題你都答錯了。在做這種題型時，應注意以下幾點：

　　　　1. 一般考做一件事情的過程，注意原文中的動詞。

　　　　2. 正確答案的順序一般與原文的敘述順序是一致的。

　　　　3. 答案在原文中往往是集中出現的。

　　這種題型在實際考試中不常出現，第四章綜合練習中有一道這種題型，請同學們注意對照練習一下。

（三）完成句子 + 搭配題

這種題型在實際考試中出現的頻率高一些，它是完成句子和搭配題兩種題型的結合。每個題目都是一個陳述句，但留有一個空格，而且都在句子的結尾。

與單純的完成句子題型不同，這種題型不是要求你寫出答案，而是從選項中選擇。也就是說，在題目中還給出一個句子結尾的選項的集合。選項的數目要多於題目的數目。

做這種題型，應按照完成句子題型的方法去做，而不要按搭配題的方法去做。主要原因是題目是有順序性的，只是在最後確定答案時，需要將原文中的詞或片語與選項相對照。正確選項常常是原文中的詞或片語的改寫。

這種題型一般比單純的完成句子題型要簡單一些。第四章綜合練習中有一道這種題型，請同學們注意對照練習一下。

（四）全文主旨題

題目要求你說出一篇文章的主旨，即整篇文章的中心意思。

這種題型也不常考，在實際考試中要嘛不考，要嘛只考一題。做這種題型要注意以下幾點：

1. 題目以四選一的形式出現。

全文主旨題都是以四選一的形式出現，題目中常有 the aim of the writer（作者寫文章的目的）、the title（文章的標題）、the main theme（文章的主旨）。

2. 最後做全文主旨題。

不管全文主旨題是文章的第一題還是最後一題，都在做完該篇文章的其他題目後，再做全文主旨題。這時，常常不需再看文章，即可直接做出來。如果不能確定，則需要看一下原文的第一段及每段話的第一句。一般全文主旨題還是比較簡單的。

國際IELTS應考叢書

閱　讀

CHAPTER　IV

IELTS 閱讀
綜合練習

READING

學 習 指 導

　　按照題型的解題技巧解題,是 IELTS 閱讀的核心。在掌握了各種題型的解題方法之後,應該做一些綜合練習,將閱讀方法和題型技巧綜合運用。

　　在做綜合練習時,應注意以下幾點:

　　1. 嚴格按老師講的閱讀方法和解題技巧去做。

　　平常做練習,不僅是檢驗自己的閱讀程度的過程,更重要的是熟悉閱讀方法和解題技巧。所以學了 IELTS 考試的閱讀方法和解題技巧,就要運用到實際測驗中,才能取得進步,而不能還用以前的老一套。

　　2. 嚴格按考試的要求去做。

　　必須在 60 分鐘之內把題目做完,而且要把答案寫在答案紙上。同學們最好選擇自己頭腦清楚的時候,選一個安靜的地點,設定時間,這樣既能檢驗自己的真實程度,也有利於適應考試的氣氛和環境。

　　3. 做完之後,要認真地檢討。

　　這是相當重要的。有的同學在做完一套題後,一對答案,發現錯了很多,大罵一聲,然後就不了了之,這是很不好的。做完一套題並不算是準備妥當,重點工作應放在試題分析上。也就是將答案核對後,要看某些題為什麼錯,為什麼沒有找到答案。要對照我們講的答題方法和規律,仔細分析這些題目。即使是做對的題目,也有必要了解為什麼"做對了"。總之,對於每一道已做的題目,分析自己為什麼對或為什麼錯,對是對在哪裏,錯是錯在何處,並按照答題方法進行驗證。同學們只要堅持這樣做,一定會逐步提高自己的閱讀和解題能力的。

一、綜合練習 **1**

Questions 1 –14

You are advised to spend about 15 minutes on Questions 1 –14 which refer to Reading Passage 1 below.

FINDING THE LOST FREEDOM

1. The private car is assumed to have widened our horizons and increased our mobility. When we consider our children's mobility, they can be driven to more places (and more distant places) than they could visit without access to a motor vehicle. However, allowing our cities to be dominated by cars has progressively eroded children's independent mobility. Children have lost much of their freedom to explore their own neighbourhood or city without adult supervision. In recent surveys, when parents in some cities were asked about their own childhood experiences, the majority remembered having more, or far more, opportunities for going out on their own, compared with their own children today. They had more freedom to explore their own environment.

2. Children's independent access to their local streets may be important for their own personal, mental and psychological development. Allowing them to get to know their own neighbourhood and community gives them a 'sense of place'. This depends on 'active exploration', which is not provided for when children are passengers in cars. (Such children may see more, but they learn less.) Not only is it important that children be able to get to local play areas by themselves, but walking and cycling journeys to school and to other destinations provide genuine play activities in themselves.

3. There are very significant time and money costs for parents associated with transporting their children to school, sport and to other locations. Research in the United Kingdom estimated that this cost, in 1990, was between 10 billion and 20 billion pounds.

4. The reduction in children's freedom may also contribute to a weakening of the sense of local community. As fewer children and adults use the streets as pedestrians, these streets become less sociable places. There is less opportunity for children and adults to have the spontaneous exchanges that help to engender a feeling of community. This in itself may exacerbate fears associated with assault and molestation of children, because there are fewer adults available who know their neighbours' children, and who can look out for their safety.

5. The extra traffic involved in transporting children results in increased traffic congestion, pollution and accident risk. As our roads become more dangerous, more parents drive their children to more places, thus contributing to increased levels of danger for the remaining pedestrians. Anyone who has experienced either the reduced volume of traffic jams near schools at the end of a school day, will not need convincing about these points. Thus, there are also important environmental implications of children's loss of freedom.

6. As individuals, parents strive to provide the best upbringing they can for their children. However, in doing so, (e. g. by driving their children to sport, school or recreation) parents may be contributing to a more dangerous environment for children generally. The idea that 'streets are for cars and back yards and playgrounds are for children' is a strongly held belief, and parents have little choice as individuals but to keep their children off the streets if they want to protect their safety.

7. In many parts of Dutch cities, and some traffic calmed precincts in Germany, residential streets are now places where cares must give way to pedestrians. In these areas, residents are accepting the view that the function of streets is not solely to provide mobility for cars. Streets may also be for social interaction, walking, cycling and playing. One of the most important aspects of these European cities, in terms of giving cities back to children, has been a range of 'traffic calming' initiatives, aimed at reducing the volume and speed of traffic. These initiatives have had complex interactive effects, leading to a sense that children have been able to 'recapture' their local neighbourhood, and more importantly, that they have been able to do this in safety. Recent research has demonstrated that children in many German cities have significantly higher levels of freedom to travel to places in their own neighbourhood or city than children in other cities in the world.

8. Modifying cities in order to enhance children's freedom will not only benefit children. Such cities will become more environmentally sustainable, as well as more sociable and more livable for all city residents. Perhaps it will be our concern for our children's welfare that convinces us that we need to challenge the dominance of the car in our cities.

Questions 1 −5

Read statements 1 −5 which relate to Paragraphs 1, 2 and 3 of the reading passage. Answer T if the statement is true, F if the statement is false, or NI if there is no information given in the passage. One has been done for you as an example.

> *Example: The private car has made people more mobile.*
>
> *Answer: T*

Q1. The private car has helped children have more opportunities to learn.

Q2. Children are more independent today than they used to be.

Q3. Walking and cycling to school allows children to learn more.

Q4. Children usually walk or cycle to school.

Q5. Parents save time and money by driving children to school.

Questions 6 −9

In Paragraphs 4 and 5, there are FOUR problems stated. These problems, numbered as questions 6 −9, are listed below. Each of these problems has a cause, listed A − G. Find the correct cause for each of the problems and write the corresponding letter A − G, in the spaces numbered 6 −9 on the answer sheet. One has been done for you as an example. There are more causes than problems so you will not use all of them and you may use any cause more than once.

Problems	Causes
Example:	*Answer*
Low sense of community feeling	*F*

Q6. streets become less sociable

Q7. fewer chances for meeting friends

Q8. fears of danger for children

Q9. higher accident risk

A. few adults know local children

B. fewer people use the streets

C. increased pollution

D. streets are less friendly

E. less traffic in school holidays

F. reduced freedom for children

G. more children driven to school

Questions 10 −14

Questions 10 −14 are statement beginnings which represent information given in Paragraphs 6, 7 and 8. In the box below, there are some statement endings numbered i −X. Choose the correct ending for each statement. One has been done for you as an example.

Example: By driving their children to school, parents help create...
Answer: i

Q10. Children should play...

Q11. In some German towns, pedestrians have right of way...

Q12. Streets should also be used for...

Q13. Reducing the amount of traffic and the speed is...

Q14. All people who live in the city will benefit if cities are...

List of statement endings

i ... a dangerous environment.
ii ... modified.
iii ... on residential streets.
iv ... modifying cities.
v ... neighbourhoods.
vi ... socialising.
vii ... in backyards.
viii ... for cars.
ix ... traffic calming.
x ... residential.

Questions 15 – 28

You are advised to spend about 25 minutes on Questions 15 – 28 which refer to Reading Passage 2 below.

RISING SEAS

Paragraph 1. <u>INCREASED TEMPERATURES</u>

The average air temperature at the surface of the earth has risen this century, as has the temperature of ocean surface waters. Because water expands as it heats, a warmer ocean means higher sea levels. We cannot say definitely that the temperature rises are due to the greenhouse effect; the heating may be part of a 'natural' variability over a long time-scale that we have not yet recognised in our short 100 years of recording. However, assuming the build up of greenhouse gases is responsible, and that the warming will continue. Scientists and inhabitants of low-lying coastal areas would like to know the extent of future sea level rises.

Paragraph 2. _____

Calculating this is not easy. Models used for the purpose have treated the ocean as passive, stationary and one-dimensional. Scientists have assumed that heat simply diffused into the sea from the atmosphere. Using basic physical laws, they then predict how much a known volume of water would expand for a given increase in temperature. But the oceans are not one-dimensional, and recent work by oceanographers, using a new model which takes into account a number of subtle facets of the sea-including vast and complex ocean currents-suggests that the rise in sea level may be less than some earlier estimates had predicted.

Paragraph 3. _____

An international forum on climate change, in 1986, produced figures for likely sea-level rises of 20cms and 1.4m, corresponding to atmospheric temperature increases of 1.5℃ and 4.5℃ respectively. Some scientists estimate that the ocean warming resulting from those temperature increases by the year 2050 would raise the sea level by between 10 cms and 40 cms. This model only takes into account the temperature effect on the oceans; it does not consider changes in sea level brought about by the melting of ice sheets and glaciers, and changes in groundwater storage. When we add on estimates of these. We arrive at figures for total sea-level rises of 15cm and 70cm respectively.

Paragraph 4. _____

It's not easy trying to model accurately the enormous complexities of the ever-changing oceans, with their great volume, massive currents and sensitivity to the influence of land masses and the atmosphere. For example, consider how heat enters the ocean, does it just 'diffuse' from the warmer air vertically into the water, and heat only the surface layer of the sea? (Warm water is less dense than cold, so it would not spread downwards.) Conventional models of sea-level rise have considered that this is the only method, but measurements have shown that the rate of heat transfer into the ocean by vertical diffusion is far lower in practice than the figures that many modellers have adopted.

Paragraph 5. _____

Much of the early work, for simplicity, ignored the fact that water in the oceans moves in three dimensions. By movement, of course, scientists don't mean waves, which are too small individually to consider, but rather movement of vast volumes of water in huge currents. To understand the importance of this, we now need to consider another process-advection. Imagine smoke rising from a chimney, on a still day it will slowly spread out in all directions by means of diffusion. With a strong directional wind, however, it will all shift downwind. This process is advection-the transport of properties (notably heat and salinity in the ocean) by the movement of bodies of air or water, rather than by conduction or diffusion.

Paragraph 6. _____

Massive ocean currents called gyres do the moving. These currents have far more capacity to store heat than does the atmosphere. Indeed, just the top 3m of the ocean contains more heat than the whole of the atmosphere. The origin of gyres lies in the fact that more heat from the Sun reaches the Equator than the Poles, and naturally heat tends to move from the former to the latter. Warm air rises at the Equator, and draws more air beneath it in the form of winds (the Trade Winds') that, together with other air movements, provide the main force driving the ocean currents.

Paragraph 7. _____

Water itself is heated at the Equator and moves poleward, twisted by the Earth's rotation and affected by the positions of the continents. The resultant broadly circular movements between about 10° and 40° North and South are clockwise in the Northern Hemisphere and anticlockwise in the Southern Hemisphere. They flow towards the east at mid latitudes in the equatorial region. They then flow towards the Poles, along the eastern sides of continents, as warm currents. When two different masses of water meet, one will move beneath the other, depending on their relative densities in the subduction process. The densities are determined by temperature and salinity. The convergence of water of different densities from the Equator and the Poles deep in the oceans causes continuous subduction. This means that water moves vertically as well as horizontally, cold water from the Poles travels at depth-it is denser than warm water-until it emerges at the surface in another part of the world in the form of a cold current.

Paragraph 8. HOW THE GREEN HOUSE EFFECT WILL CHANGE OCEAN TEMPERATURES

Ocean currents, in three dimensions, form a giant 'conveyor belt'. Distributing heat from the thin surface layer into the interior of the oceans and around the globe. Water may take decades to circulate in these 3 − D gyres in the top kilometre of the ocean, and centuries in the deeper water. With the increased atmospheric temperatures due to the greenhouse effect, the oceans' conveyor belt will carry more heat into the interior. This subduction moves heat around far more effectively than simple diffusion. Because warm water expands more than cold when it is heated, scientists had presumed that the sea level would rise unevenly around the globe. It is now believed that these inequalities cannot persist, as winds will act to continuously spread out the water expansion, of course, if global warming changes the strength and distribution of the winds, then this 'evening-out' process may not occur, and the sea level could rise more in some areas than others.

Questions 15 −20

There are 8 paragraphs numbered 1 −8 in Reading Passage 2. The first paragraph and the last paragraph have been given headings. From the list below numbered A − I, choose a suitable heading for the remaining 6 paragraphs, Write your Answers A − I in the spaces numbered 15 −20 on the answer sheet.

There are more headings than paragraphs, so you will not use all the headings.

List of headings

A. THE GYRE PRINCIPLE
B. THE GREENHOUSE EFFECT
C. HOW OCEAN WATERS MOVE
D. STATISTICAL EVIDENCE
E. THE ADVECTION PRINCIPLE
F. DIEFUSION VERSUS ADVECTION
G. FIGURING THE SEA LEVEL CHANGES
H. ESTIMATED FIGURES
I. THE DIFFUSION MODEL

15. Paragraph 2
16. Paragraph 3
17. Paragraph 4
18. Paragraph 5
19. Paragraph 6
20. Paragraph 7

Questions 21 −22

Answer questions 21 and 22 by selecting the correct answer to complete each sentence according to the information given in the reading passage. Write your answers A, B, C, or D in the spaces numbered 21 and 22 on the answer sheet.

21. Scientists do not know for sure why the air and surface of ocean temperatures are rising because:

A. there is too much variability

B. there is not enough variability

C. they have not been recording these temperatures for enough time

D. the changes have only been noticed for 100 years

22. New research leads scientists to believe that:

A. the oceans are less complex

B. the oceans are more complex

C. the oceans will rise more than expected

D. the oceans will rise less than expected

Question 23

Look at the following list of factors A – F and select THREE which are mentioned in the reading passage which may contribute to the rising ocean levels. Write the THREE corresponding letters A – F, in the space numbered 23 on the answer sheet.

List of factors

A. thermal expansion

B. melting ice

C. increased air temperature

D. higher rainfall

E. changes on the water table

F. increased ocean movement

Questions 24 – 28

Read each of the following statements 24 – 28. According to the information in the reading passage, if the statement is true, write T, if it is false, write F and if there is no information about the statement in the reading passage, write NI. Write your answers in the spaces numbered 24 – 28 on the answer sheet.

24. The surface layer of the oceans is warmed by the atmosphere.

25. Advection of water changes heat and salt levels.

26. A gyre holds less heat than there is in the atmosphere.

27. The process of subduction depends on the water density.

28. The sea level is expected to rise evenly over the Earth's surface.

Questions 29 – 40

You are advised to spend about 20 minutes on Questions 29 – 40 which refer to Reading Passage 3 below.

NEW RULES FOR THE PAPER GAME

1. Computerised data storage and electronic mail were to have heralded the paperless office. But, contrary to expectations, paper consumption throughout the world shows no sign of abating. In fact, consumption, especially of printing and writing papers, continues to increase. World demand for paper and board is now expected to grow faster than the general economic growth in the next 15 years. Strong demand will be underpinned by the growing industrialization of south-east Asia, the re-emergence of paper packaging, greater use of facsimile machines and photocopiers, and the popularity of direct-mail advertising . It is possible that by 2007, world paper and board demand will reach 455 million tons, compared with 241 million tons in 1991.

2. The pulp and paper industry has not been badly affected by the electronic technologies that promised a paperless society. But what has radically altered the industry's structure is pressure from another front——a more environmentally conscious society driving an irreversible move towards cleaner industrial production. The environmental consequences of antiquated pulp mill practices and technologies had marked this industry as one in need of reform. Graphic descriptions of deformed fish and thinning populations. Particularly in the Baltic Sea where old pulp mills had discharged untreated effluents for 100 years, have disturbed the international community.

3. Until the 1950s, it was common for pulp mills and other industries to discharge untreated effluent into rivers and seas. The environmental effects were at the time either not understood, or regarded as an acceptable cost of economic prosperity in an increasingly import-oriented world economy. But greater environmental awareness has spurred a fundamental change in attitude in the community, in government and in industry itself.

4. Since the early 1980s most of the world-scale pulp mills in Scandinavia and North America have modernised their operations, outlaying substantial amounts to improve production

methods. Changes in mill design and processes have been aimed at minimizing the environmental effects of effluent discharge while at the same time producing pulp with the whiteness and strength demanded by the international market. The environmental impetus is taking this industry even further, with the focus now on developing processes that may even eliminate waste-water discharges. But the ghost of the old mills continues to haunt the industry today. In Europe, companies face a flood of environment-related legislation. In Germany, companies are now being held responsible for the waste they create.

5. Pulp is the porridge-like mass of plant fibres from which paper is made. Paper makers choose the type of plant fibre and the processing methods, depending on what the end product will be used for: whether it is a sturdy packing box, a smooth sheet of writing paper or a fragile tissue. In wood, which is the source of about 90% of the world's paper production. Fibres are bound together by lignin, which gives the unbleached pulp a brown colour. The pulping stage separates the wood into fibres so they are suitable for paper making. Pulping can be done by mechanical grinding, or by chemical treatment in which wood chips are 'cooked' with chemicals, or by a combination of both methods.

6. Kraft pulping is the most widely used chemical process for producing pulp with the strength required by the high-quality paper market. It is now usually carried out in a continuous process in a large vessel called a digester. Woodchips are fed from a pile into the top of the digester. In the digester, the chips are cooked in a solution called white liquor, composed of caustic soda (sodium hydroxide) and sodium sulphide. The chips are cooked at high temperatures of up to 170°C for up to three hours. The pulp is then washed and separated from the spent cooking liquor which has turned dark and is now appropriately called black liquor. An important feature of kraft pulping is a chemical recovery system which recycles about 95% of the cooking chemicals and produces more than enough energy to the mill. In a series of steps involving a furnace and tanks, some of the black liquor is transformed into energy, while some is regenerated into the original white cooking liquor, the recovery system is an integral part of production in the pulp and paper industry. The pulp that comes out has little lignin left in the fibres. Bleaching removes the last remaining lignin and brightens the pulp. Most modern mills have modified their pulping processes to remove as much of the lignin as possible before the pulp moves to the bleaching stage.

Questions 29 −32

Below is a list of possible factors, A − G, which will influence the amount of paper being used in the future. From the list, choose FOUR factors which are mentioned below, numbered 29 −32 on the answer sheet.

List of factors

A. more people read newspapers

B. increased use of paper bags

C. increased book production for education

D. wider use of sign post advertising

E. increased use of fax machines

F. wider use of leaflet advertising

G. greater use of duplicating machines

Questions 33 −35

The following THREE statements are summaries of paragraphs 2 ,3 and 4 respectively. However, they are incomplete. Complete each of the statements using NO MORE THAN THREE WORDS FROM THE TEXT. Write your answers in the spaces numbered 33 −35 on the answer sheet.

33. The international community has begun to demand . . .

34. In the past, the environmental effects of pulp mill practices, were probably a price to pay for . . .

35. Some paper mills have recently modernised their mill design in order to decrease . . .

Questions 36 −40

Below is a list of possible steps in the kraft process of turning wood chips into paper. They are numbered 1 −8. Only FIVE of the steps listed below are mentioned in the passage. The steps are not listed in the correct order. Decide which steps are mentioned and write them in the correct order. Write the appropriate number for each step in the correct order in the spaces numbered 36 −40 on the answer sheet.

1. the chips are cooked

2. the fibres are bound by lignin

3. the pulp is bleached

4. woodchips are put into a pile

5. the pulp is dried

6. the pulp is removed from the black liquor

7. the chips are put into the white liquor

8. the pulp is washed

答案及詳解

PASSAGE 1 : FINDING THE LOST FREEDOM

先看文章的標題,"尋找失去的自由"。再看一眼圖,文章是和孩子的玩樂有關。文章後面的題目中沒有 Headings 題型,原文也沒有小標題,所以在答題前應把原文各段的第一句看一下。

Questions 1 –5(題型:T/F/NG)
特殊要求:要求答 T/F/NI
有利訊息:答案在原文的 1、2、3 段中找。

1. 答案:F
答案來自原文第二段中 Such children may see more, but they learn less。

2. 答案:F
答案來自原文第一段中 allowing our cities to be dominated by cars has progressively eroded children's independent mobility。erode 在這裡是"腐蝕、損害"的意思。

3. 答案:T
答案來自原文第二段中 Such children may see more, but they learn less。本題與第一題實際上是有關係的。判斷第一題為 F,那麼此題必為 T。

4. 答案:NI
容易誤選爲 F,實際上原文中並沒有明確地提到,屬於自行推理。

5. 答案:F
此題比較容易。對應原文第三段的第一句:There are very significant time and money costs for parents associated with transporting their children to school, sport and to other locations. 與原文直接相反。

Questions 6 –9(題型:Matching)
有利訊息:答案在原文的 4、5 段中找。
答案爲:6. B 7. B 8. A 9. G
詳解請見第三章中有關因果搭配題的部分。

Questions 10 –14(題型:完成句子 + 搭配題)
有利訊息:答案在原文的 6、7、8 段中找。
這種題型主要按照完成句子的方法去解題。

10. 先看題目中的關鍵詞:Children should play。從原文第六段起快速閱讀,對應第六段中的句子:The idea that 'streets are for cars and back yards and playgrounds are for children' is a strongly held belief。這時再看選項,從中找 back yards and playgrounds 的對應詞,答案應爲 vii。

11. 題目中的關鍵詞肯定是 German。繼續向下閱讀,對應第七段中的句子:In many parts of Dutch cities, and some traffic calmed precincts in Germany, residential streets are now places where cars must give way to pedestrians。仔細閱讀 residential streets are now places where cars must give way to pedestrians 這句話,意思是:居民街道現在是汽車必須讓位給人行道的地方,題目中說人行道有道路的優先權。這時再看選項,答案應爲 iii。

12. 題目的意思是:街道還應被用來……,繼續向下閱讀,對應第七段中的句子:Streets may also be for social interaction,這時再看選項,從中找 social interaction 的對應詞,答案應爲 vi。

13. 題目的意思是:降低交通的數量和速度是……,繼續向下閱讀,對應第七段中的句子:

One of the most important aspects of these European cities, in terms of giving cities back to children, has been a range of 'traffic calming' initiatives, aimed at reducing the volume and speed of traffic。reducing the volume and speed of traffic 與題目中的詞句對應上了。這時再看選項,答案應爲 ix。

14. 題目的意思是:所有居住在城市裏的人都會受益如果城市……,繼續向下閱讀,對應第八段中的第一句:Modifying cities in order to enhance children's freedom will not only benefit children。這時再看選項,答案應爲 ii。

PASSAGE 2：RISING SEAS

先看文章的標題,"上升的海"。文章後面的題目中有 Headings 題型,所以在答題前沒有必要讀原文,直接開始答題,先做 Headings 題型。

Questions 15 −20
15. 答案:G
先讀第二段的第一句:Calculating this is not easy,意思是:計算這個是不容易的,關鍵詞是 Calculating。與選項一一對應,應該對應 G。G 中的 FIGURING 是動名詞,與 calculating 詞性一致。FIGURE 的動詞意思是"計算、計算出",與 calculating 的意思也相同。本題容易誤選 H。H 中也有 FIGURES,但爲名詞,意思是"數字"。

16. 答案:H
先讀第三段的第一句:An international forum on climate change, in 1986,produced figures for likely sea-level rises of 20cms and 1. 4m,corresponding to atmospheric temperature increases of 1. 5℃ and 4. 5℃ respectively。其中有關鍵詞 figures,也有具體的數字。與選項一一對應,應該對應 H,意思是"估算的數字"。如果覺得不放心,可以再看一下第二句和最後一句。第二句中有 estimate,最後一句中既有 estimate,又有 figures。

17. 答案:I
此題較難。先讀第四段的第一句,與選項一一對應,發現一頭霧水。第二句是一個 For example,不用看。再看最後一句:Conventional models of sea-level rise have considered that

this is the only method, but measurements have shown that the rate of heat transfer into the ocean by vertical diffusion is far lower in practice than the figures that many modellers have adopted。這句比較長,也不好理解,重點看後面句子中 have shown that 之後的受詞子句。其中有關鍵詞:diffusion。

18. 答案:E
此題較難。主題句為最後一句:This process is advection-the transport of properties (notably heat and salinity in the ocean) by the movement of bodies of air or water, rather than by conduction or diffusion,關鍵詞為 advection。

19. 答案:A
此題很容易。主題句為第一句:Massive ocean currents called gyres do the moving,關鍵詞為 gyres。

20. 答案:C
主題句為第一句:Water itself is heated at the Equator and moves poleward, twisted by the Earth's rotation and affected by the positions of the continents,中文意思是:水在赤道被加熱,向兩極移動,與地球的自轉相反,並受陸地位置的影響。

Questions 21 –22(題型:單選題)
21. 答案:C
對應第一段中的句子:We cannot say definitely that the temperature rises are due to the greenhouse effect; the heating may be part of a 'natural' variability over a long time-scale that we have not yet recognised in our short 100 years of recording,中文意思是:我們不能確定地說,溫度升高是由於溫室效應。這種熱量可能是我們短短 100 多年的紀錄所不能認識到的一種自然的變化。

22. 答案:D
對應第二段中的最後一句:But the oceans are not one-dimensional, and recent work by oceanographers, using a new model which takes into account a number of subtle facets of the sea-including vast and complex ocean currents-suggests that the rise in level may be less than some earlier estimates had predicted。這句比較複雜,是一個混合句,詳見第五章中對該句的講解。該句 and 後面的句子的主幹是:work suggests that the rise in level may be less

than some earlier estimates had predicted。抓住這個主幹,不難看出,答案 D 就是它的改寫。

這兩道單選題並不難,難度主要在於原文句式複雜,而不是選項的迷惑性。

Questions 23(題型:複選題)

23. 答案:B、C、E

對應第三段中的句子: This model only takes into account the temperature effect on the oceans; it does not consider changes in sea level brought about by the melting of ice sheets and glaciers, and changes in groundwater storage,中文意思是:這個模型只考慮了對海洋的溫度的影響,沒有考慮冰塊和冰原的融化對海平面的影響,以及地下水儲存的變化。

Questions 24 −28(題型:T/F/NG)

24. 答案:NI

有的同學從文章的第一句: The average air temperature at the surface of the earth has risen this century,as has the temperature of ocean surface waters 判斷此題爲 T,實際上是錯誤理解了該句的意思。該句是倒裝句式,中文意思是:這個世紀以來,地球表面的空氣的平均溫度上升了,海水表面的溫度也一樣。其中 as 是"也一樣"的意思,並不表示原因。

25. 答案:T

關鍵詞爲 advection,對應原文第五段中的句子: This process is advection-the transport of properties(notably heat and salinity in the ocean)by the movement of bodies of air or water, rather than by conduction or diffusion, 其中 transport of properties(notably heat and salinity in the ocean)即是題目中的 changes heat and salt levels。

26. 答案:F

關鍵詞爲 gyre,對應原文第五段中的句子: These currents have far more capacity to store heat than does the atmosphere,原文是 far more,題目是 less than,題目與原文直接相反。

27. 答案:T

關鍵詞爲 subduction,對應原文第五段中的句子: The convergence of water of different densities from the Equator and the Poles deep in the oceans causes continuous subduction。

28. 答案:F

對應原文第八段中的句子：scientists had presumed that the sea level would rise unevenly around the globe，題目是 evenly，是反義詞，題目與原文直接相反。

這篇文章很難，句式複雜，而且涉及的內容很生僻。但實際上題目並不難，按照我們所講述的方法，還是能夠找到大部分題目的答案。如果非要先理解文章，再做題目，則很困難。

PASSAGE 3：NEW RULES FOR THE PAPER GAME

Questions 29 −32（題型：複選題）
特殊要求：無
有利訊息：答案在原文的第一段中找

答案：B、E、F、G
對應第一段中的句子：Strong demand will be underpinned by the growing industrialization of south-East Asia，the re-emergence of paper packaging，greater use of facsimile machines and photocopiers，and the popularity of direct-mail advertising，其中四個因素 re-emergence of paper packaging 對應 B；facsimile machines 對應 E；photocopiers 對應 G；the popularity of direct-mail advertising 對應 F。

Questions 33 −35（題型：完成句子）
特殊要求：NO MORE THAN THREE WORDS FROM THE TEXT
有利訊息：答案在原文的第 2、3、4 段中找

33. 題目中的關鍵詞為：international community 和 demand，對應原文第二段中的句子：a more environmentally conscious society driving an irreversible move towards cleaner industrial production，原文和題目的對應如下：

原　　　　文	題　　　　目
society	international community
move towards	demand

答案為：cleaner industrial production。

34. 對應原文第三段中的句子: The environmental effects were at the time either not under-stood, or regarded as an acceptable cost of economic prosperity in an increasingly import-oriented world economy, 原文和題目的對應如下:

原　　　文	題　　　目
at the time	in the past
cost	price

答案為: economic prosperity。

35. 對應原文第四段中的句子: Changes in mill design and processes have been aimed at minimizing the environmental effects of effluent discharge, 原文和題目的對應如下:

原　　　文	題　　　目
aimed at	in order to
minimising	decrease

答案為: the environmental effects。

這三道完成句子題有一定的難度,主要是原文和題目之間的對應不明顯。

Questions 36－40(題型:複選題＋排序)

注意題目要求中有 in the correct order。

通過題目要求中的關鍵詞 kraft process 先定位到原文第六段。仔細閱讀此段,注意以下幾點:

(1)一般考做一件事情的過程,注意原文中的動詞。

(2)正確答案的順序一般與原文的敘述順序是一致的。

(3)答案在原文中往往是集中出現的。

答案:4 7 1 8 6(順序必須正確)。

二、綜合練習 2

READING PASSAGE 1

OF DUCKS AND DUCK EGGS

For people who like to keep poultry, ducks offer certain advantages over hens. Ducks are immune to some common diseases found in hens and are less vulnerable to others. Some breeds of duck produce bigger eggs than hens. In addition, ducks lay eggs over a longer season than do hens.

Poultry keepers with gardens have less to worry about if they keep ducks rather than hens because the former are less apt to dig up plants and destroy roots. While both hens and ducks benefit the garden by eating pests, hens are known to damage herb and grass beds. Ducks, on the other hand, will search for insects and snails more carefully. Only very delicate plants are at risk from the broad, webbed feet of ducks.

Like all waterbirds, ducks need access to water, and duck keepers typically provide this by building a pond. Something this large is not absolutely necessary, however: ducks need only to be able to dip their heads in the water to keep their nostrils clean. If a pond is provided, though, it is important to keep ducklings away from it until they are old enough to withstand the cool temperature of the water about eight weeks.

When keeping ducks, one has to consider just how many the land will support. Generally the rule is 100 ducks per half hectare. If more than this proportion is introduced, there is a risk of compacting the soil, which can lead to muddy conditions for long periods as the rain is not easily absorbed into the ground.

While ducks offer many advantages over hens, they must be given a greater quantity of food, especially if regular eggs are desired. An adult duck will eat between 170 to 200 grams of food a day. If the ducks have access to grass and a pond, they will be able to find for themselves approximately 70% of their daily dietary requirements in warmer months but less than half that in colder times. Therefore, it is important that they be fed enough food, such as grain, every day.

Experienced duck keepers raise duckling every three years or so because it is after this period of time that ducks' egg-laying powers begin to seriously weaken. If the aim is to hatch duck-lings, keepers should be aware that not all ducks make good mothers, and that certain breeds of duck appear to be worse than others. The poor mothers abandon their eggs a few days after laying them. A sure way of making sure the rejected eggs hatch is to place them next to chicken eggs under a hen.

The eggs of ducks as food for humans have a mixed reputation. This is because of a number of cases of salmonella food poisoning in Europe in the 1970s. Although it was never conclu-sively shown that duck eggs were to blame, the egg-eating public stopped buying and many duck egg producers went bankrupt. Indeed there is a risk of salmonella poisoning when ducks lay their eggs in damp conditions, such as on ground that is constantly wet, but the same can be said for the eggs of hens. And commercial duck egg production in France and England, where the out-breaks of salmonella poisoning took place, followed the same standards as those used in the hen egg industry, which experienced no salmonella problems. (Storage of eggs, whether those of hen or duck, can also be a factor in contamination. Studies have found that bacterial growth reaches potentially dangerous levels at storage temperatures of 5℃ or greater.)

The salmonella scare was over by the early 1980s, but, at least in smaller markets like Aus-tralia and New Zealand, few producers wished to risk investment in ducks for fear of prob-lems. No large-scale commercial duck egg production exists in these countries. It has thus been left to small producers, and more commonly, home duck keepers.

poultry: farm birds(e. g. chickens, geese, ducks)

Questions 1 – 12

Questions 1 – 6
Classify the characteristics listed below as belonging to:

D   Ducks

H   hens

or

NI   if there is no information in the reading passage

Write the appropriate letters in boxes 1 −6 on your answer sheet.

Example

More vulnerable to illness   Answer: H

1. more eggs per week

2. lengthier laying period

3. less likely to uproot plants

4. dangerous to grass

5. eat more grain

6. better mothers

Questions 7 −10

Complete the partial summary below, Choose ONE or TWO words from the passage for each
answer. Write your answers in boxes 7 −10 on your answer sheet.

To prevent their ... (7)... from getting dirty, ducks should have access to water. This may
be provided by building a pond, but ducklings under ... (8)... of age should be prevented
from entering it because of the ... (9)... of the water. If too many ducks are kept on a plot
of land, the soil may eventually become... (10)... as a result of compaction. For this reason, it is advised that limits the number of ducks per half hectare of land to 100.

Questions 11 −12

Choose the appropriate letters(A −D) and write them in boxes 11 −12 on your answer sheet.

11. Salmonella food poisoning...

A. resulted from consumption of duck eggs.

B. created difficulties for the duck egg business.

C. occurred all over Europe.

D. was found in both duck and hen eggs.

12. Duck eggs...

A. have been produced in large quantities in New Zealand since the early 1980s.

B. are more at risk of salmonella contamination than hen eggs.

C. may be contaminated when laid in wet conditions.

D. should be kept at 5°C to prevent contamination.

READING PASSAGE 2

PEOPLE AND ORGANISATIONS: THE SELECTION ISSUE

A. In 1991 according to the Department of Trade and Industry, a record 48,000 British companies went out of business. When businesses fail, the post-mortem analysis is traditionally undertaken by accountants and market strategists. Unarguably organisations do fail because of undercapitalisation, poor financial management, adverse market conditions etc. Yet, conversely, organisations with sound financial backing, good product ideas and market acumen often underperform and fail to meet shareholders' expectations. The complexity, degree and sustainment of organisational performance requires an explanation which goes beyond the balance sheet and the "paper conversion" of financial inputs into profit making outputs. A more complete explanation of "what went wrong" necessarily must consider the essence of what an organisation actually is and that one of the financial inputs, the most important and often the most expensive, is people.

B. An organisation is only as good as the people it employs. Selecting the right person for the job involves more than identifying the essential or desirable range of skills, educational and professional qualifications necessary to perform the job and then recruiting the candidate who is most likely to possess these skills or at least is perceived to have the ability and predisposition to acquire them. This is a purely person-skills match approach to selection.

C. Work invariably takes place in the presence and/or under the direction of others, in a particular organisational setting. The individual has to "fit" in with the work environment, with other employees, with the organisational climate, style of work, organisation and culture of the organisation. Different organisations have different cultures (Cartwrigha & Cooper, 1991; 1992). Working as an engineer at British Aerospace will not necessarily be a similar experience to working in the same capacity at GEC or Plessey.

D. Poor selection decisions are expensive. For example, the costs of training a policeman are about £ 20,000 (approx. US $ 30,000). The costs of employing an unsuitable technician on an oil rig or in a nuclear plant could, in an emergency, result in millions of pounds of damage or loss of life. The disharmony of a poor person-environment fit (PE-fit) is likely to result in low job satisfaction, lack of organisational commitment and employee stress, which affect organisational outcomes i. e. productivity, high labour turnover and absenteeism, and individual outcomes i. e. physical, psychological and mental well-being.

E. However, despite the importance of the recruitment decision and the range of sophisticated and more objective selection techniques available, including the use of psychometric tests, assessment centres etc. , many organisations are still prepared to make this decision on the basis of a single 30 to 45 minute unstructured interview. Indeed, research has demonstrated that a selection decision is often made within the first four minutes of the interview. In the remaining time, the interviewer then attends exclusively to information that reinforces the initial 'accept' or 'reject' decision. Research into the validity of selection methods has consistently demonstrated that the unstructured interview, where the interviewer asks any questions he or she likes, is a poor predictor of future job performance and fares little better than more controversial methods like graphology and astrology. In times of high unemployment, recruitment becomes a "buyer's market" and this was the case in Britain during the 1980s.

F. The future, we are told, is likely to be different. Detailed surveys of social and economic trends in the European Community show that Europe's population is falling and getting older. The birth rate in the Community is now only three-quarters of the level needed to ensure replacement of the existing population. By the year 2020, it is predicted that more than one in four Europeans will be aged 60 or more and barely one in five will be under 20. In five-year period between 1983 and 1988 the Community's female workforce grew by almost six million. As a result, 51% of all women aged 14 to 64 are now economically active in the labour market compared with 78% of men.

G. The changing demographics will not only affect selection ratios, they will also make it increasingly important for organisations wishing to maintain their competitive edge to be more responsive and accommodating to the changing needs of their workforce if they are to retain and develop their human resources. More flexible working hours, the opportunity to work from home or job share, the provision of childcare facilities etc, will play a major role in attracting and retaining staff in the future.

Questions 13 – 26

You should spend about 20 minutes on Questions 13 – 26 which are based on Reading Passage 2.

Questions 13 – 17

Reading Passage 2 has seven paragraphs A – G.

Choose the most suitable headings for paragraphs **B – E** and **G** from the list of headings below. Write the appropriate numbers (i – x)in boxes 12 – 16 on your answer sheet.

NB There are more headings than paragraphs so you will not use all of them.

You may use any of the headings more than once.

List of Headings

> (i) The effect of changing demographics on organisations
>
> (ii) Future changes in the European workforce
>
> (iii) The unstructured interview and its validity
>
> (iv) The person-skills match approach to selection
>
> (v) The implications of a poor person-environment fit
>
> (vi) Some poor selection decisions
>
> (vii) The validity of selection procedures
>
> (viii) The person-environment fit
>
> (ix) Past and future demographic changes in Europe
>
> (x) Adequate and inadequate explanations of organisational failure

Example	Paragraph A	Answer (x)

13. Paragraph B

14. Paragraph C

15. Paragraph D

16. Paragraph E

17. Paragraph G

Example	Paragraph F	Answer (ix)

Questions 18 −23

Do the following statements agree with the views of the writer in Reading passage2.

In boxes 18 −23 on your answer sheet write

YES   if the statement agrees with the writer

NO   if the statement does not agree with the writer

NOT GIVEN   if there is no information about this in the passage

18. Organisations should recognise that their employees are a significant part of their financial assets.

19. Open-structured 45 minute interviews are the best method to identify suitable employees.

20. The rise in the female workforce in the European Community is a positive trend.

21. Graphology is a good predictor of future job performance.

22. In the future, the number of people in employable age groups will decline.

23. In 2020, the percentage of the population under 20 will be smaller than now.

Questions 24 −26

Complete the notes below with words taken from Reading Passage 2 Use *NO MORE THAN ONE* or *TWO WORDS* for each answer.

Write your answers in boxes 24 −26 on your answer sheet.

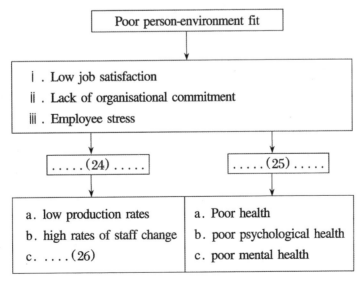

READING PASSAGE 3

You should spend about 20 minutes on Questions 27 −38 which are based on Reading Passage 3 below.

POPULATION VIABILITY ANALYSIS

Part A

To make political decisions about the extent and type of forestry in a region it is important to understand the consequences of those decisions. One tool for assessing the impact of forestry on the ecosystem is population viability analysis (PVA). This is a tool for predicting the probability that a species will become extinct in a particular region over a specific period. It has been successfully used in the United States to provide input into resource exploitation decisions and assist wildlife managers and there is now enormous potential for using population viability to assist wildlife management in Australia's forests.

A species becomes extinct when the last individual dies. This observation is a useful starting point for any discussion of extinction as it highlights the role of luck and chance in the extinction process. To make a prediction about extinction we need to understand the processes that can contribute to it and these fall into four broad categories which are discussed below.

Part B

A. Early attempts to predict population viability were based on demographic uncertainty. Whether an individual survives from one year to the next will largely be a matter of chance. Some pairs may produce several young in a single year while others may produce none in that same year. Small populations will fluctuate enormously because of the random nature of birth and death and these chance fluctuations can cause species extinction even if, on average, the population size should increase. Taking only this uncertainty of ability to reproduce into account. Extinction is unlikely if the number of individuals in a population is above about 50 and the population is growing.

B. Small populations cannot avoid a certain amount of inbreeding. This is particularly true if there is a very small number of one sex. For example, if there are only 20 individuals of a species and only one is a male, all future individuals in the species must be descended from

that one male. For most animal species such individuals are less likely to survive and reproduce. Inbreeding increases the chance of extinction.

C. Variation within a species is the raw material upon which natural selection acts. Without
genetic variability a species lacks the capacity to evolve and cannot adapt to changes in its environment or to new predators and new diseases. The loss of genetic diversity associated with
reductions in population size will contribute to the likelihood of extinction.

D. Recent research has shown that other factors need to be considered. Australia's environment fluctuates enormously from year to year. These fluctuations add yet another degree of
uncertainty to the survival of many species. Catastrophes such as fire, flood, drought or epi-
demic may reduce population sizes to a small fraction of their average level. When allowance
is made for these two additional elements of uncertainty the population size necessary to be
confident of persistence for a few hundred years may increase to several thousand.

Part C

Beside these processes we need to bear in mind the distribution of a population. A species
that occurs in five isolated places each containing 20 individuals will not have the same probability of extinction as species with a single population of 100 individuals in a single locality.
Where logging occurs (that is, the cutting down of forests for timber) forest-dependent crea-
tures in that area will be forced to leave. Ground-dwelling herbivores may return within a
decade. However, arboreal marsupials (that is animals which live in trees) may not recover
to pre-logging densities for over a century. As more forests are logged, animal population
sizes will be reduced further. Regardless of the theory or model that we choose, a reduction
in population size decreases the genetic diversity of a population and increases the probability
of extinction because of any or all of the processes listed above. It is therefore a scientific
fact that increasing the area that is logged in any region will increase the probability that
forest-dependent animals will become extinct.

Questions 27 –38

Questions 27 –30
Do the following statements agree with the views of the writer in Part A of Reading Passage

3? In boxes 27 −30 on your answer sheet write

    YES   if the statement agrees with the writer

    NO   if the statement contradicts the writer

    NOT GIVEN   if it is impossible to say what the writer thinks about this

Example :

A link exists between the consequences of decisions and the decision making process itself.
Answer : YES

27. Scientists are interested in the effect of forestry on native animals.

28. PVA has been used in Australia for many years.

29. A species is said to be extinct when only one individual exists.

30. Extinction is a naturally occurring phenomenon.

Questions 31 −34

These questions are based on Part B of Reading Passage 3.

In paragraphs A to D the author describes four processes which may contribute to the extinction of a species. Match the list of processes (i −vi) to the paragraphs. Write the appropriate number (i −vi) in boxes 31 −34 on your answer sheet.

NB There are more processes than paragraphs so you will not use all of them.

31. Paragraph A	i Loss of ability to adapt
32. Paragraph B	ii Natural disasters
33. Paragraph C	iii An imbalance of the sexes
34. Paragraph D	iv Human disasters
	v Evolution
	vi The haphazard nature of reproduction

Questions 35 −37

Based on your reading of Part C, complete the sentences below with words taken from the passage. Use **NO MORE THAN THREE WORDS** for each answer. Write your answers in boxes 35 −37 on your answer sheet.

While the population of a species may be on the increase, there is
always a chance that small isolated groups . . . (35) . . .
Survival of a species depends on a balance between the size of a

population and its . . . (36) . . .

The likelihood that animals which live in forests will become extinct is
increased when . . . (37) . . .

Question 38

Choose the appropriate Letter A – D and write it in box 39 on your answer sheet.

38. An alternative heading for the passage could be：

A. The protection of native flora and fauna

B. Influential factors in assessing survival probability

C. An economic rationale for the logging of forests

D. Preventive measures for the extinction of a species

答案及詳解

PASSAGE 1：OF DUCKS AND DUCK EGGS

Questions 1 –6（題型：搭配題 + 是非題）

1. 答案：NI

2. 答案：D
答案來自原文第一段最後一句：In addition, ducks lay eggs over a longer season than do
hens。

3. 答案：D
答案來自原文第二段第一句：Poultry keepers with gardens have less to worry about if they
keep ducks rather than hens because the former are less apt to dig up plants and destroy
roots。

4. 答案：H
答案來自原文第二段中的一句：While both hens and ducks benefit the garden by eating
pests, hens are known to damage herb and grass beds。

5. 答案：NI

此題是陷阱題，有的同學會誤選 D。有的同學從第五段的最後一句：Therefore, it is impor-
tant that they be fed enough food, such as grain, every day 得出 D。原文說，鴨子要被餵足
夠的食物，比如說穀物。"比如說"不能說明任何問題。

6. 答案：H

答案來自原文第六段最後兩句：The poor mothers abandon their eggs a few days after laying
them. A sure way of making sure the rejected eggs hatch is to place them next to chicken
eggs under a hen。

Questions 7 –10.（題型：Summary）

特殊要求：ONE or TWO words from the passage

先仔細讀摘要的第一句話，雖然有一個空格，但不難發現它與原文第三段的第一句是對
應的。此題與目前考試的摘要填空的形式很接近：摘要不太長，對應原文的兩到三段。
這道題不難，讀原文的第三段和第四段，找題目和原文的對應詞，不難確定各題的答案。
7. nostrils 8. eight weeks 9. cool temperature 10. muddy

Questions 11 –12.（題型：單選題）

這兩道單選題與目前考試的形式很接近，選項的干擾性很大。
11. B
12. C（選項中有不確定性的詞：may）

PASSAGE 2：PEOPLE AND ORGANISATIONS：THE SELEC-
TION ISSUE

Questions 13 –17（題型：Headings）

13. 答案為：iv
主題句為該段的第一句和最後一句。

14. 答案為：viii
主題句為該段的第二句。

15. 答案為：v
是幾道題中最難的，特別容易誤選 vi。先看第一句：Poor selection decisions are expensive.，應該注意到此句的關鍵詞是 expensive，強調不好的選擇決定的代價是很昂貴的，所以不能選 vi。如果不能確定，可以再看第二句。第二句是個舉例子的句子，可以不看。看最後一句，最後一句比較長，抓住主幹和關鍵詞 poor person-environment fit，確定答案為 v。

16. 答案為：iii
主題句為該段的第一句。該句比較複雜，注意看主要子句，抓住關鍵詞 unstructured interview。

17. 答案為：i
主題句為該段的第一句。

做 Headings 的關鍵是抓住該段的主題句（第一句、第二句和最後一句）。

Questions 18 −23（題型：T/F/NG）
18. YES（第 A 段）
19. NO（第 E 段）
20. NOT GIVEN
21. NO（第 E 段）
22. YES（第 F 段）
23. YES（第 F 段）

Questions 24 −26（題型：填圖填表題）

根據已知的關鍵詞 poor person-environment fit 對應到原文的 D 段中的句子：The disharmony of a poor person-environment fit（PE-fit）is likely to result in low job satisfaction, lack of organisational commitment and employee stress, which affect organisational outcomes i. e. productivity, high labour turnover and absenteeism, and individual outcomes i. e. physical, psychological and mental well-being。原文與題目的對應詞爲：

原　　　　文	題　　　　目
Productivity	Low production rates
High labour turnover	High rates of staff change
Physical	Poor health

24. 答案爲：organisational outcomes

25. 答案爲：individual outcomes

26. 答案爲：absenteeism

PASSAGE 3：POPULATION VIABILITY ANALYSIS

Questions 27 −30（題型：T/F/NG）

27. NOT GIVEN

28. NO

29. NO

30. NOT GIVEN

Questions 31 −34（題型：搭配題）

31. vi

32. iii

33. i

34. ii

Questions 35 −37（題型：完成句子）

35. may not survive

36. locality/distribution

37. logging takes place/occurs

Question 38（題型：全文主旨題）

38. B

CHAPTER V

複雜句子
分析

READING

學習指導

　　學會句子分析是提高閱讀水準的關鍵之一。閱讀理解文章難的原因之一在於句子結構的複雜。從近年 IELTS 考試的閱讀理解文章看，可以看出句子的兩個特點：

(1) 句子較長，大多數句子都在 20 個字以上，很多句子超過 50 個字。
(2) 句子結構複雜，結構複雜的簡單句、並列句、複合句、並列複合句、多重複合句、被動句、倒裝句、插入語等句型使用頻繁，造成同學們理解上的困難，由於這些句型在 IELTS 閱讀的文章中比較普遍，因此考前熟悉它們非常必要。具體而言，按時間要求做完一套閱讀題後，要從中挑一些又長又複雜的句子加以分析，學會抓主幹。這樣，閱讀速度和準確率就會提高。

　　句子結構分析的關鍵之一是抓主幹。對於複合句，抓主要子句；對於主要子句或比較複雜的簡單句，要抓主詞和動詞。抓主幹，抓主要子句的主要意思，而對修飾成分先不特別注意，這是提高閱讀速度的一個重要方法。

　　作者根據多年的教學經驗，從試題中挑選了一些較難的句子，進行結構分析，提供中文譯文，同時提供其中一些句子的主幹部分及其中文譯文。同學們應認真閱讀這一部分。相信對提高閱讀水準會有幫助的。

　　作者在提供中文譯文的時候，沒有用標準的書面語言，而是按照英文句子的結構來翻譯的。因此有些翻譯會顯得生硬，但它與英文原句的結構是一樣的，這樣是為了更有助於同學們理解英文原句的句子結構。

❖ ❖ **一、結構複雜的簡單句** ❖ ❖

　　如果句子只包含一個主謂結構,而句子各個成分都只由單字或片語表示,它就是簡單句(不管句子是長是短)。

　　有的簡單句並不簡單,也很長,複雜的簡單句包括:

　　(1) 分詞及分詞片語做定語、狀語

　　(2) 動名詞及動名詞片語做主詞、表語、受詞

　　(3) 不定詞及不定詞片語做主詞、受詞、表語、定語、狀語

　　(4) 形容詞片語做後置定語

1. To resolve a dispute means to turn opposing positions into a single outcome.

中文譯文:解決一個衝突意味着把相反的各方變成一個單一的結果。

結構分析:不定詞片語 to resolve a dispute 做主詞,動詞是 means,不定詞片語 to turn opposing positions into a single outcome 做受詞,其中分詞 opposing 是 positions 的定語。

2. Reconciling such interests is not easy.

中文譯文:調和這種利益是不容易的。

結構分析:動名詞片語 reconciling such interests 做主詞。動名詞片語做主詞,動詞一般用單數。

3. It involves probing for deeply rooted concerns, devising creative solutions, and making trade-offs and compromises where interests are opposed.

中文譯文:它涉及到探究深層次的關注,想出有創造性的解決方案,以及當利益矛盾時,做出交易和妥協。

結構分析:這是一個簡單句。主詞是 it,動詞是 involves,三個動名詞片語做受詞(屬於平行結構)。在閱讀中經常出現"A and B"或"A or B"的形式,其中 A 與 B 同義或近義,所以只要認識其中一個詞就能猜測出另一個詞的大概意思。例如:trade-off and compromises。

4. The most common procedure for doing this is negotiation, the act of communication intended to reach agreement.

中文譯文:做這件事最常用的方法是談判,一種想要達成一致的交流的行為。

結構分析:過去分詞片語 intended to reach agreement 是 the act of communication 的後置定語,the act of communication intended to reach agreement 是 negotiation 的同位語,對 negotiation 進行解釋。

5. In other words, seeing large pupils gives rise to larger pupils.

中文譯文:換句話說,看大的瞳孔會引起更大的瞳孔。

結構分析:動名詞片語 seeing large pupils 做主詞。

6. Initially, the RTA had proposed to erect a new timber fence, replacing the existing suburban fences, to act as a noise barrier.

中文譯文:最初,RTA 建議建造一個新的木屏障,代替現存的屏障,來作為一個新的噪音屏障。

結構分析:不定詞片語 to erect a new timber fence 做 had proposed 的受詞,replacing the existing suburban fences 是分詞片語做狀語,其中,existing 是現在分詞做 suburban fences 的前置定語,to act as a noise barrier 是不定詞片語做狀語。

7. The Fanwall barrier to be installed at Rhodes is the first to be erected in Australia.

中文譯文:要在 Rhodes 建造的 Fanwall 屏障是首次在澳洲建造的。

結構分析:不定詞片語 to be installed at Rhodes 做 Fanwall barrier 的後置定語,不定詞片語 to be erected in Australia 做 the first 的後置定語。

8. Yet, a father accepting responsibility for behaviour problems is linked with positive outcomes.

中文譯文:一個為行為問題負責的父親是和正面的結果相聯繫的。

結構分析:accepting responsibility for behaviour problems 是現在分詞片語做 father 的後置定語。

❖ 二、並列句及並列複合句 ❖

　　如果句子包含兩個或更多互不依從的主謂結構,就是並列句。並列句中的分句通常用一個並列連詞來連接,最常見的是 and 和 but。

　　有時,一個並列句中的一個(或更多)分句,可能包含有一個(或更多)子句,這種句子稱爲並列複合句。並列複合句句式複雜,是同學們閱讀的難點。

　　對付並列句及並列複合句的方法是各個擊破。先抓住並列連詞 and 或 but,識別出是並列句後,分別理解並列連詞前後的句子。

1. Noise generated by traffic on arterial roads and freeways is an increasing problem in Australia and there is growing concern among highways authorities in Australia about the limitations of some types of noise barriers which have been installed in this country.

中文譯文:在澳洲,由主幹路和高速公路的交通所產生的噪音是一個日益嚴重的問題。而且澳洲的高速公路主管部門也越來越關注已經安裝在這個國家的一些噪音屏障的局限性。

結構分析:一個典型的並列複合句,並列連詞 and 連接兩個句子,前一個句子是一個簡單句,主詞是 noise, generated by traffic on arterial roads and freeways 是過去分詞片語做 noise 的後置定語,後面的句子中有一個 which 引道的定語子句。

2. However, low barriers are not effective and high timber barriers have become much more expensive.

中文譯文:然而,矮屏障無效,高屏障更昂貴。

結構分析:一般的並列句,and 連接兩個簡單句。

3. Furthermore, Fanwall is maintenance free and it is not susceptible to damage by fire and vandalism.

中文譯文:而且 Fanwall 是不需要維護的,而且它不易受到火災和蓄意破壞的損壞。

結構分析:這是一般的並列句,and 連接兩個簡單句。vandalism 是一個生詞,但由於和 fire 在一起,fire and vandalism,所以應能猜出是和火災一樣不好的東西,實際在考試中能理解成這樣就可以了。

4. The parental role is central to the stress-related anxiety reported by employed mothers, and a major contributor to such stress is their taking a greater role in child care.

中文譯文：在職母親有和壓力相關的焦慮，這種壓力的主要原因是她們在照顧孩子方面具有更大的角色。

結構分析：是一個並列句，and 前後的句子都是一個簡單句。

5. Governments have encouraged waste paper collection and sorting schemes and at the same time, the paper industry has responded by developing new recycling technologies that have paved the way for even greater utilisation of used fibre.

中文譯文：政府已經鼓勵廢紙回收和分類系統，而且，同時造紙工業也通過開發新的回收技術做出了反應，這個回收技術為更大程度地利用使用過的紙鋪平了道路。

結構分析：這是並列複合句，and 前面的句子是一個簡單句，後面的句子中有一個 that 引道的定語子句做 new recycling technologies 的定語，by 是介系詞，表示"通過……的方式"的意思，後面常接動名詞。

6. Already, waste paper constitutes 70% of paper used for packaging, and advances in the technology required to remove ink from the paper have allowed a higher recycled content in newsprint and writing paper.

中文譯文：廢紙組成了用於包裝的紙張的70%。而且從紙張中去掉墨水的技術進步已經允許了在新聞紙和書寫用紙上的更高的回收滿意度。

結構分析：是並列句，and 前後都是一個簡單句，但都不簡單。and 前面的簡單句的動詞是 constitutes，而不是 used for，used for 是過去分詞片語做 paper 的後置定語，and 後面的句子的主詞是 advances，動詞是 have allowed，required to remove ink from the paper 不是動詞，而是過去分詞片語做 technology 的後置定語。

小竅門

過去分詞片語做後置定語在 IELTS 閱讀中經常出現，因為形式相同，有時容易理解為動詞（過去式），從而造成理解上的障礙。怎樣區分動詞加 ed 形式是動詞（過去式），還是後置定語（過去分詞片語）呢？有兩種方法：

(1) 看它與前面的詞是主動還是被動的關係。是主動，則是動詞過去式。如果是被動的關係，則是後置定語（過去分詞片語）。如上面例句中，paper used for

packaging，紙張是被用於包裝，所以 used for packaging 與 paper 是被動的關係，所以是過去分詞片語做後置定語。

(2)看句子中是否有其他的動詞。一個句子中，只能有一個動詞，所以，如果該句已有了一個確定無疑的動詞，那麼這個 ed 只能是過去分詞片語了。如上面的例句中，constitutes 肯定是動詞，所以 used for packaging 不能再是動詞了。

7. But the idea never died and the Frenchman Baron Pierre de Coubertin, an educator and scholar, founded the modern Olympics.

中文譯文：但是，這個思想從未死亡，而且，法國人顧拜旦，一個教育家和學者，創立了現代奧林匹克運動。

結構分析：是一般的並列句，and 前後是兩個簡單句，後面的句子中，an educator and scholar 是插入語，做主詞顧拜旦的同位語。

小竅門

閱讀文章中出現人名、地名，如果自己知道，可以翻譯出來，如本文中的顧拜旦。如果不知道，可採用首字母提煉法，如本文中，可用法國人 BPC，或法國人 B，這樣，一般是不會影響讀文章和做題目的。

❖ 三、複合句及多重複合句 ❖

　　複合句中包含有兩個或更多的主謂結構,其中,有一個(或更多的)主謂結構充當句子的某一(些)成分,如主詞、受詞、表語、定語、狀語、同位語等。充當一個句子成分的主謂結構稱爲子句。由於子句在句子中的成分不同,可分爲主詞子句、受詞子句、表語子句、定語子句、狀語子句和同位語子句等。

　　有時複合句的一個(或多個)子句可能包含有一個(或多個)子句,即子句裏套着子句,這種句子稱爲多重複合句。多重複合句句式複雜,是同學們閱讀的難點。

　　對付複合句及多重複合句的方法是,先抓住主幹,即抓住主要子句,然後再識別子句的類型,進而搞懂整句話的意思。大部分題目的答案來自主要子句,但也有一部分題目的答案來自子句。

1. Interests are needs, desires, concerns, fears —— the things one cares about or wants.

中文譯文:利益是需要、渴望、關注、恐懼 —— 一個人關心或想要的東西。

結構分析:one cares about or wants 是 the things 的定語子句。

2. Another interests-based procedure is mediation, in which a third party assists the disputants, the two sides in the dispute, in reaching-agreement.

中文譯文:另一個基於利益的過程叫作調解,在調解中第三方幫助衝突者,即衝突的雙方,達成一致。

結構分析:in which 引出的定語子句 in which a third party assists the disputants, the two sides in the dispute, in reaching-agreement 是對 mediation 的解釋,在定語子句中,the two sides in the dispute 是 disputants 的同位語,同時也是插入語結構。

3. It is often complicated to attempt to determine who is right in a dispute.

中文譯文:試圖決定誰在衝突中是正確的通常很複雜。

結構分析:it 是形式主詞,實際主詞是不定詞片語 to attempt to determine who is right in a dispute,受詞子句 who is right 是 determine 的受詞。

4. Although it is usually straightforward where rights are formalized in law, other rights take the form of unwritten but socially accepted standards of behaviour, such as reciprocity, precedent, equality, and seniority.

中文譯文:雖然當對錯在法律中被正式規定時,通常是很直截了當的,但其他的對錯採取的是非書面的、社會接受的行爲標準,例如:互惠、先例、平等和資歷。

結構分析:although 引道一個讓步副詞子句,注意本句的最後有一個 such as,是例如的意思,後面的內容往往是舉例說明,屬於不重要的內容,可不作爲閱讀的重點,socially accepted 是 standards of behaviour 的前置定語。

5. The most typical rights procedure is adjudication, in which disputants present evidence and arguments to a neutral third party who has the power to make a decision that must be followed by both disputants.

中文譯文:最典型的判斷對錯的過程是裁決,在裁決中,衝突方拿出證據和論證給一個中立的第三方,這個第三方有權利做出一個決定,衝突雙方必須遵守這個決定。

結構分析:多重複合句,定語子句中套着兩個定語子句。in which 至句尾都是 adjudication 的定語,who 至句尾是 third party 的定語,最後一個由 that 引道的定語子句是 decision 的定語。

6. Since both rapid and light rail have electric engines, pollution is measured not from the motor exhaust, but from the power plant generating electricity, which is usually located outside the city, where air quality problems are less serious.

中文譯文:因爲地鐵和輕軌都有電子引擎,所以污染不是從車輛產生的廢氣中測量,而是從產生電力的發電廠測量,發電廠通常位於城市之外,那裏空氣問題不太嚴重。

結構分析:since 引道一個原因狀語子句,主要子句中有一個特殊句型,not... but... ,意思是"不是,而是",generating electricity 是現在分詞片語做 the power plant 的後置定語,which 引道的定語子句 which is usually located outside the city 做 power plant 的定語,where 引道一個定語子句做 outside the city 的定語。

全句主幹:Pollution is measured from the power plant. (污染從發電廠那裏測量。)

抓住了這個句子的主幹,就掌握了此句的主要內容,題目常常是考文章中的主要內容,實際考試中的題目如下:

23. Where is pollution from rail transport measured?

如果你能夠把握上句話的主幹,雖然它是一個比較複雜的句子,你還是能做對這道題的,答案爲 the power plant。

7. It has already been well established that changes in pupil size are clearly associated with

changes in attitude.

中文譯文:瞳孔大小的變化和態度的變化之間有清楚的聯繫,這個觀點已經很好地建立起來。

結構分析:主詞子句,it 是形式主詞,that 到句尾是 that 引導的子句做真正的主詞。pupil 在這裡的意思是"瞳孔",而不是"小學生"。IELTS 閱讀中經常考一些熟詞的偏僻意思,稱為"熟詞僻義",如 novel,常考的意思是"新穎的",而不是"小說"。

8. However it now appears that enlarged or constricted pupils can also affect the response of the person who observed them.

中文譯文:然而,現在表明,放大或縮小的瞳孔還會影響觀察它們的人的反應。

結構分析:表語子句。it 是主詞,that 到句尾是 that 引導的子句做表語。表語子句中有一個 who 引導的定語子句 who observed them 做 person 的定語。所以,全句是多重複合句。注意句子最後的代名詞 them,指代的是 pupils。放大或縮小的瞳孔會影響觀察這些瞳孔的人的反應。enlarged or constricted 是過去分詞做 pupils 的前置定語。

9. It seems that what is appealing about large pupils in a woman is that they are an indicator of interest, which can be interpreted as sexual interest.

中文譯文:看起來,似乎女人的大瞳孔吸引人的是它們是興趣的表示者,可以被解釋為性別的興趣。

結構分析:多重複合句。it 是主詞,that 到句尾是 that 引導的子句做表語。這個表語子句中的主詞又是一個主詞子句 what is appealing about large pupils in a woman,是 what 引導的子句,that 至句尾 that they are an indicator of interest, which can be interpreted as sexual interest 是表語子句中的表語子句。表語子句中又有一個 which 引導的定語子句 which can be interpreted as sexual interest。

10. That the dilation response is in fact learned rather than innate is supported by experiments with children.

中文譯文:瞳孔放大反應實際上是習來的而不是天生的,這被對孩子們的實驗所支持。

結構分析:that 引導的主詞子句 that the dilation response is in fact learned rather than innate 做全句的主詞。全句的主要子句結構是一個被動語態,is supported,意思是"被支持"。

11. In one experiment, subjects aged 6 to 22 were shown drawings of female faces that had

different sized pupils, and asked to choose the one which was "happier".

中文譯文: 在一個試驗中, 從 6 歲到 22 歲的實驗對象看不同瞳孔大小的女性的臉的圖畫, 並被要求從中選擇更高興的一個。

結構分析: 全句主詞是 subjects, 有兩個並列動詞 were shown 和 and asked, 都是被動語態, that had different sized pupils 是定語子句做 drawings of female faces 的定語, which was "happier" 是定語子句做 the one 的定語, 過去分詞片語 aged 6 to 22 是 subjects 的後置定語。

12. Since variations in distances and city densities affect the total kilometres of travel, the annual number of trips each person takes by public transport provides a better standard for comparing its importance in various cities.

中文譯文: 因為距離和城市密度的不同影響旅行的總公里數, 所以每人乘坐公共交通每年的旅行數目提供了一個更好的比較它在各個城市的重要性的標準。

結構分析: 多重複合句, since 引道一個原因狀語子句, 主要子句中有一個定語子句, each person takes by public transport 是 the annual number of trips 的定語。

13. The challenge now is to develop policies and practices based on a presumption of shared responsibility between men and women, and a presumption that there are potential benefits for men and women, as well as for families and the community, if there is greater gender equality in the responsibilities and pleasures of family life.

中文譯文: 現在的挑戰是基於如下的假設開發出政策和實踐。一個假設是男人和女人之間的共享責任, 另一個假設是如果在家庭責任和快樂上有更大的性別平等, 對男人和女人, 以及家庭和社會, 都有潛在的好處。

結構分析: 這個句子比較複雜, 全句的主幹即 The challenge now is to develop policies and practices, 意思是現在的挑戰是開發出政策和實踐。based on 至句尾是過去分詞片語做狀語, 後一個 presumption 後面有一個 that 引道的子句(直至句尾), 是 presumption 的同位語, 在同位語子句中, 還有一個 if 引道的條件狀語子句。

14. Despite the significant increase in the number of women with dependent children who are in the paid workforce, Australian research studies over the last 15 years are consistent in showing that divisions of labour for family work are very rigid indeed.

中文譯文: 雖然有孩子的婦女參加工作的數目顯著地上升, 過去 15 年澳洲的研究一致表明，家庭工作的勞動分工實際上是固定不變的。

結構分析：despite 是介系詞，Despite the significant increase in the number of women with dependent children who are in the paid workforce 是介系詞片語做狀語。其中，who 引道的定語子句 who are in the paid workforce 做 women 的定語，主要子句中有 that 引道的受詞子句 that divisions of labour for family work are very rigid indeed 做 showing 的受詞。

15. Research studies lend strong support to the argument that there are benefits for families considering a change to a fairer or more equitable division of the pleasures and pains of family life.

中文譯文：研究表明快樂和痛苦能夠平等分擔的家庭會受益。

結構分析：that there are benefits for families considering a change to a fairer or more equitable division of the pleasures and pains of family life 是 that 引道的同位語子句做 argument 的同位語。在同位語子句中，considering a change to a fairer or more equitable division of the pleasures and pains of family life 是現在分詞片語做 families 的後置定語。

小竅門

初看起來，that 引道的同位語子句特別像定語子句。區別一個子句是同位語子句還是定語子句的方法是：that 引道的同位語子句中，that 只是連接詞，它不在子句中做任何句子成分，所以同位語子句都是完整句，而 that 引道的定語子句中，that 要做句子成分（主詞或受詞），所以 that 引道的定語子句都是不完整句（缺主詞或缺受詞）。

16. There is also higher marital satisfaction for fathers, especially when they take more responsibility for the needs of their children-fathers are happier when they are more involved.

中文譯文：特別是當父親們對孩子們的需要負更大責任時，他們有更高的婚姻滿意程度。父親們參與越多，他們越高興。

結構分析：兩個 when 引道兩個時間狀語子句。

17. Paper is also biodegradable, so it does not pose as much threat to the environment when it is discarded.

中文譯文：紙張還是可生物降解的，所以當我們把它扔掉的時候，它不會對環境造成很大的威脅。

結構分析:是多重複合句。結果狀語子句(由 so 引道)中套着一個時間狀語子句(由 when 引道)。biodegradable 是一個生詞,可以用構詞法猜測它的意思,主幹部分是 grade,意思是"級別",degrade 表示"降級",able 表示"能⋯⋯、可⋯⋯",bio 表示"生命的、生物的",所以此詞的意思是"可生物降解的"。

❖ 四、插入語結構 ❖

　　插入語也是 IELTS 閱讀中常出現的一種結構。它一般是對一個句子成分的解釋或補充説明,通常是不重要的內容。插入語的特點是左邊一個逗號,右邊一個逗號,比較容易識別。對付插入語的辦法是先略去不讀。插入語常常插在主詞和動詞之間,也可以插在其他兩個句子成分之間。有的插入語比較長,如果對插入語特別注意,會使原來句子的主要意思中斷,造成理解困難。而插入語常常是不重要的內容,所以應先略去不讀,這樣被分隔的兩個句子成分就接上了。

1. In relationships of mutual dependence, such as between labour and management or within an organisation or a family, the question of who is more powerful turns on who is less dependent on the other.

中文譯文:在相互依賴的關係中,例如勞資關係或一個家庭或一個組織中,誰更有力量的問題就轉換成誰更少依賴於另一方。

結構分析:such as between labour and management or within an organisation or a family 是插入語,同時也是舉例説明,是不重要的內容,可以先略去不讀。全句的動詞片語是 turns on, the question of who is more powerful 是主詞,受詞子句 who is less dependent on the other 是 turns on 的受詞。

2. In developing countries, where at least 16 cities are expected to have more than 12 million people each by the end of this decade, failing to give priority to public transport would be disastrous.

中文譯文:在發展中國家,至少有16個城市在這個10年結束時人口會超過1200萬,不優先考慮公共交通,會是災難性的。

結構分析：where at least 16 cities are expected to have more than 12 million people each by the end of this decade 是插入語，是一個定語子句，修飾 developing countries。全句主詞是動名詞片語 failing to give priority to public transport。

3. Buses and trains carry more people in each vehicle and, if they operate on their own rights-of-way, can safely run at much higher speeds.

中文譯文：公共汽車和火車在每個車輛中裝載更多的人，而且如果它們在自己的路上行駛，會更高速地安全行駛。

結構分析：全句用 and 連接兩個並列動詞 carry 和 can safely run，if they operate on their own rights-of-way 是個插入語，表示補充說明條件，先略去不讀，會將全句的意思掌握得更好。

全句主幹：Buses and trains carry more people in each vehicle and can safely run at much higher speeds.

中文譯文：公共汽車和火車在每個車輛中裝載更多的人，而且會更高速地安全行駛。

4. The 17th Winter Games, held in Norway in 1994, are part of an Olympic tradition which goes back almost 3,000 years.

中文譯文：1994 年在挪威舉行的第 17 屆多季奧運，是可以追溯到幾乎 3000 年以前的奧運會傳統的一部分。

結構分析：held in Norway in 1994 是插入語，從語法成分上看，它是過去分詞片語做主詞 the 17th Winter Games 的後置定語。which 引導一個定語子句，做 Olympic tradition 的定語。

五、倒裝句式

主詞和動詞有兩種順序:一是主詞在前,這和中文是一致的,稱爲自然語序。另一種是動詞在主詞之前,叫做倒裝語序。

陳述句絕大多數都是自然語序,但在某些情況下卻需要用倒裝語序。在 IELTS 閱讀中經常出現下列三種情況:

(1) 以 not only 等詞引導的句子,常用倒裝語序。

句子模式:Not only 句子1, but (also)句子2。

意思是:不僅句子1,而且句子2。

其中句子1要倒裝,句子2不倒裝。but also 之中的 also 可以省略。

(2) 比較句式,than 後面的句子可以倒裝,也可以不倒裝。

例如:下面兩個句子都是正確的。

John plays tennis better than Tom does.

John plays tennis better than does Tom.

(3)as 和 so 引起的倒裝,表示前面所說的情況也適用於另一人或事物。

如:He is a teacher, as is his brother.

他是一個教師,他的哥哥也是。

1. In a dispute, not only do the interests of one party not coincide with those of the other party, but they are in conflict.

中文譯文:在一個衝突中,不僅一方的利益與另一方不一致,而且它們是矛盾的。

結構分析:not only 位於句首,引起倒裝,前一個句子的正常語序應爲 the interests of one party do not coincide with those of the other party,現在將助動詞 do 放在主詞的前面,後面部分的 but also 省略了 also。

2. In a typical example, when viewing photographs of food, hungry subjects experience a much greater increase in pupil diameter than do sated subjects.

中文譯文:在一個典型的例子中,當看到食物的照片時,飢餓的實驗對象比飽的實驗對象的瞳孔直徑增加更大。

結構分析:比較級後面的句子倒裝,比較級實際上是比較狀語子句。than 後面的句子的正常語序是 sated subjects do, sated 是過去分詞做 subjects 的前置定語。

3. A mother's wanting her partner to do more housework and child care is a better predictor of poor family adjustment than is actual time spent by fathers in these tasks.

中文譯文：一個母親希望她的丈夫做更多的家務和照顧孩子，這比父親們在這些工作上花費的實際時間更能表示家庭的調整。

結構分析：本句比較複雜，是一個比較句式。than 之前是主要子句，動名詞片語 a mother's wanting her partner to do more housework and child care 做主詞。than 後面的比較子句倒裝了，正常語序是 actual time spent by fathers in these tasks is。比較子句中，actual time 是主詞，spent by fathers in these tasks 是過去分詞片語做 actual time 的後置定語。

4. In addition, ducks lay eggs over a longer season than do hens.

中文譯文：而且鴨子的產蛋期比母雞長。

結構分析：than 後面的比較子句倒裝了，正常語序是 hens do。

5. The average air temperature at the surface of the earth has risen this century, as has the temperature of ocean surface waters.

中文譯文：這個世紀以來，地球表面空氣的平均溫度上升了，海水表面的溫度也一樣。

結構分析：as 表示"……也一樣"，引起後面的句子倒裝，正常語序是 the temperature of ocean surface waters has。

6. Not only do we need to make the paper available to collectors but it also needs to be separated into different types.

中文譯文：我們不僅需要使紙張能被收廢紙的人得到，而且紙張需要被分成不同的類別。

結構分析：not only 位於句首，引起前面的句子倒裝。正常的語序是 we need to make the paper available to collectors。

❖❖ 六、被動句 ❖❖

被動語態由助動詞 be 加過去分詞構成,時態透過 be 表現出來。

1. Therefore, like the timber barriers, the Fanwall barrier can be built without expensive concrete footings or piles, speeding the construction time up and reducing costs.

中文譯文:因此,像木屏障一樣,Fanwall 屏障的建造不需要昂貴的混凝土地基,加快了建造時間,降低了費用。

結構分析:can be built 是被動語態,like the timber barriers 是介系詞片語做狀語,speeding the construction time up and reducing costs 是分詞片語做狀語。

2. The ancient Olympics were abolished by the Roman Emperor Theodosius in 393 AD, after Greece had lost its independence.

中文譯文:在希臘失去獨立後,古代奧運會在公元 393 年被羅馬皇帝 Theodosius 廢除了。

結構分析:were abolished 是被動語態的過去式形式。after 引導時間狀語子句。若不認識羅馬皇帝的名字,可採用首字母提煉法羅馬皇帝 T。

3. For more than 1,000 years the ancient Games were held, every four years, on hallowed ground near Mount Olympus, where the Greek gods were said to live.

中文譯文:古代運動會每四年在奧林匹斯山附近的神聖大地上舉行,超過 1000 年,據說希臘諸神住在那裏。

結構分析:were held 是 hold 的被動語態。every four years 是插入語,起補充說明作用。where 引導定語子句。

七、強調句式

強調句型的模式是：It is/was ＋被強調部分＋that/who＋其他部分（形式不變）

1. 可以強調：主詞、受詞、狀語；

   不可以強調：動詞、定語。

2. 被強調部分為人時，that/who 均可，其餘用 that。

3. 後面的句子為過去時態，用 It was，其餘用 It is。

1. It is this desire, together with its lack of fulfillment in most families, that brings about stress in the female parent.

中文譯文：就是這種希望以及它在大多數家庭中的不能實現給母親帶來了壓力。

結構分析：強調主詞 this desire, together with its lack of fulfillment in most families。

原句為：This desire, together with its lack of fulfillment in most families, brings about stress in the female parent.

八、其他特殊句式

1. Since both rapid and light rail have electric engines, pollution is measured not from the motor exhaust, but from the power plant generating electricity, which is usually located outside the city, where air quality problems are less serious.

中文譯文：因為地鐵和輕軌都有電子引擎，所以污染不是從車輛排放的廢氣中測量，而是從產生電力的發電廠測量，發電廠通常位於城市之外，那裏空氣品質問題不太嚴重。

結構分析：主要子句中有一個特殊句型：not...but...，意思是"不是……而是……"，一般 but 後面的內容很重要，是考點。

2. It is not uncommon to see several riders clinging to the outside.

中文譯文：看到幾個乘客掛在（公共汽車的）外面，並不罕見。

結構分析：not uncommon 是雙重否定，表示肯定，意思是這種現象很常見。it 是形式主詞，to see several riders clinging to the outside 是不定詞片語做實際的主詞。

3. This was because the RTA had purchased and removed a number of houses to allow the new corridor to be built, exposing to road traffic noises houses which were once located in a quiet back street.

中文譯文:這是因爲 RTA 已經購買和移走了一些房屋來建造新的連接公路,因此,將原來坐落於一個安靜的後街的房屋暴露於公路交通噪音之下。

結構分析:exposing 至句尾是現在分詞片語做狀語,在其中改變了句子的語序,正常的語序是 exposing houses which were once located in a quiet back street to road traffic noises,之所以將 houses which were once located in a quiet back street 放在句末,主要是因爲它比較長,爲了避免句子頭重腳輕。

ACCESS TO IELTS

國際IELTS應考叢書

閱　讀

CHAPTER　VI

IELTS 閱讀
原則和規律

READING

一、IELTS 閱讀八大原則

下面要介紹的八大原則是綜合了閱讀方法和各解題技巧而總結的 IELTS 閱讀總原則,非常重要,請大家仔細閱讀。

> **原則一、IELTS 閱讀的核心是帶着問題到原文中去找答案,而不是先理解文章的意思,再解答問題。**

所以,一般答完題目,別人若問文章都說了些什麼,你回答不知道、不太清楚,這是很正常的,就應該是這種感覺。

> **原則二、拒絕讀全文,但在做題目之前,先要瀏覽全文,掌握文章的大意。**

IELTS 文章大都比較長,訊息量大。一般沒有時間先把全文都仔細地看一遍。

但在做題目之前,應先看一下文章的標題、圖及圖表、小標題、每段話的第一句等。

由於在做題目前已掌握了文章的大意和各個段落的主要內容,所以很多題目可以直接先定位到原文的一個段落。這時,再仔細閱讀該段落,確定正確答案。

> **原則三、定位的三大法寶:題目中的關鍵詞、原文中的對應詞、順序性。**

很多題型做法的第一步都是:找出題目中的關鍵詞。找出關鍵詞是找答案的關鍵所在,關鍵詞應首重年代、人名、地名及其他專有名詞。這些詞在原文中都是原詞對應,特別好找。如果題目中沒有這些詞,就需要從意義上判斷,找那些意思比較特殊的詞。

找出題目中的關鍵詞以後,就要到原文中去找它的對應詞。找到了對應詞,就找到了答案,答案常常在對應詞所在的句子中。對應詞的特點如下:

(1)原詞

(2)詞性變化;例如一個是形容詞,一個是名詞。

(3)語態變化;例如一個是主動語態,一個是被動語態。

(4)同義詞

找對應詞在 IELTS 閱讀中佔有極其重要的地位。有些難題的難度就在於對應不明顯,同學們無論做對了題,還是做錯了題,都應該把各題目與原文之間的對應關係找出來,做一個總結,很多對應關係在考試中是反覆使用的。下面我們列出一些對應關係,作為例子供大家參考。

原　　　　文	題　　　　目
corporate life	company
structures	restructuring patterns
organisations	associations
a range of opportunities	support
women who apply for jobs	female job applicants
middle or senior management	management positions
predictor	indicator
family adjustment	family is adjusted
highly	great extent
participant	take part
major proportion	majority
family type	married or not
contributor to	result from
greater role	primary
rigid	little change
recruitment patterns	selection procedures
so hard for women	do not favour women
growing	increasing
women who have started up on their own	female-run businesses
significantly fewer women	male applicants exceed female
senior positions	top posts
have raised the level of grades	hold higher positions
productivity	low production rates
high labour turnover	high rates of staff change
physical	poor health
society	international community
move towards	demand
at the time	in the past

cost	price
aimed at	in order to
minimising	decrease

這裏只是作爲例子列出了一小部分,大家可以按照這種形式自己總結。

順序性也是幫助大家找到答案的一個有力的武器。80% 以上的題目是有順序性的,即題目的順序與原文的順序基本上一致。這也有助於大家確定答案在原文的位置。在所有的題型中,只有從屬關係搭配題和作者及觀點搭配題沒有順序性。另外,可能會有極少數的其他題型的題目違背順序性。

> **原則四、定位一般是兩步或三步。**

這三步是:

1. 定位到一個段落
2. 定位到這個段落中的一句話
3. 定位到這句話中的幾個詞

最好能先根據題目中的關鍵詞定位到原文中的一個段落,然後快速閱讀該段落,找到該段落中與題目相關的一句話,仔細閱讀這一句話,確定正確答案。有時,通過這一句話判斷正確答案,有時,答案是這一句話中的幾個詞。

> **原則五、首尾原則:段首段尾尤其重要,是答案經常出現的地方。**

根據筆者的統計,答案在段首和段尾的可能性在 50% 左右。這實際上也是有理論依據的。英文文章的段首和段尾通常包含重要內容,而外國人考試喜歡考重要的內容,所以,段首和段尾就成了答案經常出沒的地方。大家可以從做過的題目中自己驗證。

這個原則告訴我們:

(1) 在找答案時,重點看段首和段尾。

(2) 時間不夠了,如 10 分鐘要做第三篇文章,只看段首和段尾找答案。

(3) 瞎猜一個答案時,猜段首和段尾的內容。

> 原則六、要求考生自己寫答案的題目,答案多為原文原詞。
>   要求從選項中選擇答案的題目,答案一般是原文的
>   對應詞句。

要求考生自己寫答案的題型包括:

1. 簡答題

2. 完成句子

3. 填圖填表

4. 從原文中選詞的摘要填空

這些題型的答案絕大部分應是原文原詞,而且是原文中連續的幾個詞。只有極少的部分需要用自己的話寫出答案。所以在考試中,如果發現這些題型有很多題目都需要自己組織語言寫出答案,應首先懷疑自己找錯答案的位置。

要求從選項中選擇答案的題型包括:

(1) 找段落的小標題

(2) 從選項中選詞的摘要填空

(3) 選擇題

(4) 搭配題

這些題型的答案絕大部分應是原文相關詞句的改寫。所以,那些與原文詞句特別一致的選項應該引起懷疑。

> 原則七、不同題型的難易程度是不同的,應分別掌握。

雖然同一題型的題目也有難易之分,但一般來講,比較容易的題型包括:

1. 找段落的小標題

2. 摘要填空

3. 填圖填表

4. 複選題

5. 從屬關係搭配

6. 因果關係搭配

這些題目的特點是定位容易、對應明顯,應保證做對這些題型的大部分題目。特別是從屬關係搭配題,考試中這種題型的題目較多,一般會有 10 題以上,這種題型一般不太難,可能比較費時間。所以,在考試時,基礎較差的同學應在這種題型上多花一點時間。也就是說,與其將時間花在其他沒有把握的題型上,不如在這種題型上多花一點時

間,爭取將這種題型的題目全都做對。

有難有易的題型包括:

(1) 單選題

(2) 簡答題

(3) 是非題(T/F/NG)

這些題型有的容易,有的很難。很多同學對是非題很害怕,實際上,它並不大難。這種題型定位容易,難在有時不好判斷,尤其是 F 和 NG 之間。做這種題型時,要注意不宜耗時過多,猶豫不決,要相信自己的第一感覺,沒有強力的理由,不要輕易修改,很多同學都把原來答對的答案改錯了。

比較難的題型包括:

(1) 完成句子

(2) 作者及其觀點搭配題

對這些題型,程度普通的同學不宜耗時過多。

總而言之,40 道題中,簡單題型應佔到 20 題以上,同學們應抓住這些題目,爭取做對其中的絕大部分,這樣 5 分、6 分還是不難達到的。

原則八、採取放棄原則。

即使是基礎再好的同學,也不要指望全部答對。對於一道題,不宜耗時過多,要敢於放棄。一道單題若五分鐘還沒找到答案,可以考慮放棄。記住:所有題目的分數是一樣的,答對難題和簡單題沒有區別。

放棄不等於不答,答錯不倒扣分。所以應該寫上自己認為最可能正確的答案。

❖ 二、IELTS 閱讀答案規律 ❖

　　這裏的規律是指 IELTS 閱讀考試題目中正確答案在形式和內容上表現出來的一些規律性。同學們按照這種規律性,有時不需要閱讀原文,直接就可以做對題目,或在閱讀原文時,能大大提高找到正確答案的速度和準確率。

　　下面就是筆者總結的 IELTS 閱讀答案規律總匯:

題　　型	規　　律	正確率
Headings	正確選項對應該段落的主題句(第一句、第二句、最後一句)。	90%
Headings	正確選項對應該段落的第一句。	50%
Summary	對應原文連續的兩到三段。	90%
T/F/NG	題目中出現 must、only、all 及 always,答案不會是 True。	95%
T/F/NG	題目中出現 must、only、all 及 always,答案是 False。	60%
T/F/NG	題目中出現 fact、prove,答案是 False。	95%
T/F/NG	題目數目在 5 個(含)以上時,三種答案(True/False/Not Given)都要出現。	95%
T/F/NG	不會連續四題的答案都一樣。	95%
短問答	答案涉及數字的,會有簡單的四則運算。	95%
單選題	含有"絕對意義"的字彙如 must、always、all、will 的選項,一般爲錯誤選項。	90%
單選題	選項中含有"相對意義"的字彙如 can、may、sometimes、some、not always,一般爲正確答案。	90%
搭配題(從屬關係搭配,作者及觀點搭配)	第一題的答案往往在文章的後部。最後一題的答案往往在文章的前部。	80%

　　爲什麼會有這樣的規律呢? 任何考題的設計必須按照一定的規則,這種規則叫作"測試法"。托福考試有托福考試的規律,IELTS 考試有 IELTS 考試的規律。作者經過三

年的研究,在這方面取得了一些成果。

這些規律對於不同程度的考生有不同的利用價值:

(1)當程度較低的考生無法直接從原文找到答案或者沒有時間做完所有題目,只能猜一個答案時,應當利用上述規律,儘可能地猜到可能的正確答案。

(2)程度較高的考生可以從原文中找到答案,同時,也可以利用上述規律進行檢驗,這樣就大大地提高了正確率。

❖ 三、IELTS 閱讀十大出題原則 ❖

出題原則是指文章中的出題點,也就是說,文章中出現了這些語言現象,一般會有考題和它對應。

掌握這些出題原則,也有助於大家快速準確地找到答案。大家在找答案時,要注意找這些出題原則。

原則一、數字

文章中出現數字,一般會有考題對應。注意,有時原文中的數字是用英文表示的,而且一般會有簡單的四則運算。

例:原文:At precisely 4. 20 am on Friday the 24th of September 1993, it was announced that Sydney had beaten five other competing cities around the world, and Australians everywhere, not only Sydneysiders, were justifiably proud of the result.

題目:How many cities were competing in 1993 for the fight to hold the 2000 Games?

答案:6

原則二、下定義

原文中對某詞下定義,一般會有考題對應。下定義的方式有以下四種:

(1)判斷句

原文:Interests are needs, desires, concerns, fears- the things one cares about or wants.

題目:Headings

答案:Disagreement of interests

(2)用破折號

原文:This process is advection ——— the transport of properties (notably heat and salinity in the ocean）by the movement of bodies of air or water，rather than by conduction or diffusion.

題目：Headings

答案：The advection principle

（3）同位語

例子見下面定語子句。

（4）定語子句

原文：The most common procedure for doing this is negotiation，the act of communication intended to reach agreement. Another interests-based procedure is mediation，in which a third party assists the disputants，the two sides in the dispute，in reaching-agreement.

題目：Two common procedures used in the resolution of interest-based disputes are ...and ...

答案：negotiation，mediation

原則三、因果

原文中出現了因果關係，一般會有考題對應。而且有一種題型就是考因果關係（因果關係搭配題）。

原文：Paper is also biodegradable，so it does not pose as much threat to the environment when it is discarded.

題目：and secondly it is less threatening to our environment when we throw it away because it is ....（31）....

答案：biodegradable

常見的表示因果關係的詞，請詳見第三章中因果關係搭配題部分的講解。

原則四、轉折

轉折和因果一樣重要，原文中出現了轉折關係，一般會有考題對應，這時，應特別注意轉折詞後面的句子。

常見的轉折詞有：but、however、though、although、yet、nevertheless、on the other hand

原文：Your iron is designed to function using tap water. However，it will last longer if you use distilled water.

題目：What sort of water are you advised to use？

答案：distilled／distilled water

原則五、比較級和最高級

原文：In addition, ducks lay eggs over a longer season than do hens.

題目：Classify the characteristics listed below as belonging to：

D　　　Ducks

H　　　hens

or

NI　　　if there is no information in the reading passage

7. lengthier laying period

答案：D

原則六、舉例子

原文給一句話或一個詞舉個例子，說明這句話或這個詞很重要。舉例子通常用 for example、for instance、such as 等詞。注意，這些詞前面的句子或詞很重要，一般會有考題對應。後面的句子或詞（即例子本身）不重要，一般不會有考題對應。

原文：We need to accept a change in the quality of paper products; for example stationery may be less white and of a rougher texture.

題目：However, we need to learn to accept paper which is generally of a lower.... (35).... than before.

答案：quality

原則七、相似及遞進

表示相似關係的詞：like、as、similar to、in the same way

表示遞進關係的詞：also、besides、moreover、furthermore

原文：Therefore, like the timber barriers, the Fanwall barrier can be built without expensive concrete footings or piles, speeding the construction time up and reducing costs. Furthermore, Fanwall is maintenance free and it is not susceptible to damage by fire and vandalism.

題目：The author mentions a number of features of noise barriers. Some are listed below. Identify them by writing

　　　A. if the feature applies to low timber barriers

　　　B. if it applies to high timber barriers

　　　C. if it applies to concrete barriers

9. They are susceptible to damage by fire and vandalism

10. They do not require expensive foundations

11. They are more expensive to maintain

答案:9. A B 10. A B C 11. A B

原則八、引言

原文中引用了一個人說的話,一般會有考題對應。

原文:The Secretary of the NSW Labour Council, Mr. Michael Easson, was quoted as saying,... "what we've achieved should become the model for the rest of the building industry... great co-operation, good management, improvement in relations between employers and employees, and a feeling of optimism..."

題目:How many achievements does the Secretary of the NSW Labour Council mention in his industrial relations model?

答案:4

原則九、特殊的字

原文中括號裏的詞、引號裏的詞、黑體字、斜體字,應引起注意,一般會有考題對應。

原文:**Important**: if your iron produces droplets of water instead of giving off steam, your temperature control is set too low.

題目:What should you do if your iron starts to drip water?

答案:set temperature high

原則十、圖表

原文中若出現圖表,一般會有考題對應。

CHAPTER VII

IELTS
考前培训

READING

參加 IELTS 考試之前，要進行必要的考前培訓，做到心中有數，才能發揮出自己的較好甚至最高水準。有的同學只注重題目的訓練，而忽略了考前一些注意事項，以至於表現失常。因此，有必要將 IELTS 考前的注意事項列出來，供同學們參考。

❖ 一、考前一週 ❖

考前一週應注意調整作息時間，每天晚上不能復習得太晚。一般 10 點鐘左右就該休息了。白天可以再準備一下，針對閱讀考試可以再將本書看看。同時，看看以前做錯的題目。這一週最好安排一到兩次的自我模擬考試，安排在上午進行，與實際考試時間一致。

❖ 二、考前一天 ❖

考前一天，即星期五，就不用再做題目了。週四下午或週五上午可以去考場看看，熟悉一下環境，以免週六考試時花費很多時間找考場。晚上準備一下第二天的考試用品，也不用太早上床，以免緊張，反而入睡困難，像平常一樣，10 點左右睡覺即可。

❖ 三、考試過程 ❖

週六上午，一定按要求 8:15 到達考場，不能遲到。

9:00 – 9:30	入場
9:30 – 10:10	聽力測驗
10:10 – 10:15	休息 5 分鐘，不離場
10:15 – 11:15	閱讀測驗
11:15 – 11:25	休息 10 分鐘，離場。
11:25 – 12:25	寫作測驗
12:25 – 12:40	領取口試時間表
12:40 –	口試測驗

在考試時,要注意以下幾點:

1. 考試前,在監考老師的指導下做準備工作。

正式考試前,監考老師會指導考生填寫答案紙上的考生姓名等訊息,這時,一定要注意聽,以免填錯。如果有不清楚的,可以舉手問。考試前,還會讓大家試耳機。這時,一定要試一下,如果有問題,才可及時在考試前向監考老師提出。

2. 一定要將答案寫在答案紙上。

閱讀考試沒有專門時間讓考生將答案謄寫到答案紙上。所以,建議大家直接將答案寫在答案紙上,以免浪費時間。將答案直接寫在答案紙上有一個壞處,就是容易寫錯位置。如何避免這種事情發生呢? 一是在寫答案時,每題都與前面的題號對一下,二是平常要做這樣的練習,筆者建議大家至少在考試前一個月就要做這樣的練習,平常做題目時,就養成直接將答案寫在答案紙上的習慣。在考試時,如果發現答案寫錯位置了,要及時改過來。

3. 嚴格執行考場紀律。

即使監考老師再面容和善,他們對工作也是很認真負責的。所以,不能打開考卷時,不要打開;停止答題時,一定要停止。否則,很可能會被記錄下來,影響成績,甚至取消考試資格。

4. 不要在答案紙上留空。

IELTS 閱讀答錯題目不倒扣分數。所以即使不確定的題目,也要猜一個答案,尤其是從選項中選答案的題目,會有相當高的機率答對。

5. 不要在一道題目上費時過多。

程度再高的同學也很難答對所有的題目。不要在一道題目上花過多的時間。題目的分數一樣,沒有倒扣分數的制度,所以要敢於放棄。

6. 試題卷上可以隨便畫。

在閱讀文章時,在認為重要的內容下畫線是一個很好的閱讀習慣,IELTS 閱讀考試並沒有不準在試題卷上做標記的規定。

7. 在考試前,要關掉手機和呼叫器。

在考試時,如果你的手機或呼叫器響了,你一定會被取消考試資格。最保險的方法是把它們放在家裏,不要帶到考場去。

網站信息

★http://www.ucas.ac.uk
英國大學院校服務/申請單位(大學部)
★http://www.isuk.org.uk/index.htm
英國中學指南(中學部)
★http://www.hefce.au.uk/asmuttch.htm
英國教育系統評估
★http://www.school-search.demon.co.uk/
英國學校搜尋
★http://www.ielts.org/sample.html
IELTS 國際英語測試考題簡介
★http://www.ielts.com
留學英、澳、新的留學考試
★http://www.edunet.com/english/grammar
on-line English Grammar 網上文法練習
★http://www.edunet.com/english/practice/test-ces.html
on-line English practice 網上英文測驗